Blessed Unbeliever

Blessed Unbeliever

James P. Hurd

RESOURCE *Publications* · Eugene, Oregon

BLESSED UNBELIEVER

Resource Publications
An Imprint of Wipf and Stock Publishers
199 W. 8th Ave., Suite 3
Eugene, OR 97401

www.wipfandstock.com

PAPERBACK ISBN: 978-1-6667-5695-1
HARDCOVER ISBN: 978-1-6667-5696-8
EBOOK ISBN: 978-1-6667-5697-5

VERSION NUMBER 121322

To Barbara and our children: Kimberly, Timothy and Jennifer

Acknowledgments

Thanks to people who read early versions of the manuscript and gave helpful suggestions including Etta Erickson and Barbara Hurd. Thanks to George Callihan at Wipf and Stock for guiding me through the publishing process. Finally, thanks to the fundamentalists in my life for exercising their formative influence and providing searching questions to lead me in new directions.

California Beginnings

Chapter 1

January 1956. Edwin McIntosh stared at his newspaper. "All five were speared to death!"

Sean jerked his head up from his breakfast oatmeal. "Dad; who? What are you talking about?"

"Five missionaries were speared to death by Auca Indians in Ecuador. Nate Saint from Winging the Word was one of them. Remember when we visited WTW's hangar over at Fullerton Airport?" Edwin laid The *Register* on the breakfast nook table. "We heard Nate Saint speak at Calvary church."

Nate Saint was Sean's hero, a man who flew bush planes and conquered jungle barriers, carved new airstrips out of the jungle and air-dropped little packets of anti-snakebite vaccine into remote mission stations.

"It says here he was killed, along with four other missionaries. Dear God . . ." Edwin buried his face in his hands.

When he was a junior at Santa Ana High School, Sean had told his father, "Dad—I want to take Nate Saint's place." From then on, Edwin became Sean's greatest cheerleader in his quest to be a mission pilot.

March 1959. Grief was no stranger to Orange County General, a vast complex of white buildings near the Santa Ana Freeway. Sean sat in the emergency waiting room with his younger brother and two sisters, his arm around his mother.

When Dr. Emerson walked in, wiping his hands on his blue scrubs, they circled in a tight knot. "Mrs. McIntosh, Edwin is sinking. We have him on a ventilator but his heart's damaged and getting weaker. We're doing everything we can." He took off his heavy-rimmed glasses to wipe his forehead.

Elizabeth's hand rose to her throat and her voice broke. "He was in good health. His heart attack last year—the doctor said it was a 'warning.'

Since then, he's been exercising, watching what he eats." She wore no make-up and her tired eyelids sagged.

"I'm sorry. I'll keep you updated." Dr. Emerson wheeled around and paced out. Sean's two sisters, Joyce and Nancy, sat staring ahead Sphinx-like but his brother Paul was nervous—constantly up and down or walking out to buy snacks.

Sean turned to his mother. "Dad'll get better, won't he?"

"We are all praying so, Sweetheart," she replied.

Sean breathed fast, sucking in the antiseptic air. He remembered how his father used to drive him out to Orange County Airport where they would watch the little planes land through the tarmac's radiating heat. He remembered the turboprop whine when Bonanza Airlines' Fairchild F-27 arrived from Los Vegas. WWII had ended just fifteen years before and Edwin loved wartime aviation, although he had never piloted a plane. Father and son marveled at the Blue Angels aerobatics team and thrilled at the great blimps gliding like bloated fish to their moorings at the nearby Marine Corps Air Facility. Edwin fired Sean's imagination and aviation became his one passion.

Now, Sean heard the waiting room ceiling fan throbbing over the silence. "Dear God, please save my father. You're all powerful. You can work a miracle. You can't let him die; he's not old—you must save him." He shivered in his brown stadium jacket.

Elizabeth pulled a handkerchief from the sleeve of the blue dress she'd thrown on that morning, dabbed her eyes, then looked at Pastor Carter. "When he got up this morning he just collapsed. Even before the orderlies wheeled him into the ICU, he was starting to turn blue . . ."

He lowered his head. "We don't know why these things happen." He removed his suit coat and laid it beside him, loosening his dark blue tie. "We trust in God but it's so hard."

The hands on the eight-sided wall clock nibbled away the hours. At 2 p.m. Dr. Emerson entered again. "We've done everything we can—he's unresponsive. The ventilator is useless now."

Elizabeth started. "What? No! Dr. Emerson . . ." Her unblinking blue eyes stared at his surgical mask.

"Of course we can wait but patients in Edwin's condition rarely recover, and if they do, they often have severe brain damage." He turned his eyes toward Elizabeth. "I'm so sorry. I'll come back in a while."

Pastor Carter sat beside her holding her hand and whispering, "Elizabeth, maybe it's time to let Edwin go into God's arms." He turned to the others. "Sean, Paul, girls—you must be strong for your mother." Elizabeth gripped Sean's arm and stared up at his face. He smelled her perfume and something else—paralyzing fear.

When Dr. Emerson appeared in the waiting room two hours later, Sean flinched. This would be his mother's decision but, withered and worn as she was, would she be capable of making it?

Elizabeth rose, braced herself on the back of a chair like a warrior leaning on a shield, stared at the doctor, then caught her breath and whispered through her sobs. "After Edwin recovered from his first heart attack, he and I talked. He said he was ready. I can't imagine . . . Keeping him would be almost like going against God's will." She sank to the couch like a stone.

Dr. Emerson nodded his head and walked out but in ten minutes he returned. "He's gone; I'm so sorry. Please let us know how we can further help you."

Elizabeth and her family sat mute. After a long silence, Pastor Carter circled the family and prayed: "Father God, please comfort this dear family in their great loss. 'Yea though I walk through the valley of the shadow of death, I will fear no evil: for thou art with me; thy rod and thy staff, they comfort me . . .'"

Elizabeth, Sean and Pastor Carter left the younger children in the waiting area and filed into the sterile room to look at the silent form. Elizabeth rubbed his legs, stared at his stilled face illuminated under the harsh light. No words. Edwin McIntosh was dead at fifty-one.

Sean dropped his head into his hands. *What good is prayer if it doesn't work? Dad won't even see my high school graduation. He's the reason I'm going to Torrey Bible Institute to train for mission aviation. He's even the reason I believe in you.*

In his confusion he walked out to the hall and inserted his tall, skinny frame into a public phone booth to call Kathleen Wilberforce whom he'd been dating for three months. He longed now for her comforting arms. As he dropped a dime in the slot he wondered how she would react. He admired her calm confidence, her love of classical music and art but wondered why she had cooled recently, why she had refused a couple of times when he'd asked her out.

"Kathy, something terrible." (Sean was one of the few people allowed to call her "Kathy.") "My dad had another heart attack this morning and now the doctors say he's gone."

"Oh, Sean. Where are you?"

"He had a small one last year."

"But he's young, Sean. I'm so sorry. Are you at the hospital? Who's there with you?"

"I know I must be strong for Mom. I just don't understand why God is taking my dad away, after all our prayers."

"We must trust our God, even when things don't make any sense. God is sovereign. I'm sure your mother needs you now but Sean, as soon as you can, come over and we'll talk."

"Sure; but what's there to talk about? Dad is now past our prayers."

Chapter 2

JUST THREE MONTHS AFTER his father's death, Sean was driving to the Calvary Church beach party with his friend Lonnie Thomas. "I get tired of the Calvary kids trying to cheer me up, Lonnie. But this might be the last time I'll see them before I take off for TBI." He wheeled into Huntington Beach State Park, revving the engine of his 1950 Chevy—metallic blue, nosed, decked, hung and throbbing with twin glasspak mufflers—looking for a parking spot.

"Look at that Woodie over there with a couple boards on top," Lonnie said. "There's an open spot next to it."

"I called Kathy last night to ask if I could swing by for her," Sean said. "But she had to ride with one of the girls to bring the food. I wonder if that's just an excuse."

They stepped out barefooted onto the hot tarmac, then toad-loped the hundred yards down to the firepit, feeling the sand squish between their toes, tasting the salt air and gulping in the throat-burning Los Angeles basin smog.

Sean, six feet four, one hundred fifty pounds, all untanned and freckled, ran his hand through wiry red hair only partially tamed by butch wax. Gangly—Abe Lincoln gangly—his Hawaiian shirt rose above his navel. And skinny—self-conscious about his sharp-winged shoulder blades and spindly arms. He felt like he had few close friends in the church group, nobody to just hang out with. He stared at the girls gathered around the firepit preparing food —maxi-skirted, toenail-painted, their long hair seeded with hibiscus flowers, stooping over like goddesses of grace. Susan wore a purple swimsuit and a tiny silver chain around one ankle. Her maxi skirt covered only the bottom half of her two-piece bathing suit, revealing her bare midriff between skirt and halter top. He pulled his eyes away.

He assumed they all had stronger religious beliefs than he did. He wondered, *Why can't I just accept what Pastor Carter preaches?*

"Kathy probably won't even talk to me, Lonnie."

"Stop whining. I think she likes you," Lonnie said as they approached the group. "Great luau, Kathleen. Here's our watermelon and a six-pack of Pepsi."

She wrinkled her nose at Lonnie. "Some of the guys remembered to bring fruit or chips—maybe their mothers reminded them. Do the others think their mere presence is a gift to the world?" She smiled—not at Sean but at Lonnie.

The relentless sun sank toward the Pacific, the smog turning the coppery disc fantastic, distorted, like a rotting orange. Southern California summers heat into the nineties at midday, then cool fast after sundown. One of the guys announced, "Look, I brought some dead orange wood from our home orchard; it's chopped into firewood lengths." He lit a wad of newspapers, poured a little gasoline on it, then nursed the flame with fragrant eucalyptus splinters, inhaling the sweet smoke.

"This'll work great for kabobs." another guy said. "Why so stingy with the wood? Throw on some more orange branches."

With his light, freckled skin, Sean avoided the sun. "Late afternoons and evenings are the best," he told Lonnie, "Cooler, less chance of sunburn." He smelled the smoke from the Tiki torches standing guard around the firepit and grooved to the battery-powered radio playing "Tijuana Jail."

He looked over at Kathleen as she leaned over to grab a kabob, admiring her tawny hair that fell in waves to her shoulders. Her cover-up reached only to her hips, and when she straightened up she reached behind to tuck a protruding bit of flesh back under the hem of her blue swimsuit. *I think I'm in love,* Sean thought.

The smoky aroma of the food lying atop a woven mat of green palm leaves wafted toward him. "I hope there's lots of food. I'm starved," he said to Lonnie. Glass bottles of Pepsi Cola and Orange Crush sat cooling in a red metal ice chest. They noticed Susan had baked a lemon cake with chocolate frosting.

Sean and Lonnie peeled off their shirts and Bermuda shorts to reveal bright-colored swimsuits, then raced toward the water like seagulls. Running through the foam that was washing farther and farther up the beach, they dove into one wave after another, lunging onto the peaks and bodysurfing toward the shore. Pacific waters freeze the bones, even in summer, but the pounding waves threw them around so much they didn't notice losing feeling in their legs. As Sean stood enjoying the waves breaking over his waist and shoulders, he squinted at the sun, now sinking toward the horizon.

Lonnie yelled, "Look at that huge tsunami coming in. You've got to jump onto the peak and then swim like crazy to keep from getting sucked under."

They jumped just before the wave broke but Sean jumped too early. Instead of lifting him the wave engulfed him, filling his mouth with the taste of the roiling salt water. As he somersaulted in the power of the wave, it threw him to the ocean floor, hard. After he struggled to the surface laboring to breathe, it rolled him all the way into the shallows. Spitting out salt water, he winced from the stinging scrapes on his back and knees. As he stood gasping for breath, he saw Lonnie coasting in nearby.

When Kathleen saw Sean tumble she came running to the water's edge. Sean's heartbeat accelerated as she bent over him with her hair falling against his arm. "Sean, are you alright? Are you hurt?"

"I didn't know you cared. I'm fine—the wave just toppled me."

"Don't get angry, Sean; I just wondered if you were hurt."

After he recovered, he and Kathleen walked along the beach listening to the seagulls calling, feeling the warm breeze on their wet skin, their bare feet squishing the moist sand. Kathleen lifted her eyes to the horizon. "It is strange to think Alaska is now a state and Hawaii's about to become one. They seem so far away."

"Yeah; it's a big ocean out there."

"Sean, how are you handling your father's death? It must be so hard."

"'Handling?' How am I *supposed* to handle it? I begged God to heal him and he just ignored me."

"Oh, Sean. I am so sorry. Your proud father was looking down on you when you walked up to receive your diploma."

"That's not the same as being there." Then he changed the subject. "I heard you moved into an apartment."

"Yes. I just wanted to get away on my own for a while. I talked to a friend who just graduated from high school. She's waitressing at the Jolly Roger in Balboa Beach and told me I could apply, said it was a great job with good remuneration and tips, said I could room with her until school starts in the fall."

"So why did you move out?"

"I couldn't stay home any longer. My father's so controlling and I just had to get away. My parents are helping me pay rent, though."

"Are you accepted at Biola Bible?"

"Yes. I'm also accepted at Yale, partly because I was a finalist for a National Merit Scholarship. But I think I'll at least start at Biola. Are you still going to Torrey Bible?"

National Merit Scholar, Sean thought. *I'm just struggling to keep a B average.* "Of course I'm going. I love the idea of the east— stone buildings, thunderstorms, snow falling into your hair—I've never traveled beyond Texas. But Torrey Bible Institute makes you pass flight camp before they'll accept you into the flight program. I've worked on my own car; aviation mechanics can't be that much different. Bush flying for an overseas mission—that's all I ever wanted. And that's what Dad wanted for me." Then, "Hey, you didn't drive; can I take you home tonight?"

"Oh . . . I'd better see if any of the girls need me to help carry stuff back. Thanks, though."

Sean doubted her excuse. *She doesn't want to go with me,* he thought. As they walked in silence with the chill wavelets washing over their toes, their fantastic shadows stretched up the beach —his towering over Kathleen's. *What's she thinking about?* Sean wondered. He found out.

"Reg is at UCLA studying business and international law."

Reg—so familiar sounding! I hate when she calls him that. He knew Reggie Radcliffe had taken her out a couple times and he wondered how serious they were. Reggie wasn't tall or handsome but made up for it by his confidence, wit and his carefully combed ducktail.

"He's already finished his first year at UCLA, and now is looking for a good company to join."

Reggie grated on him like tinfoil on a tooth filling. Sean wondered if he was here at the luau. They walked up toward the firepit. *Kathy probably sees him as an older, more mature "man with a plan." Maybe they're getting serious and that's why she won't ride home with me.*

He poked at the fire with a branch and thought back to the previous Sunday's communion service at Calvary church. He'd tried to concentrate, fingering the tiny cracker in his left hand and smelling the cup of communion grape juice in his right. Pastor Carter intoned: "Bread of heaven, on thee we feed; For thou art our food indeed . . ." Sean tipped his cup to find out how long the surface tension would hold back the grape juice. He found out, then tried to wipe away the purple stain on his pants.

Glancing across the aisle, he saw Reggie and Kathleen sitting together holding their communion cups—she with her head inclined forward in prayer, he with his eyes diverted, looking down her blouse. *How disgusting,* Sean thought. *I hate him.*

Sean returned to the water's edge then looked back to see Kathleen and a couple girls gazing past him as if he were invisible. Following their eyes out to sea, he realized Reggie Radcliffe was indeed present, swimming dolphin-like, parallel to the shore far out beyond the breakers, a barely visible pustule of ego. Sean felt tired but he gathered his courage and launched out, this time swimming through the breakers and being careful not to get sucked under again.

After clearing the farthest wave, he started to tire. Then came the monster that tumbled him and this time the ocean floor was fifteen feet down. The pounding force held him under for what seemed like five minutes. He panicked, flailed about, then burst to the surface gasping. Was an undertow grabbing him? Coughing to clear his throat and lungs he didn't know if he could swim back to shore and was afraid another huge wave would catch him. Treading water and thrashing around, he yelled out but people on the beach couldn't hear him.

Even as he tried to swim toward the shore, the riptide pulled him farther and farther out to sea. He sunk again, fought back to the surface, tried to swim but the shore seemed to retreat into the distance. His arms turned to jelly and he started going under.

Then an arm from nowhere reached out and seized him. "Try to relax. I'll help you get in," Reggie yelled. Sean flailed, trying to keep his head above water. Reggie one-armed him in a vice grip around the chest and took strong strokes with his other arm. Sean didn't want to be rescued by Reggie but he had little choice now.

They made slow progress. The riptide pulled them seaward but Reggie swam parallel to the shore, trying to get out of it. "I can get us there; just don't fight me." Then he turned toward the beach, pulling the terrified Sean along behind him like a whipping antenna.

The other kids stood on the shore watching the drama. One large wave overwhelmed them but Sean held on, Reggie held on and they surfaced. Like a slow-motion movie they inched forward, riding the waves as they broke.

They reached waist-deep water, dragged themselves onto dry sand then fell together on the beach exhausted.

The kids ran over to where they lay gasping—Kathleen got there first. "Sean. I didn't know you had ventured so far out. Oh, Sean—think what could have happened. I'm so happy Reginald was there for you."

I'll bet you are, Sean thought.

Then she turned her eyes to Reggie, knelt beside him and rubbed his back. "Reginald—that was a beautiful thing you did. Where did you learn lifesaving? How did you have the strength? If you hadn't been there, Sean would have drowned. I don't know how you managed to drag him in. God must have given you extra strength."

Reggie gave her a weak smile. "I just did what I had to do . . . I'm kinda hungry—what's for dinner?"

Sean's mind churned. *How stupid to go out so far. I sure underestimated the strength of the tides. Now Reggie has embarrassed me in front of all the kids. I wish I had drowned.* It was then he knew he'd lost Kathy forever.

Soon Susan yelled down from the firepit. "Hey you guys. Grab a skewer and load it with vegetables. Here's bacon, too. We're not doing it for you."

People began gathering to wait for the usual dinner prayer. They bowed their heads as Kathleen prayed a spontaneous prayer of thanks. (Calvary Church was big on spontaneity.) She wasn't just pretty and intelligent, Sean thought; she possessed the requisite fundamentalist piety.

People loaded skewers, then everybody stood around roasting kabobs. The girls had piled pyramids of steaming hot rice on banana leaves, along with sweet corn they'd roasted unhusked in the coals. Everybody sat around on blankets eating the kabobs and gnawing the succulent corn right off the cob.

After a while Susan said, "You all can roast marshmallows while I cut the cake. There's mango juice in the cooler, you guys, more Pepsi and orange." Calvary Community Church was no-alcohol. A couple of the guys imbibed but never here, never with their church friends.

The friendly dark fell fast as the seaward breeze swept away the smog. People ate cake and sucked the sticky marshmallows off the wire roasting sticks. The two-horned moon hung low and the air chilled but the bonfire shot out its light to warm their legs. Someone started "Michael, Row the Boat Ashore." They sang at church; they sang here also.

The evening grew late and people started to leave. Sean watched Reggie and Kathy walking toward the parking lot—he was taking her home. He and Lonnie followed, walking up to their car. "Lonnie, I think I've lost her for good."

"Oh, stop complaining. I'm tired hearing about Kathy. She'll come back to you if it's God's will. Anyway, there're other girls around."

"I doubt it. God must be ticked at me or he has plans I don't know about."

God's will? Do I believe that? His adolescent insecurities had overwhelmed him, especially since his father's death. A Grand Canyon opened between his childhood beliefs (faith in a caring, all-powerful God) and his recent experiences (anxiety, lack of confidence, failure with girls). Now his heart throbbed like a torn muscle—he had lost the girl he cared for. And how could he go to Torrey Bible if he was losing his faith in God?

Chapter 3

IN 1959 THE AIRLINES were fast. But from sea to shining sea the railroad still pressed her ear close to the beating heart of America. Because Sean McIntosh and his family were vacationing with a relative in New Mexico, he waited for the Santa Fe Super Chief in Albuquerque. Thrilled at the prospects of his trip, he wasn't thinking much about what his mother, brother and sisters were feeling. Elizabeth stood beside the tracks and hugged him a long time, reminding him of his dad's advice: "Son, always remember whose you are." But did Dad mean the McIntoshes or God?

Thus began his journey to Chicago's Torrey Bible Institute. He waved to his family from the window as the great train started moving. His sisters waved and smiled but his brother Paul just stared. He had given little thought to his mother's desolation after the loss of Edwin and now, just three months later, her son. He noticed her brave smile and wet cheek.

A porter, uniformed and capped in Atchison, Topeka and Santa Fe livery, guided him to his private compartment, a luxury paid for by his uncle John. "They charge me whenever someone steals a towel or a water pitcher. I gotta treat passengers good because most of my money I get from tips." He'd apprenticed in the golden age of trains and should be a conductor by now, he told Sean, "but most of 'em 're white. I been workin' this line thirty-two years and if you ride enough, you'll crash. Once we rammed a freight train in Iowa and I got throwed to the floor."

Now the train was laboring over Raton Pass (elevation: 7800 feet) and Sean stared out his window. It had been over four hours since he'd boarded and the smell of the diesel exhaust stoked his excitement. He'd read that right here at Raton Pass in 1878 the ATSF company had gotten into a shooting war with the Denver and Rio Grande Western over railroad rights. ATSF won. As the Santa Fe Chief rounded a curve, Sean caught a glimpse of its 3600-horsepower diesel-electric engine with its red and orange war-bonnet paint scheme.

He couldn't believe he was on his way to Chicago—Carl Sandburg's "city of the big shoulders." He left his sleeping compartment and canvassed the train, browsing the faces, seeking human contact. Continuing forward he entered the Vista Dome car with its seats set high under a glass, camel-hump canopy—informal, conversational space offering a panoramic view of the passing world. It was the 1950s and he noticed that most people still dressed up for train travel.

Lurching toward the far end of the swaying car, he saw an efflorescence of beauty sitting with her parents. With her brown eyes and brunette pageboy hair, she needed no makeup. A strand of tiny pearls circled her neck and a silver bracelet graced her white wrist. Poised and confident but not worldly—a brightly coiffed flower.

She looked up and saw him staring. "My name is Margaret—not Margie, Margaret. These are my parents, Mr. and Mrs. Donaldson." She smoothed her crinoline-stiffened white skirt that complemented her blue sweater and white false collar.

"Hello. I'm Sean McIntosh, going to Chicago to start school. Are you traveling as far as Chicago?"

"Lovely," Mrs. Donaldson interjected. "Won't you join us for dinner?"

Shocked, Sean agreed and then followed them down the aisle. He inhaled the bouquet of smells pouring from the dining car with its white, starched tablecloths and polished silverware. After they sat down he discretely turned a plate over—the Mimbreño China stamp proclaimed it a custom design for the ATSF railroad. Sean thought about his mother's coarse crockery dishes and the oilcloth table covering for ordinary meals, with a *serape* thrown on top for Sundays.

"They say the duck's delicious," Mr. Donaldson told him, so Sean ordered duck. He worried that he carried little money—his mother had packed him a two-day lunch for the trip. The Donaldsons paid his meal; he didn't even think of offering to pay the tip. He never saw Margaret or the Donaldsons again.

The Santa Fe Chief crossed the corner of Colorado at La Junta, then hurtled across the scrolling Great Plains through sleepy little towns. Sean watched the sun's shiny disk disappear behind the Rockies, leaving an orange glow. Soon, moonlight illuminated the cattle grazing the sparse pastures—one cow for every fifteen acres, he'd heard. He remembered Carl Sandburg's lament:

> The buffaloes are gone.
> And those who saw the buffaloes are gone.
> Those who saw the buffaloes by thousands and how they pawed
> the prairie sod into dust with their hoofs, their great heads down
> pawing on in a great pageant of dusk,
> Those who saw the buffaloes are gone.
> And the buffaloes are gone.

Sean sensed the watching eyes of those disappeared ones as the train sped by—ghosts viewing the machine that had stolen their land and culture. When the porter came back to make the bed, Sean over-tipped him.

Later that evening Sean threaded his way down the stairs to the club car where he bought Coke and potato chips and sat down in one of the narrow booths. A girl appeared and slid in opposite. She looked like one of James Fenimore Cooper's women: "all sappy as maples and flat as a prairie." With longer, tousled hair and radiating a faint perfume—was it gardenia?—she appeared to be in her early twenties, long legged and lank as a heron, wearing a white blouse, green Capris and black flats. Not ugly or brazen, she wasn't stunning either, just meat and potatoes. With a touch of lipstick and eye shadow, she wore a patina of respectability.

"What's your name?"

"Sean. Are you here with family?"

"I'm Desiree. Do you like train travel?"

"Yes."

"I hate it. Slow, noisy, too much swaying back and forth. What's your work?"

"I'm going to college in Chicago. Where are you traveling?"

She didn't seem to mind the questions. "I'm going to Chicago too."

"Student?"

"No."

"Oh—what's your work?"

"I'm a stripper." She lifted her eyes from the table and smiled at him.

After that, conversation sort of lagged. Sean felt her magnetism, imagined her working an excited city audience. He fantasized asking her, "Could you show me the first sixty seconds of your act?" Or, "Do you give private performances?" But his inner fundamentalist tether restrained him—he knew he should eschew this type of woman, the type King Solomon warned about in Proverbs. Anyway, he didn't know what to say to her. She walked off without ordering anything.

Later, Sean realized she was trawling. Did she know he slept in a private compartment? Maybe. Her job would require knowing. Like many men, Sean considered himself immune to any seductress.

He walked back to his compartment and lay supine on the bed, pulling up his knees to fit. When he couldn't sleep, he sat up and stared out the window. The passing night hypnotized him. He watched the purple Great Plains morph into flat prairies—vast expanses thinly punctuated with siloes soaring above the grain fields. They sped through Dodge City, Hutchinson, Newton and then Kansas City.

He awaited the dawn wide-eyed. Back home in California, the sky would lighten long before the sun's rays flashed over the high Sierra Nevadas. Here, the train rumbled toward an enthusiastic sun springing out of the distance full bloomed like a bright flower, spreading its radiance everywhere.

Sean ate his last packed sandwich, then returned to the Vista Dome car. He noticed a group of guys sitting together in one corner talking, smelling of testosterone. One guy wore jeans, polished black boots and a white T-shirt with the gold Semper Fi insignia.

"Them Air Force guys are a bunch of f–ing wimps; shouldn't even call 'em military," Semper Fi said. His muscles rippled under his tee shirt. Marine recruits, Sean guessed, just out of Camp Pendleton.

"Yeah; their boot camp training's a joke. I'd give anything to fight an Air Force guy in combat training."

Semper Fi described how to kill someone. "You grab the guy from behind, put your hand over his mouth, run your knife into his kidney and rip upwards so he doesn't scream. If I had my knife, I could kill you right now."

"Cool."

Sean heard nothing about loyalty to President Eisenhower or about defending our great Constitution. They'd all been baptized into a band of brothers ready to kill for their commander and for each other.

Apparently Marine boot camp also taught linguistics—Sean learned a new set of colorful anal-genital metaphors. *Should I be taking notes?* he wondered. Semper Fi begged his friends, "Guys, you have to f–ing help me clean up my f–ing language before I get the f– home. My mother'll be happy to see me but she would freak out at this s–t." His friends laughed.

Jackbooted Semper Fi's talk troubled Sean. *He's a worldly, profane, vulgar fighting machine with a warped set of values,* he thought, *rejecting everything his mother taught him. I'm just a naïve prig in a tough world, inexperienced and old-fashioned. He's joining a killing unit; I'm going to fly airplanes to save the world for Jesus.* He felt morally and spiritually superior, like the Temple Pharisee who pulled his righteous robes around him. Yet he admired Semper Fi's coarse worldliness.

On the way back to his private compartment, he paused to eavesdrop on two guys—both college-bound, he guessed. One was dressed all tweedy with a sports coat, white button-down shirt and a butch-waxed crew cut. When he stood up Sean noticed the dark, belt-in-the-back Ivy League slacks, the brown brogues—the whole outfit evoking an upscale department store ad.

Before he left home, Sean had seen a *Santa Ana Register* article about dressing for college. Three pairs of dress pants, three sports coats, six or eight white shirts and the same number of ties, wingtip shoes and a Fedora hat. But he had no extra money to buy new clothes. He hadn't even thought about *winter* clothes and his parents hadn't suggested any.

Sean had worn tee shirts and jeans in high school or an informal collar shirt or a shirt with a little alligator on the pocket. Converse tennis shoes. He seldom wore a tie but was proud he knew how to tie one in a Windsor knot. He looked down at his brown stadium jacket with its familiar feel and smell—as comfortable as his own skin. But it hung short on his tall frame and now seemed inadequate. Not even a red tag on the back of his nothing-brand jeans. He wondered, *Did I bring the right clothes?* He feared that California casual wouldn't cut it in the East.

Tweedy wasn't focused on his clothes, though. "My dad knows boys will be boys," he said to his friend. He told me, "I know you'll mess around with the girls; just take it easy." They both laughed.

Clearly, he's not looking forward to drinking from the font of knowledge, Sean thought, *but rather he's looking for a hunting ground with few game rules where he'll find great sex.*

Sean walked back and hid hermit-like in his sleeping compartment, staring out the window as the train shot across the prairies with their snapshots of Americana—red flashing lights and crossing guard barriers, miles of wheat, backyards, junkyards, dying main streets. When the train sat at a crossing, he felt alien eyes staring at him like zoo visitors so he pulled down the shade.

Gazing out across the vast lands he imagined every pastured field an airstrip. He longed to "break the bonds of earth" and escape into the clouds. TBI enjoyed a reputation as the best school for mission bush flying but one great obstacle lay ahead—flight camp—two weeks of assessing his aptitude for mechanics and piloting. Twenty-two men were coming to flight camp; a maximum of twelve would survive. He was determined to be one of them.

The Santa Fe Chief rumbled through Iowa, then clickety-clacked over the long steel trestle across the Mississippi, the great river that flowed ten thousand years before Sean was born. This was the first time he'd traveled east of Texas, the first time he'd seen the Mississippi. Eternal, changeless, it took no note of his crossing. They rolled into Illinois—Galesburg, Chillicothe, Streator, Joliet.

The last few miles stretched long as the train crawled through Chicago's vast rail yards. For the first time in his life Sean saw towering piles of black coal. Now he knew he was in "The East." He felt the West receding behind him, remote and irrecoverable.

All the travelers he'd met were about his age but on different tracks. The "brightly coiffed flower" helped him realize that people are kind to strangers. The Semper Fi guy caused him to marvel at how six weeks of brutal training can transform a down-home boy into a hardened killer. The Ivy League students reinforced Sean's stereotype of "worldly" people. The stripper—itinerant, bold, predatory—shocked him; he'd been unprepared for the yellow-toothed, lustful devil nibbling at his own soul. Years later, Sean would soften his judgment of her—doubtless she was as much victim as perpetrator. He would later see her as afflicted with a wasting disease, bereft of grace, trafficking in the fleshly desires of lonely men, nature's child thrown up on the barren shores of modern anonymity.

Over the final miles he wondered, *Who am I now, free from the scrutiny of my family and friends? I'll soon find out. I wonder if I'll ever see Kathy Wilberforce again.*

Chapter 4

KATHLEEN WILBERFORCE WAS THE second child of Ben and Jane Wilberforce. Born and reared in Calvary Community Church, she had grown up as a model fundamentalist. At eleven years old, Pastor Carter baptized her, an expected event that signaled her desire to follow Christ. She shivered as the cold baptismal waters washed over her blue dress that clung to her legs when she exited the pool.

Blossoming into womanhood, Kathleen grew up sheltered by strong moral principles and invigorated by a robust youth program where spring banquets, Easter sunrise services, Christmas parties and youth meetings bonded her to the group.

In high school, along with playing flute in the Orange County Regional Orchestra, she took private piano and organ lessons. Terminally brilliant, her English teacher had told her, "Kathleen; you have an IQ of one-seventy," an embarrassing fact she shared with no one.

When Kathleen was fifteen, Sean McIntosh appeared at Calvary Church. She appreciated his Bible knowledge and interest in overseas mission. And she knew her father would approve. One Sunday she approached him. "Sean, would you like to go to hear my piano recital?"

"I'd like to but I don't have my driver's license yet."

"That's OK. I have my learner's permit and Mother will go along."

Katheen, wearing a gold bracelet, drove up Sean's driveway in the family Buick. Her mother Jane sat in the passenger seat wearing her cloche hat and black sheath dress. Sean slid into the back seat smelling the fine leather upholstery and feeling embarrassed in his brown jacket and Converse tennis shoes. At the recital, Sean listened while Kathleen played a couple of Mozart pieces unfamiliar to him. *I feel underdressed,* he thought. *When I was reading comic books she was learning to play the classics.*

He stared at Kathleen's mother whom Kathy talked about all the time. Jane Lockwood Wilberforce, born in Rhode Island and graduated from Wellesley College, played the piano herself, loved reading the classics and dabbling in watercolor.

Kathleen had told Sean, "She' a dedicated lactivist and I was breast-fed until I entered kindergarten. [Sean blushed.] But then my little brother Sammy came along with Downs Syndrome and Mother was forced to focus on him. When he needed a life-threatening heart operation, she abandoned her plans to open a piano school."

Kathleen talked to Sean every Sunday at church and after he got his driver's license, she went with him to a couple of church parties and then on a Balboa Harbor sailboat cruise where they sucked in the bracing saltwater air and heard the captain yell, "When the boom comes around be sure to duck." Sean was fascinated with her but Kathleen, not so much with him.

Everything changed for Kathleen when Reggie Radcliffe arrived at Calvary Church in spring of 1959. She loved his black eyes and spontaneous smile. He talked about worldly things—movies, fancy restaurants, travels to Hawaii. He impressed Kathleen's mother who told her, "He's immaculately groomed, self-assured, worldly wise. Everything he touches seems organized and animated."

When Reggie Radcliffe was a child, his mother, Gladys Radcliffe, felt her life spiraling out of control. Her husband Lloyd would slap her and when Lloyd gave Reggie hard spankings they left welts. After they divorced, Lloyd disappeared and Gladys worried about Reggie's future as he approached high school.

Then Gladys discovered the hopeful radio messages of Charles Fuller on the Old-Fashioned Revival Hour and opened herself to God as best she knew. After they moved to Stanton, California, she suggested to Reggie, "Let's go Sunday to Calvary Community Church." After combing and waxing his ducktail, he went along reluctantly. He wore a white tee shirt (always ironed) and kept his hands in the back pockets of his new jeans with their precisely rolled cuffs and little red Levi tag above the back pocket. His black penny loafers gleamed in the sun. He soon grew to love the young people's events and especially the cute girls; however, he was less thrilled with Calvary's arcane fundamentalist doctrines and lofty lifestyle standards.

One Sunday after church, Reggie walked up to Kathleen. "Would you like to drive to the beach with me next Saturday?"

Kathleen hesitated, said she would let him know. Reggie enjoyed a certain reputation. She asked her mother. That afternoon Jane walked out to where Ben was mowing the backyard grass, even though most fundamentalists frowned on "working on Sunday." "Ben, you know the new guy at church, Reggie Radcliffe? He asked Kathleen to go out with him."

"I don't think so—I don't trust him, heard things about him. I don't want Kathy to date him." He turned back to mowing. Jane knew he wouldn't change his mind.

Ben and Jane Wilberforce had met at USC—Jane, the cultured sophisticate, Ben, the down-to-earth manly man. After they had been married two years, they went on a whim to a Billy Graham meeting in the Los Angeles Coliseum. After all, everyone was going. That very night Ben walked down front, met with the counselor, filled out the card and turned fundamentalist. Shunning his former dissolute life, he became fiercely disciplined, shedding his bad habits like crap flying out of a manure spreader.

At first, Ben's earthquake-like change pleased Jane. No more drinking. cursing, gambling, no more late nights away. But along with Ben's moral reform came a rigid dogmatism that scared her. Soon Ben (and Jane, reluctantly) joined Calvary Community Church. She chafed at Calvary's strict lifestyle expectations and did not feel guilty when she enjoyed an occasional glass of wine with her non-Calvary friends.

Ben confronted his daughter. "Kathy, I hear Reggie wants to take you out. I've asked around, talked to people, talked to your mother. We don't think you should go out with him. We've heard things about him."

Kathleen said nothing. Her father was so controlling. She embraced Calvary's parochial doctrines and lifestyle standards but longed to explore a wider, more sophisticated world, the world her mother lived in. *I know my father hates Reginald.* (She always referred to him as "Reginald.") *But why should he control me? Father wouldn't like anyone I dated, except Sean. And Sean is so immature, naïve—and boring.*

She felt a magnetic attraction to Reggie, and told Susan, "Reginald lives untethered, spontaneous; he does fundamentalist differently than most Calvary people."

"I don't know, Kathy," said Susan. "I'm not sure he does fundamentalist at all. He went to Orange High School and one of my friends told me about a couple girls he ran around with, girls who carried a reputation. One of 'em was a *Mexican*" (spoken in a low, embarrassed voice).

"But it can't hurt to go out with him just once. And Mother approves."

The next time Reggie asked her out, she said yes. *Am I going with him just to spite Father?* Kathleen wondered. *Maybe.*

Ben was too busy with his attorney practice to notice. Two weeks passed before one of Ben's friends at church happened to mention "Reggie and Kathleen."

Returning home, Ben confronted Jane as she was fixing dinner. "Did she?"

"Did who? What?"

"Did she go out with Reggie?"

"I was going to tell you . . ."

"What? You *knew* she was going out with him and you didn't tell me? I told you we don't want Kathy dating Reggie."

"Oh, Ben—I knew you would be angry but Kathleen's older now and needs to make some of her own decisions."

"Oh? That's because you like Reggie. You'll be sorry if she keeps dating him." He wheeled on his heel and walked away, straight to Kathleen. They had an ugly interchange—Ben, warning her of moral decay and holy hellfire, Kathy, quiet but stubborn in her decision.

Kathleen longed to free herself from her father. The week after graduation she was shopping for new shoes at JCPenney in Santa Ana when she ran into her high school friend Valerie, a girl a couple years older than she who shared her Christian values.

"Valerie, I feel guilty but I need to get away from Father for a while. I'm thinking of moving out."

"Oh? I waitress at the Jolly Roger in Balboa and they always need more help. I've got an apartment in Costa Mesa, not too far from the restaurant. So if they hire you, maybe you can move in with me and share costs. It's a little cramped but maybe we can cook dinners together. It'll be fun."

Chapter 5

AT THE BEGINNING OF hot smoggy summer, Kathleen moved to Costa Mesa with Valerie. Ben objected and Jane cried but they ended up helping her with the rent. Against her father's wishes, Kathleen continued dating Reggie. Her conversations with Sean dwindled—she never told him she was falling for Reggie but she knew he knew. By the time of the luau at Huntington Beach, she'd decided to stop dating Sean altogether. She felt bad for him but he just wasn't as exciting as Reginald—the sharp dresser who was so relaxed and confident.

Kathleen liked Reggie's red 1947 Ford almost as much as Reggie. Its two hundred twenty-one cubic-inch flathead V8 engine sounded great through the twin chrome pipes and when he floored it you could smell burning rubber. He drilled holes in the floorboards to install seatbelts, hung furry white dice from the rearview mirror and drove down to Tijuana to get white and beige tuck-and-roll upholstery. Kept a cloth handy to dust the dashboard. Vacuumed the carpet once a week. Stored a little notebook in the glove compartment where he recorded oil changes and maintenance performed (he reorganized his glovebox items every month). When he got the oil changed he would tell them to blacken the floormats. In the trunk he carried window cleaner and a can of Carnuba car wax. After it rained he would wipe the whole car down with a chamois.

His beautiful chick-magnet car had bagged him a couple of high school girlfriends. For Reggie, girls were the wildlife of the world and he resented the game rules. He always played catch and release and soon lost respect for them, called them "skags."

Reggie lived in the UCLA campus dorms and interned at O'Melveny & Myers law firm in downtown Los Angeles but most Saturdays he would drive down to Kathleen's Costa Mesa apartment to pick her up—always on time. By midsummer they were going out two or three times a week—eating on Olivera Street, with its smells and tastes of chili rellenos, enchiladas and deep-fried chimichangas; surfing the waves at Newport Beach; catching Hollywood Bowl concerts. Once they even rode the Angel's Flight Funicular up the steep rails from Hill to Olive Street.

One weekend they were standing in line at Disneyland for the Jungle Cruise ride when Reggie turned to her. "Do you wanna go see *Ben Hur* at the drive-in?"

"The one with Charlton Hesston?"

"We could go Saturday."

"Oh, I don't know, Reginald. You know what Pastor Carter says about going to the movies . . ."

"Come on, Kathy. He didn't forbid it; he just said it wasn't the greatest idea. And remember, he said we need to make our own choices." (Gaslighting Reggie—using a strategy borrowed from Eve's tempter to get what he wanted. What Pastor Carter had actually said was, "We need *God* to help us make good choices.")

"Besides," Reggie said as he slipped his arm around Kathleen's waist, "it's a drive-in, not a theater." She told herself she should be making her own decisions, so she agreed to go with him.

Reggie—so worldly, so sophisticated. At Calvary Church, "worldly" was not a good thing—members were supposed to be separated from the world. But Reggie's attention flattered Kathleen and all the Calvary girls envied her. She was taken by his self-assurance, impressed by his clear goals, flattered by his interest in her. Besides, Reggie attended church and even took communion, so she assumed what most lovers assume—that they shared similar values.

Sometimes they would come back to her apartment and cuddle while they watched *The Red Skelton Show*. He stayed later and later. They found lots to talk about and his deepening caresses aroused her.

One night in July, after they had parked above Laguna beach to watch the luminescent waves glowing with their blue algae, they drove back to her apartment. "Where's your roommate?" Reggie asked, looking around as he installed himself on the soft couch and parked his feet on the coffee table.

"Overnighting with her parents in Brea." She went to pour Pepsis.

"Wait; I brought something else." He pulled a couple of wine bottles out of a paper sack.

"I'm not sure we ought to be drinking alcohol, Reginald." Pastor Carter preached against alcohol but without Ben's knowledge Jane Wilberforce would enjoy a glass with friends in restaurants. She'd even shared a glass with Kathleen once or twice.

"Do you have a nipper?" Reggie asked.

"What?"

"It's the thing to cut the seal."

"No."

"Never mind; I'll take care of it."

He walked into the small kitchen and found a steak knife that worked. And since Kathleen had no corkscrew he used an ice pick to get the cork out, dropping tiny fragments into the liquid. Sieving out the pieces of cork, he carefully filled two glasses and set them on the coffee table, taking care that they sat parallel and in the center of their coasters.

The wine lubricated the conversation. They refilled, lost count of the glasses. Their hungry arms needed each other.

All Kathleen's fundamentalist training pointed toward chastity. She'd read the little pamphlet, "For Girls Only" and knew that before marriage you drew the line at petting. Petting, as the little pamphlet explained in exciting detail, came in two categories—light and heavy. "Light" meant caressing the breasts. "Heavy" meant below the waist. All petting was off-limits for fundamentalist young people. She assumed Reggie respected these same values.

His caresses became more urgent. "I love you," Reggie said.

"I love you too," she replied. She was convinced that she and he meant it.

He began exploring, crowding the fence, testing her defenses. Kathleen knew girls were supposed to be the gatekeepers, the enforcers who set limits. And she assumed Reggie would honor the bright boundary lines she'd been taught to respect since childhood.

But Reggie began coloring outside the lines, advancing into uncharted territory. "Reginald; what are you doing?" she asked. Reggie just smiled and let his hands do the talking.

He made her feel secure, enfolded and excited. She thought she had strong boundary lines but tonight she felt the lines blurring, shifting and then melting away. Her frontal cortex grew busy inventing a rationale for what the little lizard part of her brain wanted. *I can stop any time,* she reasoned. *Reginald respects me and won't push me too far . . .* Gradually, she released her young, unpracticed heart.

That night Reggie didn't go home.

In the morning he got up, dressed and gave Kathleen a patronizing kiss. "I've got to go, Honey. I'll call you tomorrow." Then he walked out.

Kathleen sank into her easy chair with a throbbing headache, confused and crying. *What was I thinking? I violated Father's wishes going out with Reggie. And Mother—I can't bear to disappoint her. I'll never tell either of them.*

Reggie called her the next day—"Hi, Kathy; can we get together this weekend?"

She knew she bore as much guilt as Reggie did. But he acted as if sex wasn't a big deal. She was angry he had violated her, had not even asked her. "Reggie, I never want to see you again." She slammed the receiver down before he could answer and stared across the bleak landscape of her future—without Reggie.

Sean's First Year

Chapter 6

Saturday, 18 July 1959. At 1:30 p.m., one hour late, the Santa Fe Chief pulled into Chicago's opulent LaSalle Street Station. Sean read on a plaque that the station was built in 1903 and was featured in Alfred Hitchcock's recent movie, *North by Northwest.*

Schoolboy-confident, he stepped off the train and for the first time in his life felt hot, dripping humidity. His shirt clung to his skin as he clutched his suitcase and duffle bag and waded into a sea of people—boys selling the *Chicago Tribune*, red caps hustling luggage, parents herding their children. He looked around and thought, *There's sure lots of people here I don't know.*

The huge city—vast, industrial, commercing with the whole world. He wanted to experience it all. He'd read Carl Sandburg's "Chicago" poem at school:

> Hog Butcher for the World,
> Tool Maker, Stacker of Wheat,
> Player with Railroads and the Nation's Freight Handler;
> Stormy, husky, brawling,
> City of the Big Shoulders . . .

He flagged a Checker cab. "Torrey Bible Institute, LaSalle Street, please."

The cabbie nodded and after a short ride, pulled over. "That there's the institute."

Sean over-tipped the cabbie, got out and found himself staring up at TBI's welcoming stone arch. Built on Chicago's near north side, TBI stood as a fundamentalist citadel of right doctrine and right lifestyle, gated and ghettoed to seal out the world's wild winds, fortressed against Chicago's secular metropolis like a jealous older woman who whispers, "Distrust the world. Seize the old certainties. You bloom best in the old soil." TBI also sealed out dangerous modernists such as Norman Vincent Peale of New York's Marble Collegiate Church, of whom fundamentalists said, "[St.] Paul is appealing but Peale is appalling."

He walked through the great entrance arch inhaling the old stone smell along with the spirit of TBI's founder, R.A. Torrey, the nineteenth-century shoe-salesman-turned-preacher who had said, "Expect great things from God; attempt great things for God." Sean expected and was going to attempt. The year was 1959, he was eighteen and all things were possible.

But he wondered about the depth of his faith. He had checked "born again" on his application, meaning he was a committed Christian. He'd walked forward in a few revival meetings and had been baptized at age twelve. But was he here for a Christian education or for aviation training? He'd sucked up fundamentalist Christianity with his mother's milk but he assumed everyone here possessed more faith than he did. In truth, he felt only fundamental-ish. He wondered if even TBI's faculty could quiet his doubts.

Climbing the stone steps into Cromwell Hall's lobby, he spit his spent chewing gum into a wastebasket and presented himself to the woman at the desk.

"Hi. I'm Sean McIntosh, here for flight camp."

"Welcome. Please let me check." Her brow wrinkled behind her horn-rimmed glasses. "Oh . . . flight camp isn't here," she told him. You're supposed to be out at the airport."

"Really? How do I get out there?" He hoped he wouldn't arrive late.

She made a couple of calls. "I think we'll overnight you here and tomorrow the airport van can run you out." She picked up the phone. "I'll call Ma Graham; she'll find you a room."

Soon Ma Graham walked in. A small, gray gust of a woman who wrapped her long hair in a bun at the nape of her neck, she wore a darker, flowered dress, sensible black shoes, no jewelry and walked bowlegged. The dorm mothers slept in the residence halls at night to shepherd the students. (It was the fifties and colleges still practiced *in loco parentis.*) He liked her at once—an urban incarnation of his own grandmother.

They exited Cromwell and walked across the "quad"—an accidental, cobblestoned space bereft of grace, hemmed in between brick walls and displaying not a spear of grass. The institute sat crammed upon a single city block and Norbert Hall loomed ahead, a five-story building smelling of old moist brick, that housed male students. "How was your long train trip?" Ma Graham asked. "I hope you like it here."

"I liked sitting in the observation car and watching America go by the window."

To Sean, reared in progressive California, Norbert Hall looked like an ancient pile of bricks. The entryway with its waxed linoleum floor seemed well-maintained but smelled musty.

"Not many students are here summers," she said as they took the stairs to the second floor. "There's the bathroom, on the right."

Then they entered a high-ceilinged room—plastered walls, heavy dark wood trim, a corner sink and mirror. "I've laid out a couple of towels and a washcloth. The dining hall serves supper at 5:30. They don't like you to be late. My room is near the elevator if you need anything." Then she smiled and disappeared.

Sean surveyed the bunk beds, two study desks, two dressers and a glowing globe hanging from the ceiling. No telephone or TV. Clothes hooks but no closet. A couple electric outlets. He'd never seen such an old building with its (unused) gas light sconces still protruding from the walls. Ma Graham had told him TBI prohibited heating elements—coffee pots, hot plates, space heaters—although he later learned some guys bootlegged them in.

The unscreened window stood open, sucking in the hot, moist air. He leaned out and peered into the quad below where a couple students sat on cast-iron railings along a basement stairwell. One yelled something unintelligible up at him.

The floor squeaked as Sean walked down the hall, then took the stairs down to ground level and out the door. A huge pile of coal that foretold winter's cold sat mounded up in a corner lot. Several multi-story buildings stared down on him. To the east he saw Cromwell Hall that held administrative offices and classrooms; to the west, a driveway exiting onto Wells Street. To the southeast stood Hargreaves Hall, a newer, ten-story brick building that housed the single women students.

That evening Sean ate dinner with just a few summer school students in the vast dining hall then returned to his room and read his Bible some. Bible smart, he had memorized verses, entered Bible competitions, pasted verses on his bedroom wall. On his Torrey application, Sean had affirmed he believed in the "verbal, plenary inspiration" of the inerrant text. His father Edwin had once assured him, "Sean, the Bible cannot have any errors because God wrote it." End of discussion. He went to bed early but with the heat, the unfamiliar humidity and the wail of distant sirens, he turned and tossed on sweaty sheets. *Everybody I know lives two thousand miles away,* he thought. But he thrilled at the thought of flight camp.

The next morning he awakened with a sore jaw caused by clenching and grinding his teeth, a habit he'd developed in high school. Nerves, he guessed. The hazy Chicago air sieved the Sabbath sun that poured through Sean's open window and caressed his face.

TBI sent over the airport van to carry him out to the school's Maple Plain Airport. His stomach churned. Flight camp—one single chance to make the aviation program. The next two weeks would decide his whole future. But he felt confident, knowing God had called him here and would give him success.

Chapter 7

I laugh to see your tiny world, your toys of ships, your cars.
I rove an endless road unfurled where the milestones are the stars.

—Gordon Boshell

After two weeks at flight camp Sean McIntosh and fellow candidate Aaron Byler stood in Maple Plain Airport's ready room scanning the list of students accepted into the three-year program. "It seems short," Sean said.

Always excited about aviation, he had pursued no goals except flying. He realized all that had brought him to this place so far from his home, the place that held so many of his hopes. His father would be thrilled. He scanned down the list of accepted students—

Downton, Earl
Hardy, Dan . . .

Sean thought back to the first day of flight camp when he'd arrived a day late. He had disembarked from TBI's van in front of Maple Plain's big hangar and walked in grasping his two suitcases, casting his eye on the sky.

Mr. Norman Richards greeted him. "Welcome to Maple Plain, Sean. I'll show you your bed." Thirty-something, square-jawed, clean-shaven with glistening dark brown hair, Richards stood in sartorial splendor, wearing a crisp, collared shirt, beige cotton pants and black shoes. A serious man on a mission.

Richards led him up the steel stairs to the loft above the hangar where twenty-two cots sat in two neat rows. "It's all temporary—after two weeks the accepted students will find their housing elsewhere." Inhaling the faint smell of solvent, Sean parked his suitcase on his assigned cot and laid his

Bible next to the pillow. Richards turned to the guys who were already settled in. "Men, meet Sean McIntosh."

Surveying the room, Sean recognized one person—Dan Hardy, a high school friend from California. Black-booted and confident, he smirked. "Hi, Sean. Welcome to TBI's All-weather Airmaple Plainport and Country Club."

Sean smiled. "Dan—I'm glad you're here; I'm a little late." Most of the candidates seemed about his age; a few were older. In two weeks, the instructors would winnow these down from twenty-two to twelve or fewer. Unlike his high school where Sean remembered feeling like chopped liver in a steakhouse, here he felt like an equal among friendly guys all sailing in the same boat.

"The Army built this hangar in the 1940s," Richards said. Sean noticed the exposed steel trusses supporting a half-Quonset roof. Richards walked him to the railing and gestured out over the gray hangar floor below, clean enough to eat from. "That T-6 there is a WWII trainer with a 600-horsepower Pratt & Whitney radial engine. We use that blue and white Comanche next to it for cross-country flights. And the Seabee with its pusher prop over in the corner is a WWII amphibian that leaves the ground only reluctantly. Those little floats support the wingtips on the water." Sean stared—could those stubby wings lift anything into the air?

He couldn't believe he was standing there. For years he had dreamed one bright dream—flying. He'd hung around airports and imagined every farmer's field a potential airstrip. But today, reality. His pulse quickened.

Descending the stairs, Sean ducked as he entered the door into the ready room, its dark wood walls smelling of new lacquer. Richards pointed to the bulletin board. "We'll post the successful candidates here."

Sean stared at the blank space. *In two weeks, I'll see my name there.*

They approached a tall man, sober and stiff —Richard Nixon stiff—who stood in one of the offices. "This is our chief pilot, Mr. Van Dixon. He came to Maple Plain Airport from the Air Force Academy because, he says, he got tired looking at the backs of cadets' heads."

Van Dixon looked at them without smiling. "Hello, Sean." And then to Richards, "Did you see the food van pulling in yet?"

Sean shook his hand thinking, *If I mess up, he'll eat me like a baby marshmallow rabbit.*

They exited the admin building into a languid July day that smelled of new-mown grass. Cumulus clouds floated above the flight line where a few planes were tied down. A dozen plastic lawn chairs sat lined up on the trodden grass. Richards said, "The flight students eat lunch here and listen to Paul Harvey on the radio." (Sean remembered the famous voice: "Paul Harvey . . . Good day.")

A yellow Cessna 140 sat on the flight line beside a twin-engine Apache and beside these, three yellow J–3 Cubs, their wings rocking in the breeze. "You'll fly one of the J–3s with Mr. Latham." Sean didn't mention he'd never flown a plane.

They looked out across the wind-rippled grass field where little yellow cones marked out the runways. A huge yellow segmented circle sat in the distance, signaling traffic patterns for incoming pilots. "In twenty-knot winds, the windsock inside that circle there stands straight out. The J–3s are a handful in that kind of wind."

The next morning the candidates ate a hangar breakfast where the smell of pancakes mixed with the smell of grease and solvent. The guy next to Sean said, "Hi; I'm Aaron Byler from Pennsylvania. Where're you from?"

Sean put down his fork. "Pennsylvania? I've never been anywhere east of here. I'm from California." He didn't mention he'd never heard of anyone named "Aaron."

"I thought so. You have a California accent. And I've never traveled west of Illinois."

"There's no such thing as a California accent."

"Oh yeah? Well, maybe I just imagined it." Aaron smiled as he brushed back his careless, sand-colored hair that peeped from under his trademark red "Queen Dairy" bill cap. "Weird to think half of these guys won't be around after next week."

"Yeah, I was thinking the same thing. I'm nervous about mechanics, even the flying, but I feel so focused, feel like I was born for this."

After breakfast they walked over to the maintenance building—a low, white wooden structure with heavy sliding doors, just big enough for three or four of the smaller aircraft. Richards introduced them to Mr. Masterson, an artifact from WWII days. He was a no-nonsense, blue-collar kind of guy in his fifties, a bit on the pudgy side, with roundish head and fat neck. He stroked a thin moustache over a never-smiling mouth. His checked shirt was stuffed inside jeans held up by a thick belt with a brass buckle. He'd served as a wartime aviation mechanics instructor at Purdue University and now was chief mechanic here at Maple Plain.

For the next two weeks Sean felt like a tourist in a foreign country—airplane maintenance presented an exotic landscape with all the road signs in an unknown language. That first Monday, Masterson gathered the candidates around a long table and introduced them to a "turnbuckle." (Sean had never heard of it.)

"This brass tube has an eye-screw at each end for tensioning aircraft control cables. I want you to safety-wire this." He gave each of them a turnbuckle, twenty-four inches of stainless-steel safety wire and a page of opaque diagrams and instructions.

Sean looked over at Earl Downton, one of the farm boys he'd just met. Dexterous, confident in his green John Deere cap, he plunged in at once, the turnbuckle task seemingly as familiar as his nose. Sean thought, *He's safety-wired turnbuckles on thrashing machines since he was five. I hate him.*

After a few minutes Sean had coiled a tangled ball of safety wire somewhere in the vicinity of the turnbuckle and placed his work atop the crumpled instructions. Mr. Masterson peered down at it. "You done?" He wrote something in his little notebook, then turned to give the guys their next task—riveting aluminum ribs.

Before lights out that evening, Richards gathered the men for prayers. Sean looked around and asked himself if any of the other guys doubted their faith. If so, they weren't showing it.

Next morning, Mr. Lance Latham led the first group of men out to one of the J-3 Cubs on the flight line and stood under the wing with his hand gripping the strut. "Gentlemen, this is an airplane." They wrote it down.

Sean towered over Lance Latham who stood shorter than average with his styled black hair, button-down shirt, crisply pressed pants and black flight boots. Neatness gone to church. He'd flown in Peru for JAARS, the air arm of Wycliffe Bible Translators. As serious as a heart attack, he smelled of cologne and seemed oppressed by an unaccountable sadness.

He led the guys around the yellow, fabric-covered plane. "The J-3 weighs 680 pounds empty. Punch your thumb in the fabric. If it dimples, the fabric's rotted. Always look underneath the plane for any tears." Sean ran his hand over the sleek, lacquered skin. "Climb up on the wheel and look into the gas tank," Latham said. "This wire in the cap shows you how much fuel is in the tank. Make sure it's not sticking." Sean bounced it up and down.

He peered at the sixty-five-horsepower Continental engine with its black, finned cylinders bulging out from the cowling like the eyes of some huge prehistoric insect. Then Latham stooped down under the engine cowling. "Here's the gascolator. Drain a little gas to see if there's any water in the fuel. Airplane engines don't like water." (Spoken dryly, without the hint of a smile.)

The day it was Sean's turn to fly he poured himself into the J-3's rear canvas sling-seat and buckled up, grinding his teeth so hard his jaws hurt. He could almost feel the ceiling liner against his head but his height helped him see ahead better. Latham hauled himself into the front seat and closed the bottom part of the split door.

Since the J-3 had no electrical system or starter, Mr. Masterson came out to hand-prop the plane. "Throttle closed, switch closed," he ordered. He pulled the prop through three or four times. "Prime, switch open, throttle cracked." Latham pumped the primer twice, reached up to turn the magneto switch to "both," then opened the throttle a little. Masterson swung his leg, then pulled the prop down sharply. The engine belched, coughed out a bit of gray smoke, then settled down to a tractor-like clacking. Sean inhaled the sweet smell of exhaust.

The J-3 had no intercom, so Latham bellowed, "Taxi 'er out but keep the control stick back in your lap. Steer with the rudders and push with your heels to brake. Easy on the turns—it'll want to swing around." Latham advanced the throttle and Sean pulled the slack stick back. They started moving but he couldn't see anything except Latham's haircut. "S-turn so you can see ahead," Latham yelled. Sean S-turned, smelling the sweet-cut grass through the open window, then veered to the left. "Keep your feet on the rudders. It won't steer itself."

Since a brisk wind blew from the south, they taxied out to the head of runway one-eight, checked engine operation and control movement, then moved into position for takeoff. Latham said, "She'll want to swing left. Keep 'er straight with the right pedal so we don't end up in the weeds."

As Latham closed the side window and firewalled the throttle, they accelerated amid the smell of oil and burnt avgas. As the controls came alive, he felt Latham's slight control movements under his own hands and feet. Sean overcontrolled on the rudders and the plane lurched right, then left. But the tail soon rose, then the nose lifted. They bounced into the air and began climbing.

Mr. Latham turned his head and yelled, "Keep the nose about four inches above the horizon to climb. Look left and right—hold both wings the same distance above the horizon." Sean sat rigid, his sweaty left hand on the throttle and his right hand clamped around the control stick. When he leaned, he felt like the airplane would tilt sideways. He tried to avoid moving the stick to keep from banking. They leveled off under scattered clouds. "And keep looking around for other airplanes," Latham yelled.

Far below lay a sparkling, crazy-quilt patchwork—roads, railroads, woods, cornfields and a small lake reflecting summer's light. "The J-3 tops out at eight-five mph on a still day and with a headwind the cars pass you on the expressway," Latham said. Sean couldn't see the horizon well but pushed the stick front, back, sideways, trying to keep the plane level. If he even thought about diving, climbing or banking, the airplane responded.

"You're overcontrolling. Just relax and let the plane fly itself."

Right.

After they flew around the practice area twenty minutes or so, Latham said, "Let's head back to the airport. On your approach to land, reduce power and establish a glide at sixty mph. The nose will ride about eight inches below the horizon." When they throttled back to descend, Sean felt the plane falling out from under him. "Use the trim control to trim the nose up," Latham said. They sunk down, turned ninety degrees and lined up on the south airstrip. "Just before we cross Thorndale Avenue, waggle your head to check for cars." He waggled. The J-3's wheels touched the smooth grass, swerved, then rolled to a stop. As Sean taxied back to the gas pump, Latham said, "Be sure to keep up your speed on final approach. You don't want to run out of altitude, airspeed and ideas. And you need to relax more."

Two weeks passed quickly; then came decision day. Lowering, bulbous clouds scudded overhead, threatening rain. After the men ate a quiet breakfast, they sat around talking for an hour or so out on the flight line. Nobody mentioned the soon-to-be-posted acceptance list.

Then Aaron Byler walked over to where the men sat. "Richards just told me he posted the names."

Adrenalin rush. This was it, the day Sean had dreamed of since he was in Santa Ana Junior High School. This day, he was convinced, God would begin fulfilling his life plan. He knew he'd messed up on the turnbuckle assignment and was a little tight in the stomach flying the J-3, but he felt confident. He had to make it; he had no other plans. He'd always felt he was special, adored as he was by his parents and other adults. His Bible teaching told him he was chosen. How could he not be chosen?

The heavens opened and the rain drenched them, revealing Aaron's muscles through his wet shirt. Sean asked himself, *What would it take to have muscles like that?* They processed into the ready room where his shoes sloshed on the wood floor. He and Aaron would face their common destiny together.

Sean's jaw tightened and his hands sweated. He felt like he was back in junior high school looking at the list of guys who'd made the basketball team. He thought of the years of his life, his early faith, his longing for aviation and for overseas missions. He missed his father, longed for him to be here at this, his greatest moment.

Twelve names were posted. He scanned down the list.

Downton, Earl

Hardy, Dan

Landis, Stan . . .

His name should appear next. It didn't. He hadn't made the cut. Aaron hadn't either. He felt nauseated, like he was drifting in a dystopian dream world where all the love, all the joy, was gone forever. His blossoming dream disappeared, ripped up root and branch. *I thought sure I'd get in but I didn't.*

When they walked out they saw that the rain had come and gone, leaving the hangar roof steaming with humidity. Neither spoke. Sean felt like his whole future was a gray slate—dreary, and devoid of joy.

Soon they climbed into the TBI van and rode back downtown in silence—what was there to talk about? Sean's only goal was to become a missionary pilot and he'd just washed out of flight camp. His beautiful vision stalled, spiraled down and crashed.

When the van rolled into TBI's quad, the guys disembarked into the sultry Chicago air and walked over to search for their temporary dorm rooms on Norbert Hall's fifth floor. Sean turned to Aaron. "Latham was my instructor; you had Richards. I wonder which instructor washed the most guys out?"

"Earl and Dan passed flight camp so easy—they're naturals," Aaron said, "Why do some guys make it and some not? Is it aptitude? What else are they looking for?"

Sean inhaled the waxed smell of the wood floor as he stretched out on his bed—wistful, reflective and just sad—actually, devastated. He was a glass-half-empty kind of guy who tended to focus on his troubles and failures rather than on his successes. *Am I just fated to fail? Should I continue trying? Was aviation my own selfish ambition or God's will? Where is God in all this, anyway? And what now? I've never considered anything except flying.*

His thoughts drifted back to the beach luau with his Calvary Church friends—it seemed a long time ago. He thought about his family, all the people who were cheering for him. Kathleen Wilberforce was now two thousand miles away and anyway, she was dating Reggie. How could he compete with Reggie? Reggie had organized his whole world, laid out his future following a track that would lead him to wealth and worldly success. Kathy had slipped away from him like a short thread slipping through the needle's eye. He flopped on the bed and tried to sleep.

Chapter 8

SEAN LAY SLEEPLESS IN his Norbert Hall room, ruminating about his spectacular flight camp failure. But, against all expectations, the reluctant sun rose the next morning. He tried to cheer himself up. He was in Chicago! A city of shining skyscrapers and endless possibilities, a city where fortunes are made, a living, breathing city trafficking with the whole world. Nobody knew him here. He could leave behind the awkwardness and loneliness of high school and start over.

These first days, talk frequently turned to faith. Once when they were hanging out in Aaron's dorm room Sean asked him, "When did you get born again?"

He frowned. "Well, I guess I don't know. I joined the Mennonite church when I was sixteen, got baptized and confessed my faith. So I guess that coulda been when." His response shocked Sean—Aaron wasn't speaking the language of fundamentalism. How could he be saved? Later that night, he continued. "Sean, 'born again' talk is foreign to my Mennonite people back home in Pennsylvania. Besides, they think it's prideful saying that you know you're born again, and pride is one of the worst sins."

For the first time Sean entertained the possibility that some people other than fundamentalists could be committed Christians.

What would Kathy think of the Mennonites? *I guess I should forget Kathy.* He wondered if he should start dating some TBI girls. Who? He couldn't think of anyone nicer than Kathy. But as the months passed, he became convinced he would never date her again.

Failure bonds people and he and Aaron became fast friends. They started running around with other guys who were determined to commit sophomoric acts of mischief. For the first time in his life Sean felt accepted by a fellowship of friends. Regardless of his failure, maybe he would stay awhile at TBI. He considered choosing a different major. He could still become a missionary, perhaps a Bible translator. Aaron said to him, "Why don't we take some summer school, say, I and II Corinthians?" They signed up and, thanks to no interest, effort or study, Sean received the first two Cs of his life.

Then August arrived and the days turned muggy—a stifling, dripping humidity. Sean stood with Aaron in front of Norbert Hall looking across the quad, filling his lungs with the moist air. Dan Hardy walked toward him, wearing his black flight boots. *When will I be worthy of wearing black flight boots?* Sean wondered.

Since Aaron had already signed up to room with someone else, Sean approached Dan. "Do you need a roommate for the fall?"

"Hi Sean. Oh; I'm already rooming with Earl." He walked away.

Of course. Earl and Dan both made the flight camp cut, so they would live here and commute out to the airport. Sean turned to Aaron. "You know, all breathing life separates into two species—the flyboys and the groundlings—and we're slithering along here earthfast."

Then Fulton Buford walked up. "S-Sean, w-w-would ya'll like to room with me?" Every time he opened his mouth, Fulton stuttered in a Deep South drawl. But his friendliness endeared him to everyone. *We love people for their weaknesses, not their strengths*, Sean mused. Fulton had blond, untamed hair and rough, white hands. He never walked; he loped. His red, white and blue tee shirt with "Freedom" written on the back was a gift from his father. He fingered his pocket watch that had a silver chain looped to his belt.

Dear Fulton— kind and gentle, even a teeny bit effeminate—the guys didn't do much with him but the girls loved him. From deep Louisiana, a recent convert from Mormonism, Fulton had swallowed fundamentalism whole and now wanted to get all the Bible he could get. He dreamed of becoming a minister and thus had enrolled at TBI.

Many Northerners still nurtured certain stereotypes of Southerners—poverty, low education, low culture. The guys teased him: "First time you've seen paved streets, Fulton? How do your new shoes fit, Fulton? Can we show you how to turn on the electric lights, Fulton?"

Fulton took all this with good grace—he seemed the most decent human being Sean had ever met. Sean remembered making no close high school friends and now he longed for acceptance. He could overlook Fulton's parochial habits. "Sure, Fulton; let's sign up." They roomed together for the next two years.

Several weeks had passed when Sean received good news. He found out he could enroll at the downtown campus in pre-aviation and reapply for the mission flight program in two years. He thrilled as his dead dream stirred to life. Henceforth he would become a model student. Even though he felt "fated to fail," he couldn't afford to blow his second shot at flight camp.

Like the mothers of most teenage guys, Sean's mother had always washed his clothes so at TBI he needed to ask somebody how to run the washing machine and dryer. The first time he tried he fed two quarters into the washer, winced at the fumes when he opened the bleach bottle, then poured a glug down the washing machine chute before turning the water on— bleaching a big white spot on his expensive blue shirt.

Fulton showed him how to iron clothes. The first time he tried, he smelled burnt cloth—he'd perforated the collar of one of his dress shirts. Fulton told him, "S-Sean; w-why don't you send your shirts out like ah do? It's not e-expensive." After smelling scorch a couple more times Sean gave up and like most of his dormmates sent his white shirts out to launder at twenty-five cents apiece. They came back washed, ironed, starched and fresh-smelling.

One night, Fulton said to Sean, "Hey; l-l-let's go over to Jim's room. I reckon we could ask him to play his sax for us." Jim Whitman, a senior at TBI, served as the Norbert Hall resident assistant. So they and a couple of the other guys stomped down the stairs to Jim's room.

As Sean deposited himself into Jim's easy chair, one of the guys asked, "Jim, why is TBI so *ruley*?"

Jim explained that the rules encouraged a Christian lifestyle. He intoned the list: "No smoking or alcohol, even in the summer. No facial hair or long hair on men. Good table manners, collar shirts, no jeans, shined shoes (no tennis shoes). Girls can wear only a touch of makeup, no short hair, no facial jewelry, no pants. Their skirts must reach at least down to the knees."

Sean took all these practices for granted—it mirrored the world of his childhood. Most of these rules reflected American middle-class lifestyle norms but TBI elevated them to a test of biblical fidelity and Christian piety. Sean rarely worried about clothes—he usually wore a collar shirt and slacks—but he carried a little brush for his treasured white suede shoes.

Another guy asked Jim, "I don't understand girls. I don't know . . . What do they want, anyway?"

Jim Whitman closed his eyes, pretending to ponder the opposite gender. "It's hard to say . . . Men seem so simple—they really only want one thing. [No one in the room dared ask what that "thing" was.] But girls are different. They want security, want a man to adore them, want a home, children—a whole bunch of things."

Sean didn't ask Jim if girls liked sex. He assumed sex was something guys wanted, something girls reluctantly gave.

Then the talk shifted to theology. As he walked to Jim's little fridge and helped himself to a coke, Fulton asked: "Jim, how does 'p-predestination' work, anyway? If God knows everything in advance, knows if ya'll are chosen or not chosen w-why does it matter what ya'll do?" As the carbonation from the coke reached his nose, he winced—he'd never drunk Coke in his Mormon childhood. He raised his eyebrows and looked at Jim.

Jim Whitman sat his own coke down on the table. "Fulton, from our side of heaven, we choose, and if we choose Christ, we have confidence that God's Spirit moved us and that we're chosen. We need to listen to God telling us what to do. We can't just wait for God to move us to do something."

"G-God works in mysterious ways," Fulton said.

As they got up to go, Sean kept quiet. These sessions with Jim made him feel accepted—he loved hanging out with the guys. However, it tightened his stomach, raised dark questions in his mind. He ducked as he exited through the door into the hallway.

One day that October Sean sat in the TBI barber chair toweled, shorn and smelling of menthol. His friend Doug walked by the door and yelled in, "Just cut everything off above the neck." A small joke but Doug's jibe thrilled him. He was making friends here, something he'd found difficult to do in high school. He could start over. This possibility numbed the pain of his doubts and failures.

That evening Doug recruited some guys. "Hey, let's grab Langston and shave his moustache off." Langston Brooks, one of the few colored students at TBI, approached life as a cross to bear. As serious as a heart attack, he wore a clipped moustache—a topographical feature rare at TBI and considered by some to be ostentatious.

Sean, Fulton, Doug and two other guys took off chasing Langston who ran down the Norbert Hall stairs and into the men's bathroom. Doug held the door and yelled, "We've got him."

Fulton shouted, "H-hold him; A-Ah've got the razor."

Sean led the charge into the dark bathroom. He heard a whoosh in the blackness, then his face felt sticky and menthol-cool. "Hey, what's happening?" Sean and Fulton ran out of the bathroom, all shaving-cream-flecked.

It was a sting! Doug and Langston stood there laughing. "Hey, you guys look great."

But as Sean stood rubbing the shaving cream off, the peripatetic Dean Clarence Winters—the guys referred to him as "six feet of snow"—appeared like an epiphany. Fulton turned to run but gave himself away: "Lawd have mercy." Several of the guys swept up the stairs or into the adjacent halls. Winters pursued one boy into the gymnasium but an old war wound had given him a persistent limp and he soon gave up the chase. Sean stood stapled to the floor.

Winters challenged him. "What's going on here?"

"Dean Winters, we were just playing a little practical joke. We didn't mean anything by it."

"Sean, you know better. This kind of behavior might keep you out of the aviation program." Winters was not happy. His mouth twitched and his whole head turned beet red. Then he turned and limped away.

Sean left, licking the shaving cream off his lips. Totally worth it, he thought.

Chapter 9

September 1959. Despite her shame over her liaison with Reggie, Kathleen Wilberforce decided to move into the Biola College dorm in downtown Los Angeles and start her freshman classes. Biola—an acronym for "Bible Institute of Los Angeles"—stood at the navel of 1950s California fundamentalism professing strict doctrine and holding Puritan-like lifestyle standards that made no allowance for worldly entertainments (dancing, movies) and no allowance for sexual immorality.

Kathleen's spirit hurt. Here, she was looking for answers, searching for an elusive forgiveness after her lustful lapse. She would pace the residence halls where the low sconce lighting illuminated narrow hallways. Always alert and on guard, she feared the women's dean would find out about her great sin.

Kathleen knew she'd knocked the bar off its pins, failed the test, disappointed and angered her God. Her teachers didn't help. They whispered God's grace but shouted out his judgment—good teachers but they insisted on God's perfect standards for a fallen humanity. In class, her mind wandered. She felt numb, cut off, as if she'd fallen to the bottom of a narrow pit with no way out. She learned a lot of Bible but nothing that spoke to her pain. She had failed God, sensed his anger, did not know how to reconcile.

She never told anybody at Biola about Reggie—not the women's dean, not her counselor, not her dorm mother—she just couldn't. She decided to work this through for herself, always paralyzed in fear that someone would find out.

But how could people *not* find out? One day she exited the dorm and walked across campus. The Biola girls were standing around like celibate showcase mannequins with their starched blouses, tight skirts and quaffed hair. Were they talking about her? She felt like Hawthorne's Hester Prynne, felt as if she were wearing a big red badge: "Fallen Woman."

She'd told Reggie she never wanted to date him again but he continued to wear her down, stalked her cougar-like, tried to breach her defenses. A couple of times Reggie drove down from UCLA to Biola but she refused to talk to him. She knew she was also at fault but Reggie had betrayed her trust. Worse, he never showed any regret for their brief union. The flames of her burning heart extinguished, leaving only cold ashes. She accepted no dates and sought solace in her friends and in her flurried activities.

At first, this worked. But when September turned into late October, Kathleen became distressed. She'd missed her period a month ago and now her next period was not coming. One morning she vomited into the toilet, the sour taste lingering in her mouth.

After another week she visited her doctor, alone.

"Kathy, we'll have to take a urine test, then wait a bit," Dr. Nesland told her.

"I don't have any urinary problems."

"They inject your urine into a mouse. If you're pregnant, your urine has hCG in it and it'll make the mouse start to ovulate. If it does, you're pregnant."

"No, really. Is there any way you can tell? I don't think I am."

"Yes, really. This test will tell. We need to check you out."

She returned in a few days. "I just came because I wanted to make sure . . ."

Dr. Nesland had delivered Kathleen, seen her throughout her childhood. He hated to be the bearer of bad news. "We got your results back. You're pregnant, Kathy."

"I wanted to see you to make sure I was just imagining things." She stared uncomprehending at his medical certificates on the wall.

"No, Sweetheart—you're pregnant."

Silence.

Then, "Impossible. I was only one time with my boyfriend."

More silence.

This is what happens to bad girls, Kathleen thought as she sat disconsolate in her dorm room that night, *girls who are promiscuous or careless.* Then she told herself God was punishing her for giving in to Reginald. God had very high standards and she had violated them. *But how could the beginning of a precious new life be a punishment from God?*

When she would walk across campus she felt all eyes on her, felt like everybody knew her great secret. She imagined their scorn and condemnation. She dreaded talking to her parents, especially her father, but she could not continue to hide her condition. That same night she left Biola and drove home for the weekend.

After the family dinner, Ben Wilberforce retired to his study as usual—he was working on a big liability case. Kathleen and her mother sat on the couch looking out the plate glass window at the fading fall sun, making small talk. Then, "Mother, I have something I need to tell you."

Jane turned to search her eyes but Kathleen's head was bowed. Silence.

"Mother, I've missed my period twice now."

"Kathleen, you should go to the doctor. You must be ill."

"I did, Mother; he said I'm pregnant."

"Wha . . . That can't be . . . I . . . You . . . That's impossible!"

"It's true, Mother. Nobody else knows." [Eyes averted.]

For the first time in years, Jane Lockwood Wilberforce was at a loss for words. After several minutes Kathleen lifted her teary eyes. "I can't stay at Biola and I know you and Father won't want me back home. O Mother, I don't think Reginald saw having sex as anything special. I do not want anyone to know I am pregnant." She shifted around and pulled her legs up under her. "Please don't tell Father."

Silence. Jane grimaced, digging her long fingernails into the arm of the couch. In that moment, Kathleen knew her confession had breached the hedge around Jane's hygienic life-garden. She had big plans for her little girl, daughter of her heart, daughter of her dreams—plans like an advanced college degree, music performance, a godly husband, children.

Kathleen stared into Jane's vacant, still-dry eyes and realized that Jane's own ordered world was evaporating like a California coastal fog. She saw all her mother's highest hopes for her daughter draining away.

Kathleen knew her mother was thinking about damage control, about how she could bring her well-tended sanctuary back into perfection. She was probably thinking to herself, h*ow can I ever face Ben again?*

Then, "Kathleen, I assume it's Reginald. Have you told him?"

"No."

"I doubt he will be thrilled. I hate to suggest it but have you considered an abortion?"

Kathleen started. "Mother, what? You're suggesting I kill my own baby? You don't even care about it? It's your grandchild. Besides, abortion is illegal."

"Kathleen, listen. You've got your whole life ahead of you—your music, your education. It's so important you make the right decision here. We can go to Mexico . . ."

"I can't believe this conversation, Mother. I won't kill my baby just for your own convenience."

"Of course you won't, Sweetheart, but I'm thinking about your future. Or perhaps you could stay at Biola as long as possible. Try to finish out the semester. When you must leave, how about staying with your Aunt Helen in Seattle where you would avoid prying questions from friends and relatives. Have you considered putting the baby up for adoption?"

"Adoption? How could I abandon the product of my own body? Mother, you are worried about your *own* reputation." And then, "Why didn't you give *Sammy* away when he was born Mongoloid!" She ran sobbing up the stairs to her old room.

Pierced, Jane slumped on the couch, her mind reeling. She had spent her life managing things, mending fences, airbrushing her family's image. Now, not only had her fences crumbled; Kathleen had rejected her.

Kathleen knew it wasn't just her baby; it was also Reggie's. She resolved to urge him to take responsibility, so she arranged to meet him at Andrees in Laguna Beach where it was unlikely they would run into anyone they knew. Reggie smiled to himself when she called and said she wanted to get together but he grew curious. She'd said she never wanted to see him again. Maybe she was softening. He drove down from UCLA, walked in to Andrees and saw her sitting at a far table against the window—solitary, sober, her hair falling across her cheek. He slid in opposite, then arranged his silverware, straightened his napkin and aligned the salt and pepper shakers.

Kathleen sat silent for a long time, listening to Reggie prattle on as she stared outside at the drizzle falling out of low gray clouds that mimicked her sagging spirit. They ordered food. Then, "Reginald, I know you and I have different viewpoints on what happened but I needed to meet with you now."

"Oh, sure. It's great to see you, Kathy. I'm sorry for what happened and I appreciate that you think we should back up a little and start over."

"Reginald . . . I need to tell you something but don't know how to say it."

"That's OK; I know you've just begun at Biola and you've gone through lots of adjustments."

She raised her head. "No, that's not it. We are in a very different situation now."

"Well, yeah, separated in two different schools and all but we can still telephone, still get together once in a while."

"Reginald, I'm going to have your baby."

He jerked back and widened his eyes like someone had just punched his face. "W-what? No . . . You're kidding, aren't you?"

"I've missed two periods and Dr. Nesland confirmed I'm pregnant."

"Is he sure?"

"Yes."

The waitress came to refill their drinks. They both ignored her. Reggie sat silent. Her news had shocked him into thoughts deep enough to drown in. "Kathleen—er, were you with anyone else?"

"No, Reginald, of course not. Only with you."

She could see his mind racing. Probably wondering how he could have a child—it would complicate his plans for finishing school and starting his career. Silence for several minutes and then, "Well, you should have thought about that when you gave in to me." [Gaslighting again—blaming Kathleen for his own lust.] "I can pay for an abortion. We'll find someone who can do it—maybe in Mexico. No one will ever know."

Kathleen flinched, narrowing her angry eyes. "Abortion. I can't believe you'd say that—not even concerned about your own flesh and blood. Never! Rather than destroy this precious life, I'd rather lose my reputation and live as a single mother."

"Shhh," he smirked. "People around will hear us. Calm down and we'll get this worked out." To him, her pregnancy presented a problem needing a solution. Reggie was good at working out solutions.

"Look, I want to do my part here. We could get an apartment, move in together, maybe get married." He knew she never had wanted that. But maybe the baby would force her hand, open her up to loving him, draw her to him. He still wanted to be with her.

Now Kathleen fell silent. How could she make a life with Reggie? How foolish to have gotten tied to him. Then, "No, Reggie. You have no idea what you're asking. You have no concern for my feelings. I don't know what to do but making a life-long decision based on an emergency—I can't, I won't do it."

Not much more conversation. They parted with nothing decided. She walked out to her car in a light drizzle that dampened her sweater.

During the long, wet drive back to Biola, Kathleen realized Reggie had no interest in the baby. His off-the-cuff ideas about an abortion, about living together, disgusted her. *He cares for nobody except himself,* she thought. *How stupid to have gotten involved with him. I played a dangerous game and lost.*

Late that night she sat in her dorm room alone, the guilty moonlight leaking in her window. What *about* seeking an abortion—it would be a quick fix. Nobody talked about these things in public. Kathleen remembered a *Santa Ana Register* story about a Chapman College woman who delivered her newborn baby in a public restroom, then abandoned it.

But how could I do that? I would never forgive myself. She put her hand on her womb to palpitate the new life growing within her. Ashamed and heartbroken as she was, motherhood awed her. She, a woman-vessel, carrying new life within. She lay supine and hugged her pillow to her breasts.

By November Kathleen was showing much more. Her skin turned clammy at the thought that she would be discovered at Biola. For the first time in months she realized she needed her mother's support. She drove over to Anaheim and walked into her childhood home.

"Mother, I am sorry I was angry with you. I know you will always be there for me."

"Oh, Kathleen. You know we want what's best for you. Why don't you move home?"

So, explaining to the dean that she felt ill and depressed, she left her Biola dorm room and moved home. A brilliant student, she arranged to do her classwork from there, returning to pick up and drop off assignments and papers. She would go back to take her final exams and earn her fifteen semester credits.

Neither she nor her mother told her father she was pregnant; he assumed she'd moved back from Biola because she was sick. But one day he stumbled across a note from Kathleen's doctor.

Kathleen was out, so he confronted Jane. "Jane—what did Kathy go to Dr. Nesland for?"

Jane blanched. "Oh, Ben. I was going to tell you but it was so hard. She went in for an hCG test."

"What's that for? She doesn't have low iron, does she?"

"I thought if I told you, you might get so angry and force her away from home forever."

"Why would I do that over a doctor's visit?"

"We're going to have a grandchild, Ben. I do not think she's told anybody except Reginald and now she's not even talking to him."

"She's pregnant? [His head jerked up.] Who's the head of this household anyway? I have a right to know what's happening to my own daughter and you have an obligation to tell me. Reggie? I can't believe she gave in to him! Ben was furious— angry at Kathy for ignoring his advice about dating Reggie; angry at Reggie for venting his brute lust upon Kathy, Ben's beloved daughter; angry she'd given in to him; angry Jane neglected to tell him; angry at himself for not protecting her and in general, angry at the world.

"Reggie's a terrible person. Why did Kathleen refuse my advice?"

"Ben, we can't fix this now. Kathleen told me she would never marry Reginald. We must support Kathleen and help her work through this. I still hope she'll put the child out for adoption as soon as it's born. You mustn't be angry with her or you'll drive her away forever."

Ben then spoke to Kathy, controlling himself with great effort: "Kathy, I don't understand why you did what you did but you can't make any radical decisions now."

Kathleen flinched—he had found out. But in a way she was relieved her secret was out.

"Father, I . . ."

He put one hand on her shoulder. "Please, no long explanations. Just stay here at home—we'll try to work with you." No hugs. His lips pursed and his neck turned red as he turned and strode away.

Kathleen felt trapped. She needed her parents but could not live with them. Her father was still frowning and closed-mouthed after a month, so Kathleen told her mother, "I just cannot do this. I need to live somewhere else, need to think and plan. I need to work. I'll try to move back in with Valerie."

Jane wept when her daughter moved back to Costa Mesa with Valerie and returned to work at the Jolly Roger. Kathy stopped talking to her old Calvary Church friends. They wondered where she'd gone but her mother said nothing.

Chapter 10

"O F-FAT. D-DEVOTIONS IN five minutes." Fat—an exquisite epithet expressing disgust, disappointment and lament for the boredom of life. Fulton tried to rub the sleep out of his eyes. "You get dinged if you sign in late." He and Sean sprang out of bed at 7:25 a.m., giving them plenty of time to get down to mandatory men's devotions at 7:30. Sean threw on his collar shirt and jumped into his slacks, ran to the little corner sink to comb his hair, rubbing some of the chlorine-laden water on his face. He and Fulton joined other guys running down the stairs and over to the cold basement under Moody-Sankey Auditorium where they scribbled their initials on the sign-in sheet just before the buzzer rang.

Having elevatored down from his tenth-floor Cromwell Hall office, Dean A. Franklin Puckett entered the room wheezing. He used the "A" initial instead of his first name, Adolph. (WWII and the Nazis were still a fresh memory.) An introverted man, he hummed to himself when he walked. His wrinkled dugs showed under his white shirt and his chronic asthma modulated his croaking voice. In short, he had the charisma of a baked potato and as much assertiveness. But as he neared retirement, his moral probity and fatherly manner earned him the respect and love of all the guys.

Morning devotions segregated the men from the women. Today, Puckett was giving his annual masturbation talk. "If you're having trouble, come see us and we'll help you stop; we'll work with you. If you can't stop we'll have to ask you to leave TBI." Sean wondered how many takers he got. Which was the worst TBI sin—masturbation or atheism?

Devotions ended at 8 a.m. As they walked out, Dan Hardy mumbled, "Ninety-seven percent of the guys here masturbate and the other three percent are liars."

TBI labored to segregate its students from the worldly social norms of the day. So, piety and lifestyle rules. Fundamentalist morality demanded prescribed dress codes, limited entertainment options and strict sexual control.

At first Sean thought everyone followed the rules. But then he saw guys playing with prohibited "Euchre deck" cards (regular face cards), betting a nickel a hand. The RAs were supposed to watch for this but they usually turned a blind eye.

Sean never smelled cigarette smoke on campus but Dan Hardy told him, "Sometimes a couple guys buy a pack of Camels and smoke them up at Lincoln Park. I know guys who stash a bottle of beer in their rooms and pour it into coffee cups. But Ma Graham makes routine room checks, sniffs for tobacco, looks for empty beer bottles. Plus, the room cleaners come in about once a week and they'll rat on you. You could get kicked out of TBI."

After devotions the guys walked straight over to breakfast in Cromwell basement's sprawling dining hall. Sean came with a couple days of facial growth, hair standing askew. Some of the girls wore scarves.

He filled his lungs with the food smells as he sat down in one of the bow-backed chairs at the long table. Institutional silverware lay at each setting and large serving plates held bacon, toast, oatmeal and bananas. Seven hundred people ate three meals a day here.

Ma Hutchins stumped by, omnipresent in her flowered dress and red face as round as a tomato. She squinched her eyes behind thick glasses but never smiled as she circulated between the tables, enforcing proper decorum. An earnest, patient woman who'd worked at TBI for twenty-five years, she ran the dining hall like a military mess unit. Sean watched her portly figure as she made the trip across the vast dining hall, a lengthy journey. Wearing her long graying hair gathered back in a tie, she flourished indestructible as crab grass but lived somewhat dehydrated of the sap of human kindness. Veritable, unforgettable Ma Hutchins.

Leaving the dining hall, Sean walked over to Dr. Moreau's class, Introduction to the Bible. Several of Cromwell Hall's classrooms overlooked LaSalle Street—high ceilings, dark wood trim and stained hardwood floors smelling of wax and holding a hundred secrets.

Robert Moreau, a Dallas Seminary man, emphasized Reformed doctrine and, like all the TBI teachers, held a high view of Scripture. Throughout the semester he patiently painted the vast panorama of Bible history—Garden of Eden, Tower of Babel, Noah's flood, call of Abraham, the Exodus, the kings and battles, the prescient prophets and the exile of the Hebrew people. Today, he was laying out the great vision of the prophet Daniel and his suffering under King Darius. He taught earnestly, staring owl-like at each student in turn. A devoted Apocalyptician, Moreau waxed eloquent on Jesus's return, the millennium, the Great Tribulation. Sean knew this vocabulary from his childhood and loved the class.

Next came New Testament Survey. Mr. Claude Bailey, trained at St. Paul's Biblical Seminary, seemed unprepared, staring down at his notes for the first ten minutes of each class. Fifty-something, balding and overweight, his ham hands hung down from short arms and his armpits dripped sweat as he paced back and forth. He wore tan slacks, black shoes, always a white shirt, and suspenders, which he would snap. He must have assumed that if he expended enough energy, spoke loudly enough, students would get it. However his earnest exertions never translated into good teaching.

The cool fall air wafted in the open LaSalle Street windows. Bailey moonlighted as a fire department volunteer and when he heard a siren's wail, he would rush to the window to check out the passing engines.

The students tried to get him distracted by asking about his California high school in Oceanside. "Yeah, one of the visiting teams poured tar all over the bleachers," he would say, smiling. "Another time, some guys got a Caterpillar tractor and a chain and pulled down our big palm tree . . . The guys loved to stand around watching the girls draw blood on one another when they fought with their heavy steel locker keys."

Sean learned a lot about Bailey's high school adventures but not much New Testament. Students saw Bailey as a turtle on a fencepost—nobody could figure out how he got there.

That evening Sean and Aaron walked into the dining hall and smelled the steaming bowls of bird's nest stew sitting atop the long tablecloths.

People sat at assigned, mixed-gender tables. The girls wore dressy dresses and the boys wore white shirts and ties, slacks and dress shoes (no tennies). The rationale—if students dressed formally, they would learn better manners. TBI worked to prepare students to perform well in higher-class company, thinking it a testimony to Christian virtue. Although no one ever said so, it was partly about class uplift. The girl seated next to him turned to Sean. "Do they think everybody comes from small farm towns and need to be taught city ways?"

"Look over at the flyboys," Sean said, "They sit apart like the upper class with their dark aviation glasses hanging from their belts and Dan Hardy wearing his black flying boots. They always remind me I washed out of flight camp."

The room quieted as Clarence Winters stood up at the deans' table near the kitchen to offer a prayer. The girl whispered to Sean, "Once, somebody taped a dead fish to the underside of the deans' table and it took Ma Hutchins and her crew two days to trace the stench."

Meals were served family style. Tonight, Sean was the "runner" for his table, meaning he needed to trek across the huge room to refill serving bowls from the open counter near the kitchen—bird's nest stew, tuna casserole, mashed potatoes, string beans and lots of white bread with jelly and margarine.

After the meal, a designated "cleaner" used a knife to scrape the crumbs off the tablecloth onto a dinner plate. A "stacker" organized all dirty plates and tableware, while the "runner" loaded them on a cart and trundled them back to the kitchen.

Sean liked the food, different foods from what he ate at home. His mother's cooking was efficient, practical and basic. Here, he ate high-carbohydrate food—potatoes, pasta, stews, soups—food that gave him seven cavities his first year. Desserts were often rice pudding or cookies.

Sean explained to one of the girls why he was carrying an apple. "It's not for me. Several guys carry out their apples and give them to Greg, one of the Norbert Hall guys. He gives them to his fiancée at the Clark Street Rescue Mission."

As the calendar turned to November Sean had never felt such cold. He sat shivering at his dorm room desk staring at the blind-eyed windows of the slum apartment building across Chestnut Street that showed faded paint and rotting window casements.

They went to bed. In the middle of the night flashing lights woke Sean and Fulton up and they ran to the window. A rain-snow mix beat against the dirty brick walls of the Chestnut apartments. Police cars stood at the curb while, illuminated by weak streetlamps, a few dead-eyed men hung out of the upper story windows, smoking. Two ambulance attendants carried a white-sheeted guy away on a stretcher while the police questioned the residents.

"I wonder what happened," Sean said. "Is the guy dead?"

Sean and Fulton descended the stairs and walked across the street to talk with a Negro man sitting on the rusted railing, smoking and shivering. Fulton asked him, "W-what happened?"

The man raised his head. "I was sleepin' here in my basement apartment when I heard a loud thump. I jumped up and runned to the door and saw this guy lyin' all crumpled up in my stairwell. He weren't movin.' He fell from up there [he raised his eyes]. Or somebody pushed him. Drunk." He turned his head away to take a drag on his cigarette.

Sean looked up to where the birds had limed white the ledge of an open window, then looked down into the stairwell. The police wouldn't be too impressed; they worked dozens of these cases. He wondered, *How can people live here? I guess most don't have a choice.* He felt like he'd stumbled into the apocalypse and became convinced that Chicago embodied "The World" the Bible warned against. But where was God? Did he even care?

November came and the Norbert Hall steam radiators spluttered. Fulton told Sean, "I-I'm gonna take the train home to Louisiana for Thanksgiving and warm up."

"I guess I'll just stay here," Sean said. He missed his family, dreaded staying in the dormitory alone, wondered how his mother would do without Edwin on Thanksgiving. But he had no money to travel home.

The talk turned to girls. "I still like Kathy, even though she's not writing," Sean said. "But I think I might have lost my chance."

"Well, you just g-gotta be patient. I dated a girl a couple of times who's doing nurses' training at Swedish Cov Hospital. I heard n-nurses make great wives. I hope I can see more of her after Thanksgiving."

That evening Sean sat in his room missing his father, ruminating on his flight camp failure, thinking of losing Kathy, thinking about his struggle with his faith. *I can't sit here all night*, he thought, so he trudged over to Cromwell Hall and waited in front of the elevator which had a brass panel overhead—"Otis Traction Elevator." He told Moses, the operator: "Could you drop me off at the WTBI radio studios on the eleventh floor?" After he exited, he slipped into the quiet observation room where he sat alone. It smelled fresh and clean. Cocooned in the quiet room, he looked through the big plate glass window down at the vacant radio studio where the glowing red light meant *On the Air*. Listening to the programs, he mouthed the words of the songs. Breathing deeply, he relaxed and almost fell sleep.

WTBI broadcast the great fundamentalist preachers—Donald Grey Barnhouse, Alan Redpath, J. Vernon McGee. They carried "Songs in the Night" from Western Springs Church. Sean liked the song, "Just a little talk with Jesus," but they never played it—maybe its phrase "feel a little prayer wheel turning" sounded too Buddhist or something. Neither did they play the stirring hymn, "God of Grace and God of Glory" because its author was the flaming modernist, Harry Emerson Fosdick. WTBI, like TBI in general, seemed insular, self-righteous—holding her skirts tightly about her to avoid the false doctrines and corrupting muck of the world's dirty byways. Sean began to suspect that TBI set an impossible standard, acted like it was achievable and criticized those who could not reach it. Despite the soothing music, he sensed his faith was slipping away. He felt his arms flailing, felt himself being pulled off the great rock of fundamentalist certainty and sucked down into a chaotic sea where he would find no mercy but only the great, thrashing Leviathan who lusted for human souls.

Chapter 11

THE TUESDAY BEFORE CHRISTMAS Kathleen Wilberforce left the Jolly Roger late, a falling mist dampening her waitress uniform as she exited her car and ran toward her apartment building, grimacing and cramping. She barely made it to the bathroom, where she vomited. The cramping increased.

Later she returned to the toilet and sat there, cramping and retching. She felt a knot in her stomach, looked down and saw pink. After waiting a while with no more blood or cramps, she went to bed but couldn't sleep. "O dear God, what's happening? Please protect my baby!" Valerie had already gone home for Christmas and she dreaded going to Dr. Nesland again.

The next night she again felt strong contractions that forced her to return to the bathroom. Then she slept for two hours.

The contractions started again, so she went to pee, felt a terrible pain, retched, then knelt on the tile floor and dropped a bloody discharge onto a folded-up green bath towel.

She stared for a minute, then vomited again. The afterbirth came and she was still bleeding, still trying to staunch the blood with a large towel.

After a long time, she picked up the tiny thing in the towel and wiped the blood and slime off. Staggering into the kitchen, she laid it on the table, sterilized a butcher knife in the stove burner, then sawed off the umbilical cord.

It was a tiny little girl, barely ten inches from head to toe but well-formed in every detail. Perfect hands and fingernails. Ten tiny toes. You could see little baby hairs forming. She looked just ready to open her eyes.

Kathleen stared for many minutes. "You have come too early," she spoke as she bent over her, "and I bear the blame." Her salty tears fell on the still form.

She wept long, sobbing without restraint. "I am so sorry," she cried aloud. "My poor little girl. I am so sorry; it is not your fault." Piercing, wracking cries of lament. *But no one hears,* she thought, *not even God.*

Panic. *What should I do? No one's here to help.*

Two hours passed with sickness and weakness. Then she got up and found a tiny, pink onesie—a gift from her older married sister—and slipped it on the baby, whose still form almost disappeared inside it. Then, placing her on a new, folded dishtowel, she laid her in a rectangular plastic container she'd found in the cupboard.

Staring at the container-coffin, she breathed over and over a secret name she'd given to her baby. After another hour passed, she sat down and wrote, her hot tears staining the paper:

> Dear _____ [Here she wrote her baby's special name],
>
> You are beautiful. Your life hardly started and now it has ended. No one will ever look upon your face but I. May God and all his holy angels receive you into his kingdom for eternity. I weep for you; I miss you terribly; I am so sorry; you bear no blame; it is my fault. I wish I could join you. I long for the day I will see you again. May God carry you into his presence.
>
> Your forever mother,
Kathleen Wilberforce

Kathleen plucked a white carnation from a vase on the kitchen table, laid it on the baby's breast, pinned the note to her onesie, then closed the container and stared long at the little girl still visible through the translucent lid. She sat down again for a long time. The weakness and bleeding continued but was lessening. In her grief, she obsessed about caring for this helpless child.

Then she decided.

Finding a flashlight and a large serving spoon, she exited her apartment carrying the plastic container into the chill pre-dawn that gave just enough light to find her way. She almost fainted but her purpose drove her on.

Behind the apartment the orange grove furrows still lay wet from the night's rain. Clutching the small box, Kathleen inhaled the orange-blossom-scented darkness as her feet sunk into the moist soil oozing around her slippers. Her beating heart leaped and the hairs on her neck rose when she heard a baleful, grating sound. Just branches in the wind, she decided.

Stopping at a navel tree with its sharp scent of early orange buds, she lifted the low-hanging branches and used her spoon to scoop out a hole in the soft ground. Laying the box in the black hole, she memorized the distorted outline of her daughter, then filled in the hole by hand, the guilty dirt sticking to her fingers. *What am I doing?* she thought. *Is this even legal?*

But this was a sacred moment, a moment to say a last goodbye to her precious, barely formed daughter. This hallowed spot—how could she remember it? She gathered ten stones to erect a small cairn over the grave. Lingering long, kneeling on the damp earth, she tried to pray but found nothing to say; she could only sob.

A strange, secret burial with a sole mourner. Who would she tell? Nobody. Valerie would know she'd miscarried. But no one would ever know her special baby-name, never hear of this secret grave, the dark ritual, the deep lament—not Valerie, not even her own mother. She would grieve this loss the rest of her life—the day she lost part of her body, part of herself. *Why did I lose this baby?* she wondered. *I think it's God's punishment for having sex before marriage. How will I ever find forgiveness?*

On Christmas Eve day she telephoned home. "Hello, Mother. I am feeling ill. I am so sorry to miss Christmas Eve but can I come over tomorrow morning?"

"Kathleen—we're missing you here, with the Christmas tree, the decorations and all. So good to hear from you. What a blessed time of the year."

"Oh, Mother, that's wonderful. But I'm tired and have a bad stomach."

"Kathleen; what's wrong? Do you have a fever? Are you eating well? Shall I come?"

She refused all her mother's caring questions, hung up, closed the curtains and curled up fetus-like on the couch for the rest of the day.

Tortured dreams. Her little girl sat up in the box, looking at her with downturned lip. Demon voices mocking her from the censuring darkness, intoning eternal condemnation. Visions of devouring angels and their muted, mournful music chanted in a minor key, meaning judgment. Tentacular flashes of lightning, meaning judgment. Loud screams, meaning judgment. Accusing faces, meaning judgment. She jerked awake, breathing fast, wiping cold sweat off her face and arms.

On Christmas morning she dragged herself out of bed, drove over to her parents, then walked weakly to the porch. *I don't know how I can stand it,* she thought, *but I want to be with my family today.*

Somehow, going home consoled her. She felt like she was seeing her family for the first time— her older sister and husband, excited little Sammy, Father smiling to see his family united and always Mother who presided over the beauty and specialness of the day—she realized how much she loved them all.

Kathleen's mother sat at the piano and they gathered to sing as they always did on Christmas Day— "O Come All Ye Faithful," "O Little Town of Bethlehem"— she knew the words by heart. Father prayed a prayer of thanks for the birth of Christ. They opened all their gifts, then at 2 p.m. ate a huge dinner which Kathleen only nibbled at.

After they cleared the dishes away, Kathleen's sister needed to go to work so she and her husband gave goodbyes and left. Father retired to his study where he sat digesting both his dinner and a book about the rapture. Kathleen found herself sitting on the couch near her mother whose face contorted in worry. "Kathleen, you're so withdrawn, no appetite. Are you alright? Do you feel any better today?"

How do I even start? Kathleen wondered. She looked away, then back at her mother. Her eyes watered and her stomach knotted. She was glad she hadn't told her mother on the telephone.

"Kathleen; there *is* something wrong. What is it?"

All at once she dropped her bomb. "Mother . . . I miscarried Wednesday night."

"What? Oh, Kathleen; and you're here today? Was anyone with you?" Her face contorted and her eyes watered.

"No—Valerie is home with her parents." Kathleen drew near and spilled out all her emotions on her mother's shoulder, just like she used to when she was five. Then silence, both holding each other, both sobbing.

"Have you seen the doctor yet? Was it a boy or girl?"

"I wanted to call you but I was afraid and wanted to tell you in person."

"Oh, Sweetheart, I am so sorry. I wish I could have been there with you. Did you keep the little fetus?" Mother always came right to the point.

"A girl. I'll see the doctor on Monday, Mother."

"Can I see it?"

"No. I'm sorry, Mother. Please, no more questions; I never want to talk about it again."

Her mother probed to find out more about the fetus and afterbirth but Kathleen sat mute.

On Monday Kathleen went back to Dr. Nesland. Her breasts pained her because her milk was in—abundant, superfluous milk, cruel milk her baby would never taste. She told him she had disposed of the fetus and afterbirth.

"You should have brought them in; perhaps we could have found out why you miscarried. But I can at least give you a shot to stop you from lactating." He acted like it was no big deal.

"Dr. Nesland, please do not tell my parents or anybody about this." Kathleen felt the physical pain but more, the wrenching in her soul. She cycled through many emotions—disappointment, guilt, self-pity, depression, anger.

When Valerie got back, Kathleen told her. She gasped, opened her mouth. "Kathleen—why didn't you phone me?" She wrapped her arms around her.

Kathleen buried her face on Valerie's shoulder and whispered, "Well, you went away for the week and anyway, I did not want to tell anyone, except Mother." Valerie's perfume made Kathleen feel faint.

She felt too ashamed to move back home and she couldn't face the Calvary people or Pastor Carter, so she stayed in Costa Mesa and continued working at the Jolly Roger, trying to save some money. She needed time to sort out her feelings, sort out her life. She wept for days.

Jane Wilberforce faced a dilemma—whom should she tell if anyone? Kathleen had not given her permission but she couldn't bear this alone, so the next Sunday when she saw Gladys Radcliffe at church, she told her, "Kathleen miscarried. She asked me not to tell anyone but . . . I assume Reggie told you."

"What? Oh, I'm so sad for her. Is she sure it was Reggie? He hasn't told me anything. He came home for Christmas, said he'd met with Kathleen. But he's back at UCLA now. He called me last night. I wonder if Kathleen told him yet. Is she OK? When did it happen?"

"Christmas Eve day. She's taking it hard. She thinks God is punishing her for what she did."

"Oh no; God doesn't work that way. Poor girl, mourning for her lost little one." Gladys said she wouldn't tell anyone—except Reggie. Jane reluctantly agreed.

Gladys called Reggie who seemed surprised and relieved. But when Reggie called Kathleen, she refused to talk to him.

Chapter 12

It was 9 p.m. on an early December night of Sean's first winter in Chicago.

"I'm going out for food," Sean told Fulton.

"A-Ah need to stay here and study."

Sean exited Norbert Hall into a grey landscape.

Ice chunks filled the cracks in the slippery sidewalk and the bitter winds off Lake Michigan blew right through his light stadium jacket. A man stared through the bleared glass of an upstairs window in the apartment across the street. Some bricks were crumbling, others missing. Icicles hung from the window ledges. He turned to head over to Clark Street to "The Hole in the Wall"—a tiny, brightly lit space with a Dutch door that opened onto the sidewalk. He leaned over a bit to look in, inhaling the smell of grease pouring out of the deep-fat fryer. A short man with a sweaty face and dirty apron handed him out a hamburger. He scarfed it down where he stood with his feet turning numb.

On the way back a fringe of hoar frost formed on his jacket collar. He'd almost reached TBI when a guy stopped him. About fifty years old and wearing a heavy sweater, the burden of his years lay heavy on him as he gazed over at Hargreaves Hall.

"Could I find a woman for the night up there?" He stared out of a bleak alcoholic face, slurring his words.

"I'm not sure that would be a good place to look . . ."

This kind of easy morality shocked Sean—he wanted to wrap his righteous robes around himself and turn away. But this sexual world also fascinated him.

The next morning Sean launched out to buy some white shirts. A light snow sprinkled his overcoat, already besmirched with little "Chicago freckles"—gray industrial ash. He licked the sooty taste off his lips. The locals took Chicago freckles for granted—just one more tax on city living.

Compared to the choking, throat-burning smog of Southern California, Sean preferred Chicago freckles.

Several men passed with heads erect—upwardly mobile in their fine-ly-cut suits and Homberg hats protecting their cropped hair. *They're on a different mission,* Sean thought.

People called Chicago "The Windy City" for a reason. Scraps of yesterday's newspapers dampened by last night's snow blew across the sidewalk, along with spilt soft drink cups and cigarette butts. Soaring office buildings leaned over him, blocking the weak sun. He passed closed doors and shuttered windows. Pitiful sidewalk trees struggled to gulp sunlight and moisture. Chicago's dreary world dragged Sean's spirit down on this cold winter day.

As he reached the "L" he noticed the rattle-can-sprayed graffiti where gangs had marked the rusted steel trusses. Ice hung from the edge of the platform. Several overcoated people stood looking down the tracks, clapping their gloved hands. An express train thundered by. Nobody talked except a couple of buskers illegally trying to sell candy and cigarettes. With his inadequate shoes and socks, Sean was losing feeling in his feet.

He boarded his train smelling the steamy warmth and the smoke from old men's cigarettes. Noticed people hanging on the grab-poles. Enjoyed the speed and clatter, the precarious, creaking turns. He'd read that in 1895, steam engines powered Chicago's first city trains. Now, with 102 miles of track, the electrified "L" formed the second-busiest rapid transit system in the nation with its long bony fingers stretching out in all directions, stitching the city together.

Sean looked around at a sprinkling of riders, most with their faces buried in the *Chicago Sun-Times*. A couple of tardy school kids clutched their books. An old woman in a print dress slumped against the frosty window. Young, mute, colored men sat staring at their hands which grasped their splayed knees. The occasional person sat singing or talking to himself. The democratic "L"—carrying rich and poor, old and young, speakers of many languages. He got off, then walked a couple of blocks west to Marshall Fields where he bought two shirts, the kind with slits for cufflinks.

After he returned and entered the arch he swung by his P.O. box and spun the dial with his chilled fingers, not expecting anything. He pulled out a letter with no return address, postmarked Anaheim, California. His heart leapt. He'd written to Kathy's home address and asked that the letter be forwarded but she hadn't answered. Could this be from her? When he ripped it open, he was disappointed—it came from his high school friend Lonnie Thomas. Lonnie said he'd enrolled in business school and was working weekends on his father's egg ranch. Said Kathleen's father told him she'd left Biola.

Why did she leave Biola? Sean wondered. *Is she maybe going to transfer to UCLA to be with Reggie?*

Sean was thrilled when December came and Sean's mom sent him a plane ticket home for Christmas. Northwest Airlines had just introduced their Boeing 707s and Sean was excited for his first ride on an airliner. Finding a window seat he buckled in and turned the air vent to blow on his face. On takeoff, the powerful engines threw him back as the plane accelerated along O'Hare's runway two-seven right and launched into the western sky. Once aloft he stared down at the tiny barns and grain elevators, the vast prairies. A couple of hours later he marveled at the sharp Rocky Mountain peaks passing far below. As they approached California, the sun slowly surrendered its last light and the enveloping darkness suspended him in time and space. Then the plane sank down toward the million lights of the Los Angeles basin and turned toward L.A. Airport.

Sean's whole family met him at the gate. He smelled his mother's perfume when she gave him a joyous hug. "Hi, Sean; it's so good to see you. Welcome home!" Joyce and Nancy each gave him a smile and hug. He loved talking to his family on the one-hour trip home, loved wheeling into his driveway. They avoided mentioning Edwin. But Sean sobered when he remembered he would never see his father again. How he longed to share his TBI life with him. And he wondered about his mother. Edwin McIntosh had a good union welding job and had left Elizabeth some savings and a decent life insurance payout but Sean knew she had to watch her finances carefully. Some of Elizabeth's family helped her out periodically. Sean felt guilty she'd bought his airline ticket, guilty that he wasn't around to help her more, but she always urged him to finish his studies at TBI.

Now in the kitchen, he slid his feet under his mother's table, a table that had seen hundreds of happy family gatherings. Compared to many of his friends, his house was plain—board and batten walls, living room linoleum, a tiny kitchen and breakfast nook. Yet he loved every square foot. Here he was accepted; he'd never doubted it. He walked into his bedroom—a mother-guarded shrine, unused since his departure for college. He felt as if he'd been gone for years and yet everything remained in place, including the framed Bible verses his mother had hung on the walls when he was an infant and a picture of his father. He stared, still struggling to comprehend his father's death.

Elizabeth arranged a drop-in for Sean that Saturday night. He felt strange meeting high school friends, most of whom were going to college here in Southern California. He looked around for Kathleen. She wasn't there and people didn't seem to know anything about her. Reggie wasn't there either.

An hour later, Sean was working on his third cup of coffee and fifth brownie bar when Reggie showed up with Maddie Allen, a Calvary girl Sean had dated once in high school. Sean tensed and turned away—he had no desire to talk to Reggie, still felt humiliated about Reggie saving him from drowning, still felt resentful over him stealing Kathy away.

Reggie pursued him. "Sean, did you know Kathleen and I broke up this fall?"

His heart leapt. "No; how was I supposed to know? I've been out of touch with the Calvary kids."

The next day Sean called Kathy's home and Jane Wilberforce answered. "Oh, hello, Sean. No, Kathleen is still living down in Costa Mesa." She gave him her number. "You know she dropped out of Biola?" Her voice was measured, sober. She offered no further information.

"Yes, I heard. Please tell her I called and I'll try to contact her." But when he called he got no answer.

Sean loved the return flight to Chicago. The huge four-engine jet sprung out of the Los Angeles basin, turned east and cleared the coastal range, then after four hours began its descent into O'Hare. He forced himself to refocus from small-town Santa Ana to Chicago's metropolis. He shivered walking back to TBI from where the airport shuttle bus dropped him off. The ancient city overwhelmed—vast and uncaring. And yet he still looked forward to the possibility of flight training, hoping TBI would accept him the second time around.

Chapter 13

FEBRUARY *1960*. SEAN WAS working TBI maintenance when one day the supervisor sent him over to wax the Sweet Shop floor, along with Darrell Reardon. As they entered, Sean gazed at the lofty, embossed ceiling and the chrome-backed chairs with their vinyl-covered seats arranged around Formica tabletops. The black and white linoleum floor tiles were filthy with tracked-in snow. This was his first time in the Sweet Shop with its ice cream and soda fountain because he never had extra money to buy anything. They stacked the chairs on top of the tables, started mopping, and soon the whole area smelled of hot wax.

"Hey; let's sit down and rest a minute," Sean said as he pulled a chair off the table.

"Nope," Darrell said. "Once the boss caught me lying down and I can't risk getting caught again."

When other students walked by the window Sean asked himself, *Do these people work at all? They eat in the Sweet Shop, go places, buy new clothes.* Sean never resented his own poverty; he was on a mission. But would that mission ever materialize?

Another day Sean was working with the crew in Cromwell Hall washing classroom furniture in a huge tin vat. *Why do we have to wash the chairs and desks?* he wondered. Nobody did that at home. Was it just busy work, maybe? The hands on the wall clock nibbled away the minutes. One of the guys would count down until quitting time: "We've got fifty-five minutes . . . thirty-two minutes . . . nineteen minutes left . . ."

"Stop it." Sean said. That makes the time go even slower."

"Well yeah, whatever."

Sean lifted another chair into the vat. TBI flight training seemed so far in the future. What made him think he could get through flight camp the second time if he failed the first time? Even if he made the cut, some guys usually washed out the first year. But the hot coals of his hope burned under the ashes of failure.

He had saved up his modest wages because Aaron had convinced him they should go out to Palwaukee Airport for a flight lesson once a week. When Sean got off work that day, he and Aaron rode the "L" to the end of the line. It was a race against the sinking sun—they could not fly after dark. "We've got to hitchhike from here out to Palwaukee," Aaron said. They reached the airport a half hour before the sun disappeared over the horizon.

Palwaukee, a small grass-field airport, featured J-3 Cub trainers—planes with no electrical system, hence no navigation lights and no night flying. So sometimes the guys barely got in a half hour of flying.

But Sean loved it. Loved sitting in the canvas sling-seat, the control stick vibrating in his hand. He worked hard to not overcontrol, straining to see around the instructor who sat ahead of him.

One time when they took off, he saw a plane lying tail-high in the snow just across the airport boundary road. Several severed electric wires dangled from where the pilot had hit them and plunged to his death. Sean thought, *What if that had been me?* But of course that would never happen to him. *You can't crash and die when you're twenty years old,* he told himself.

Another day Sean and Darrell were delivering a small cherry dining room table to Dean Darla Dickenson's apartment across LaSalle Street where she lived in a second-floor walkup. Dickenson was the women's dean and, like the woman herself, the whole apartment screamed discipline and order—like a China shop that needed bulling. Darrell told Sean, "Dickenson's a great intimidator. I heard that once she made Dean Puckett cry." Sean had heard the stories. *I guess TBI needs tough people like Dickenson,* he thought.

A little ferret of a woman, Dickenson would walk ramrod-erect in her tweed suit, starched, high-collar blouse, dark stockings with the seams string-straight and sensible low black heels. Word was that the president had hired Dickenson because she oozed efficiency and possessed a sharp eye for detail. Indeed, she was the perfect women's dean.

They pushed the table through her door and put it down on the plush carpet. A Chippendale chair sat at a polished wood writing desk that held a typewriter with a sheet of paper rolled in it. Sean saw only a couple of chairs. *Probably doesn't entertain much,* he thought.

The living room featured crown molding under the plastered ceiling and a crystal chandelier. He told Darrell, "Wow; it's compact but decorated fancy. Old furniture, lots of polished wood." The beauty and order braced him. He straightened up.

"I wonder if Dickenson has any social life," Sean said. "Maybe church or inviting a friend in for tea sometimes." A couple of paintings hung on the wall (placid nineteenth-century pastoral scenes) alongside a plaque: "Be not drunk with wine but be filled with the Spirit." One photograph—framed, small—pictured an older and younger woman. Her mother and sister? Sean wondered.

On a wide shelf next to her typewriter, a cloth concealed something bulky and angular. "I wonder what this is, Darrell."

"Better not touch it. There's a reason it's covered."

Sean hesitated, then pulled up a corner of the cloth, revealing a small TV. These were prohibited for students, and staff were discouraged from having them. Sean smiled. Maybe Dickenson was human after all.

Walking back to campus they said hello to a guy sitting on a bench along Chestnut Street. "Hey; you've got a Chicago freckle on your forehead," Sean said, pointing. The man smiled.

As they walked away, Darrell said, "Sean; that guy's a Catlicker. He got that spot of ash on his forehead in his church today—Ash Wednesday—it shows repentance from sins. I guess they don't believe too much in God's grace and love." Sean had never heard of Ash Wednesday.

Later that month he and Darrell were pushing a dolly with a large desk on it across the bumpy quad over to Hargreaves Hall, getting drenched in a hard rain. Rather than tracking mud in through the lobby, they planned to take the freight elevator. Amid the quad's cobblestones lay a steel trap door with "No Parking" painted on it in big red letters. When Darrell pushed the "up" button on a nearby post, an alarm sounded and the steel doors clamshelled open, shedding rivulets of rainwater. After the elevator platform stopped at ground level, they rolled the table onto it and descended to the basement steam tunnel.

Sean wiped his hot, humid face and looked overhead at the multiple steam pipes hissing and spitting through the torn insulation. After another elevator lifted them into the reception area of Hargreaves, they checked in at the front desk, then continued up to the eighth floor.

Cloistered Hargreaves Hall stood as a mysterious, gated, guarded nunnery, making the girls that more remote and exciting in the minds of the boys across the quad. Darrell told him, "No guys enter these halls unless they're cleaning or maintenance." When they pushed the dolly out onto the floor, he yelled, "Man on the floor."

They heard a muffled voice—"Grab 'im!" Then giggles.

A girl walked past them down the hall in her bathrobe, self-conscious with her unmade-up face and hair in curlers. Sean's eyes darted back and forth, hoping he'd meet someone he recognized. What if a girl walked out partially clad?

They entered one of the bathrooms ("Maintenance here") to clean the sinks and stools. Much nicer than the men's bathroom and smelling of lavender, it featured unfamiliar dispensers hanging on the wall and padded benches. *Do girls need more rest?* he wondered. Although he'd grown up with two sisters, girls were to him an other-gendered mystery.

On an earlier delivery to Hargreaves, Sean had placed a note and a small bouquet of flowers in Maria Martinez's room, a girl he knew from his class on the book of Job: "Hi, Maria; guess who?"

The next afternoon Sean and Darrell needed to hand-truck a filing cabinet up to the president's office. They entered Cromwell Hall, punched the elevator button and waited until Moses opened the scissor grating and steel doors.

At that moment the maintenance supervisor came up and called Darrell away to clean up a spill in the dining hall. Sean felt awkward riding alone in the elevator with Moses. He hadn't met many Negro people, couldn't think of anything to say. "Hi; twelfth floor please."

"Sure." Then silence. Moses had been there a long time. He knew he had a job to do and it didn't include entertaining the riders with conversation.

When he reached the twelfth floor, Moses jiggled the lever up and down to align the elevator with the floor then opened the doors. Sean trucked the cabinet out and down the hall, then knocked at a door with a brass plaque: "R. Albert Clearson, President." Sean wondered why so many of these men used only a single initial for their first name.

"Come in," Dr. Clearson said. Sean trundled the cabinet into the office, looking around at the heavy wood trim, wainscoting and subdued sconce lamps that shed amber light on the thick carpeting.

The office seemed almost funereal, far above the frenetic to-ing and fro-ing of students far below. Books lined the walls—multi-volume, embossed-cover commentaries by Lightfoot and Scofield; biographies of D.L. Moody and R.A. Torrey; works of theology (but none by the three B's: Bart, Brunner, Bultmann, who were thought to be too liberal). Over by the mullioned window stood a large world globe covered with tiny red pins. TBI's missionaries around the world, perhaps?

Sean had never met the president—he'd just heard his chapel sermons—stentorian, authoritative, doctrinal, expository and most of all, fundamentalist. Clearson sat rotund in the rarified atmosphere of his lofty eagle eyrie, looking Ebenezer Scrooge- like but minus the whiskers. He was typing a manuscript on his typewriter amidst a sea of books, many of them open, with his little desk lamp illuminating a notepad. He wore a dark blue suit, white shirt and a navy tie anchored with a little silver cross. About sixty years old, Sean guessed, with thick, graying hair and plump hands.

"Excuse me, Dr. Clearson; I'm delivering your file cabinet."

"Thank you." Clearson stopped typing, took off his reading glasses and squinted. "Just put it in the corner there. Careful you don't scratch the woodwork. What is your name?"

"Sean McIntosh. I'm pre-flight, hoping to go to flight camp next year."

"Good; are you from the Midwest?"

"No; California." He maneuvered the filing cabinet into place, wondering what Dr. Clearson thought of profane, ungodly California. He was petrified Clearson would discover his weak beliefs.

"Well, welcome," Clearson said. "I hope TBI serves you well as you prepare for Christian service."

"I hope so, sir."

Sean stood in awe, knowing he was in the presence of a person apart, a winner of spiritual victories, a knower of arcane theologies and elucidator of obscure biblical passages—God's older brother, so to speak. He imagined Clearson could answer any question about the Bible and Sean boiled with many questions. But he feared Clearson's best answers would not satisfy his own heart and mind. He was terrified Clearson would discover his dalliance with atheism. Trailing the hand truck behind him, he exited, flustered.

As he hauled the hand truck back to the maintenance shop, the military draft wore on his mind. The cold war was at its height— Russia was building a hydrogen bomb and he'd heard that the U.S. had two hundred military "advisers" in southeast Asia. Would America sleepwalk into another war? Sean ran into Aaron crossing the quad. "Did any of your Pennsylvania friends get drafted yet?"

"I don't know of any," he said. "I spoke to my bishop and he wrote my draft board. Then they reclassified me I–O, Conscientious Objector, because I was in the Mennonite church."

"Wow; they classified me I–A in September, right after I started TBI."

Sean hesitated to talk to the dean about the draft for fear the conversation would turn to his beliefs about God. But he had to deal with his I-A draft status. The next day he walked into Dean Winters' office who said, "Sean; we'll have to send them a letter and explain you're in missionary training."

Three weeks later, Sean ran into Aaron at the P.O.'s. Sean pulled out an official-looking letter from his mailbox, opened it at once, then yelled at Aaron. "Remember I told you I was I-A? They just re-classified me as IV–D, 'ministerial student.' I guess I won't have to go to Vietnam."

"Vietnam? Where's Vietnam?"

Chapter 14

In his second semester at TBI, Sean discovered the Second Gender. He worked with Myrtle each week to produce the *TBI Trumpet*, the student newspaper. One evening she walked into the dining hall a little late. Sean, along with seven hundred faculty and students, turned to notice her skirt riding one and a half inches higher than her knee. He glanced over at the flyboys' table—their eyes were glued on her.

It was the sixties and across the country women's hemlines were relentlessly rising. Sean looked over at Darla Dickenson who sat at the deans' table. Dickenson, in her mid-thirties and eternally single, lived convinced that she alone defended the barricades guarding TBI's high morality against the decadent outside world. Her pursed lips made tiny vertical wrinkles above her mouth. An articulate older student described her to Sean: "She holds charismatic power, strikes fear in student hearts and terror in the hearts of the men's deans. She's got guts for garters, chills the very seed in the ground she walks on." Sean read between the lines. Using her middle finger to push her thick-lensed pince-nez up onto her nose, Dickenson squinched her eyes at Myrtle.

That evening Sean and Fulton sat in their room talking about Myrtle. "I get fixated on her hemline," Sean said. My eyes get heavy. If I try raising them, they just fall to her legs "Fulton, why do girls wear what they wear?"

"A-Ah've wondered the same thing. Ah sure don't know." Fulton jumped down from the upper bunk bed. "Girls are d-different from boys; like alien-different. Different interests, even different morals, ah think."

"Girls don't feel the same attraction guys do. They're more moral," Sean said. He did not think girls eager for physical contact. Or perhaps just not eager for contact with *him*. He longed to get closer but feared rejection. Sean had known a few "loose girls," but considered most girls pure as the driven snow, bastions of virginity wearing impenetrable armor.

"Course they feel the attraction," Fulton said. "But they're just pickier."

Before lunch the next day, Fulton and Sean walked over to the campus post office. "H-hey; here's a note from S-Sue," Fulton said. Sue had come to TBI from South Carolina—open to the world, friendly, bankrolled by her daddy, a classic Southern "bowhead" without a care in the world.

Fulton whispered, "The note says God told her we should get engaged." He beamed but looked puzzled.

"Fulton—get a grip. How can God tell her such a thing?"

"But what should ah write her?"

"You just need to write back: 'Great. When God tells me the same thing, I'll get back to you.'"

Sean never received such notes. He looked in his box and saw an orange card which he exchanged at the window for a shoebox wrapped in brown paper and twine. Surely it contained Mother's home-baked chocolate chip cookies (a boxed mix but Mother-baked). If you received a "care package" from home, people expected you to share it out with your roommate and friends. He searched in vain for a letter from Kathy but she hadn't written since her break-up with Reggie and leaving Biola. Sean's mom said she didn't know much more. What was going on?

Then Maria Martinez walked by, a vision of loveliness in her blue pastel dress and black, shoulder-length hair. Sean followed her as she walked to her P.O. box and stooped over to pull out several letters.

"Hi, Maria; get anything interesting?" He caught a whiff of her perfume as she looked up at him.

"Hi. Mom wrote and a friend from church. I miss my home church and my friends back in Fresno."

"Fresno? You're from California?"

"Sort of. Our family moved there from Mexico right after WWII. My dad worked for a while in the apricot orchards in the Valley [spoken with her eyes cast down]. Where are you from?"

"I'm from Santa Ana, down south. You're the first girl I met here from California."

"Oh—That's nice. Did you get anything, Sean?"

"Yep. My mom sent me a box of cookies, at least I think that's what it is. When I open it, I'll send you one through the P.O.'s. How'd you do on Laster's exam?"

"OK. I never knew you could get so much out of the suffering of Job."

"Yep. He sure goes deeper than my Sunday School teacher ever did. "I'm glad I caught you. If you're free Sunday night, would you like to go to Elm-LaSalle with me?" Sean held his breath; this was the first time he'd asked Maria out.

"Hmmm . . . I usually go with the girls to Torrey Church . . ."

"Well, Elm-LaSalle's closer and Pastor Tommy has great sermons. My RA from Norbert Hall's going to play his saxophone."

"Well, I guess I could try out Elm-Lasalle."

"Great. Say I pick you up after supper, about 6:30?"

"OK. Well, bye; I've got to get to class."

Sean was thrilled. He hadn't known if Maria would go with him. Maria—exotic, fun-loving, so different from Kathy.

When Sean stopped by Hargreaves on Sunday evening to ring up Maria, the desk girl looked at him sideways, always alert for trouble or deception; then she rang upstairs and asked one of the girls to get Maria.

Sean sat down and waited . . . and waited . . . After more than half an hour down she came, unapologetic but looking radiant, her black eyes glowing like coals in a banked fire. She stood just under five feet tall, her brown skin betraying her Monterrey, Mexico birthplace. "Hello, Sean."

They walked up to Elm-LaSalle Church, four blocks north of TBI, arriving late. Most TBI students had little money so on dates you walked everywhere, including to church. Pastor Tommy (young, attractive) preached a good sermon.

After evening service some of the college kids met in one of the small rooms for coffee and cookies. They got a little crazy. As Maria passed by, Sean slapped her on the rear end. She did not protest.

Later that week Sean strolled into Dr. Laster's class and sat down next to Maria. From Alabama, Laster was an earnest man with an earnest drawl: "Today, class, remember the theme of the book of Job—'Whah do the righteous suffah?' Sean wondered why TBI hired some men, men whose publishing record overwhelmed their teaching ability. His voice hypnotized Sean, though—as soon as lecture started he would nod off.

After class he and Maria talked about movies. They both knew the titles of avoidable, trashy movies but Maria said, "*Sleeping Beauty* just came out. How could that be bad?"

"I dunno. It's a Disney animation." So they hatched a plan to go see it.

To go out together, they both needed their deans to sign off because of TBI's attempt to protect their young people from inappropriate destinations. For "destination" they both wrote down "restaurant." It got approved.

On Friday night, Sean buzzed in at Hargreaves to pick Maria up. "I don't know, Sean," Maria said. "We're not actually going to a restaurant."

"Maria, I told you not to eat supper. We're sort of going to a restaurant." Sean, whose morals sprung from the spirit and not the letter of the law, reassured her. "It's just a rule, not biblical." (He reasoned that movies didn't exist in Bible times.) "Besides, it's a cartoon movie."

"But it doesn't matter. What if Dean Dickenson finds out about it?"

"She won't find out. We'll be back well before curfew."

They headed over to Clark Street and ordered burgers at the Hole in the Wall. Behind the small Dutch door stood the same sweaty man flipping burgers over the same steaming grill. Nobody ever took a girl there; people stopped to buy burgers to go. But this had to count as the "restaurant" part of the date, so they ate standing up.

Bussing to the Uptown Theater on North Broadway, they bought tickets and a bag of popcorn. Sean didn't try anything with Maria—he assumed most TBI girls maintained unbreachable boundaries. After the show he hurried to deliver her back to Hargreaves Hall before 10 p.m. curfew.

Later that spring some frat brothers from the University of Chicago invited some TBI guys over to a Delta Kappa Epsilon party. Some TBI girls lied on their sign outs and went along. Sean took Maria.

In the frat house's great second-floor common room, everybody danced to turntable music. Sean had never danced before and felt embarrassed but Maria led him through some steps, including a new dance, The Twist. Maria seemed in her element, which shocked and excited him.

As they danced, Maria said, "Sean, *The Diary of Anne Frank* is out. I would love to go see it but I guess we can't."

"Yeah. Too bad. Can't risk it. I heard it's an awesome movie. I don't know why TBI prohibits all movies. What could be wrong with a movie about Anne Frank?"

It got later. A couple of the frat guys disappeared into side rooms with their girlfriends. Most TBI guys weren't used to alcohol and some got a little drunk. Sean felt out of his element and regretted bringing Maria.

The TBI deans always held their fingers pressed against the pulse of the institute. Darla Dickenson told Dean Winters, "I received a tipoff that some TBI students are going to a frat party over at the University of

Chicago." (TBI had its moles—people who took it as their spiritual calling to rat on others, sniffing out unrighteousness.) So that night Winters and Dickenson planned a raid. They parked two blocks away and walked up to the unlocked main door. Bursting into the hall swat-team-like, they ran up the stairs to the common room, looked around and started taking down names.

TBI students scattered like water droplets in a hurricane. Sean and Maria ran down the hall, escaped out an emergency exit door and down the rusty fire escape steps which pivoted to lower them to the sidewalk. Glancing up the steps at another escaping couple, they saw Dean Winters standing haloed in light, specter-like, peering out the open door into the dark, not daring to pursue anybody because of his limp.

Sean didn't think Winters had seen them so they fled back to TBI like bank robbers, grateful the busy pedestrian traffic on the city streets had dwindled to almost nothing. Because they wanted to avoid campus security, they ran down Chestnut Street instead of entering through the arch. "Maria, here's the locked gate—I'll hold your foot so you can grab the top of the chain-link fence." As she scrambled over, he looked up at her brown legs. Then he jumped up and swung himself over. They skulked along the stone walls of Norbert Hall until they saw a security guy coming with his flashlight.

They ran a bit, then shrunk down in a recessed doorway. The guy's footsteps grew closer as he hummed a tune, "Victory in Jesus." The flashlight illuminated the macadam, switching right, then left. Just as he walked past the alcove he swung his flashlight and his head to the right, away from them.

They waited a minute, then breathed out their relief. "Let's run to the other side of the quad, Maria. We can't buzz you in to Hargreaves; it's after curfew. We'll take the freight elevator down to the tunnels." They ran across, turned down an alleyway, then watched as the pavement opened to receive them onto the platform and lower them to the steam tunnels.

Gulping in the humid air from the noisy pipes, Sean whispered, "I work maintenance and know where the Hargreaves elevator keys are. Wait here." When he returned, they ran to the end of the tunnel where Sean's key unlocked the elevator. Maria said a hurried goodbye to Sean, then disappeared inside. He watched the elevator numbers light up until they stopped at her floor. Then he left to return the keys to the maintenance office, ran back through the tunnel, rode the freight elevator up to pavement level, then ran across the dark quad to Norbert Hall and safety.

In devotions the next morning Dean Puckett's face sobered and his marsupial cheeks quivered—"We know about the U of Chicago frat party." He explained how it violated TBI policy and then explained the dangers of worldliness, alcohol, etc.

They'd caught a few guys and a couple girls at the party. The dean would interview each student alone and ask who else was present and one student would throw another under the bus. The penalty—one week's suspension from TBI. Puckett warned the guys that if the deans later learned they were at the party they'd receive harsher discipline.

Sean was worried that someone would turn them in. If they did, his TBI days were done, even if Winters never found out that his Christian faith was slipping away. But nobody ever ratted.

A week after the party Sean asked Maria to go bowling. "Sean, I've never bowled, but I guess I could try," she said.

They both needed permission from the deans. Dean Winters looked at Sean from under a furrowed brow. "Students usually don't go bowling; they serve alcohol there. But maybe this can be a test case. I'll sign you off, then Dean Dickenson will need to sign Maria off. Let us know how the place is."

Maria walked up to Dean Darla Dickenson's office to present her petition. To Dickenson fell the burden of protecting the women students' virtue. Before the spring banquet, the girls had to kneel before her. If a girl's dress didn't touch the carpet she would send them back to let the hem out. She'd written a little book on female morals—*If I Were a Mother.* TBI girls thought of her as a perpetual virgin, like the mother of Jesus, and felt grateful she wasn't *their* mother.

Maria handed her the slip. Dickenson asked lots of questions, then, "I'll let you know tomorrow."

That night Sean told Fulton, "Getting permission for a date here is worse than applying for a marriage license."

Fulton said, "T-that's nothin.' Ever hear of Bob Jones in South Carolina? They prohibit mixed dating. When you enroll you gotta register your race. Then you can't date anybody from a different race. My cousin dated this friend from my c-church, Miuko. Her w-white soldier father met her Chinese mother during the war and she's mixed. When she enrolled in Bob Jones she wrote down 'Chinese.' But when s-she wasn't getting any dates, she w-went back and said she wanted to change."

"What? She couldn't do that, could she?"

"The dean of women told her, 'Well, you can change this once but you c-can't change again.' So Miuko wrote down 'white.'" Fulton smiled.

"I never heard a TBI rule like that," Sean said. "Course TBI doesn't have many non-white students, either."

"Well, I know a white girl here who dated a Guatemalan guy," Fulton said. "Last month this couple g-got secretly engaged. People talked. We're in the North but even up here they want to keep the races pure. That's why you're having trouble getting permission to take Maria out."

"Ridiculous. That can't be the reason."

"Yep. I-I bet it is."

TBI enforced all sorts of rules. These didn't seem onerous to Sean—he'd lived by them since childhood. No alcohol—he walked through TBI's arch never having tasted alcohol. No smoking—he never even tried a cigarette. No dancing—he was the only student in Santa Ana Junior High School who didn't learn the Bunny Hop. No gambling—he'd never bet even a penny at any card game; indeed, he never used the dangerous "Euchre deck" with its face cards—kings, queens and jacks. No movies—the night he and Maria snuck out was the first theater movie of his life. So, the rules didn't bother him—until now, with this delay in taking Maria bowling.

The next day, Dean Winters called Sean in and stared at him, his face as red as an apple. "I need to rescind your permission, Sean. Dean Dickenson mentioned that Maria's been struggling with some things at TBI and she should wait a while to date."

Did they hear about us going to the movies? Sean wondered. *Or the frat party? No—they would have called me in earlier. But Winters has the power to kick me out of TBI if I date Maria.*

When Sean told Fulton that Dickenson had axed his date with Maria he said, "Maybe it's b-because she's Mexican." Fulton knew that, even though the idea of race was a biological fiction, racial segregation was unspoken doctrine not just at TBI but in most of the U.S. in the 1950s.

Sean stared at him. "Really? It never crossed my mind. "At Santa Ana High School I hung out with a couple Mexican friends. My friends here know I dated Maria a couple of times and they never said anything."

"Well, no one talks about it but ah bet they're trying to prevent mixed dating."

How can I keep seeing Maria? Sean wondered.

Chapter 15

SEAN WOULD TALK BIBLE for hours with Bennie Delarosa who lived on his same dorm floor. From Brooklyn, Bennie's bronzed skin contrasted with Sean's pale face. "I come from a whole family of Catholics," Bennie told him, "but Dad turned Protestant after a friend took him to Brooklyn Tabernacle. They call that church 'non-denominational, intercultural.' The choir sure impressed him. He soon left the Catholic Church and joined the Tabernacle. Dad's glad I'm here at TBI to get more Bible."

One April afternoon Sean and Bennie sat in their shirtsleeves on the black pipe railing along the basement steps next to Cromwell Hall. While aimless people wandered Chicago's streets, homeless men lined up at Pacific Garden Mission soup kitchens and Cook County Hospital patients languished in dark corridors, the two guys sat on the railing debating free will, eternal security and biblical inerrancy. They never talked about homeless and hungry people—they weren't on their radar.

Sean shifted his seat on the railing. "Hey, Bennie, will you help me bake a cake for Fulton's birthday—it's today."

"Sure; let's go buy the ingredients."

They walked down to Sam's grocery. How about this yellow cake mix?" Sean asked. "You just need to add milk and an egg."

"OK, but it needs chocolate frosting. Look—you can buy frosting in cans so you don't have to mix anything." They added a six-pack of Pepsi, then carried everything back to the dorm.

Sean ducked through the door into the tiny Norbert Hall kitchen—linoleum floors, cream-colored cabinets, one table with two chairs, fridge, stove and a sink drawer holding a few utensils. Taped to the fridge, a large sign read, "Keep this refrigerator clean. Mark your stuff and dispose of it. Housekeeping throws everything out at the end of the month." Sean opened the fridge. "Whew; smells sour. This is where food comes to die."

The fridge was everybody's responsibility, so no one paid any attention to it. Sean wondered what the girls' fridges looked like.

He poured the cake mix contents out into a mixing bowl, then added milk and an egg. Looking over at Bennie he thought, *He seems so certain about his faith.* He trusted Bennie, so for the first time, he told him his doubts. "I dunno, Bennie. The church kids were friendly but I didn't make any close friends in high school, didn't have anybody to do stuff with. I prayed a lot, asked God to give me friends but he didn't. Never dated any serious girlfriends. Then my dad died this spring."

Bennie was surprised at Sean's tone. "Sean, I'm sorry about your dad. I didn't have that many dates in high school either. But I knew God was in control, always with me."

"Yeah, but what about me losing Kathy? I've never prayed so hard but Kathy slipped through my fingers; she's gone. Where is God in that?"

"Sean, have patience. God will come through for you yet."

Sean stirred the batter. "I failed flight camp. If God gave me this one passion, why did he let me fail? Does God even care?" Bennie fell quiet, didn't know what to say. He turned to butter the cake pan.

"Oh, fat." Sean said as some of the egg white dribbled onto the counter. Sean had picked up language that circulated in TBI's sacred halls—"All God's people said . . . fat." Or, "Get thee behind me Satan—and push." (Expressing the desire to resist temptation but more, wanting to "enjoy the pleasures of sin for a season.") At a Bible institute with such high ideals, hypocrisy and sarcasm and even cynicism proliferated.

Unlike Sean most TBI students accepted all the fundamentalist doctrines, or at least didn't object. No questions, just memorizing a fixed corpus of truth. "Bennie, theology's so boring; nobody asks questions, there's no debate. And what about the doctrine of total depravity? How can people be totally evil? I mean, everybody, even a criminal, has a little good in them."

"Yeah but our good deeds don't cut it with God. We've gotta realize that all our righteousness is filthy rags in his sight since he's so holy."

Like an epiphany, Bruce Jenkins materialized out of nowhere. Bruce, a former Navy man, had seen a lot, done a lot—alcohol, gambling, women—and wore a long-sleeved shirt to cover a girlie tattoo on his right bicep. But his navy buddies had invited him to a Navigators Bible study group onboard ship that earthquaked him into Christian conversion. So now he acted like a dried-out drunk, preaching in his nasal voice to whoever would listen.

He glanced at them putting the cake in the oven and then launched into his favorite subject—Calvinism. Bruce never said hello; he just embedded himself like a tick into the conversation. TBI was high on Calvinism, the teachings of the sixteenth-century Protestant reformer, John Calvin. "God knows the end from the beginning," he said loudly. "God knows who's going to be saved and who's going to be lost."

He spoke with a perpetually stuffed nose. And he had the kind of breath toothpaste couldn't cure. Bennie, spittle-flecked from Bruce's assault, asked him, "How does Calvinism's 'limited atonement' work?"

"Well, Jesus died only for those who would be saved. God is sovereign so if he wished to 'create some vessels suited unto destruction' I can't argue with him. Makes sense, Christ dying only for the elect, not for everybody. But you and I can *know* we're elect, chosen by God."

"So . . . how's a person supposed to pray if he isn't one of the elect?" Sean asked, baiting him.

"Well, I guess he should praise God for condemning him for all eternity," Bruce snorted. (Was the snort for emphasis or just post-nasal drip?)

Sean laughed but then sobered when he realized Bruce was stone serious. He stared at Bruce who, after delivering his Jeremiads, turned on his heel and left as abruptly as he'd come in.

Bruce is an energy vampire, he mused, sucking joy out of people with his crapulous claims—supplying a good example of why Sean was losing his own faith. "How could I ever believe in a God like that?" Sean asked Bennie. "Even if I believed like Bruce, I wouldn't tell anybody."

"But our ways are not God's ways," Bennie said. "Some things we just can't understand." Sean wondered what Kathy thought about limited atonement. He'd ask her sometime.

They turned the oven on and poured the batter into a Pyrex baking dish. When Sean opened the oven door he smelled burned grease. They popped the cake in. "I hope it's the right temperature."

"It says 350 degrees at twenty-five minutes . . . What time is it now?" Bennie had no idea what to say to Sean about Bruce or how to erase Sean's doubts.

The guys sat down while the cake baked. Sean turned to Bennie and at last confessed his secret. "Bennie, I don't understand prayer. I can't see how all the Bible can be inerrant. I've never felt further away from God. I think I'm becoming an atheist."

"What? Why would you do that?"

"I don't believe in God anymore. I'm just trying to be honest."

"Maybe you need to meet with a pastor or something."

Sean didn't answer; he puzzled over so many other questions. Most modernist churches (Presbyterian, Lutheran, Methodist) allowed that the Bible could have some imperfections but fundamentalists believed it was inerrant, without errors of any kind.

"Bennie, sometimes the writers of the New Testament, and even Jesus, quoted from the Greek Septuagint translation of the Old Testament. Does that make the Septuagint inerrant or just the parts they quoted from? And even the gospel writers translated Jesus's Aramaic words into Greek. Is the translation inerrant? It's a muddle."

Bennie explained, "In Dr. Meacham's John and Acts class, he says that the Bible contains no errors in science, history, geography, names, dates, events. If you had been there making a movie, you would have filmed exactly like it says. Sean, it's all true history—all the kings mentioned in the Bible, all the battles, the Exodus, the conquest of Canaan, even Jonah and the whale. (Well; it doesn't say 'whale' in the story; it says, 'big fish')."

"But what about scientific statements? The Bible was written before science. Solomon's great basin measured thirty cubits in circumference and ten cubits across. Bennie, that can't be right. Circumference equals πd. Ten times π equals 31.4 cubits."

"Well, maybe the ten cubits measures the outside of the lip and the thirty cubits the inside. Or maybe it's an estimate."

"But what about Adam and Eve?" Sean asked, switching the subject. "No one's ever found the Garden of Eden. And archaeologists discovered evidence of people farming as early as ten thousand years ago. How could creation have happened *six thousand* years ago?

"Sean, if you count back the Bible genealogies to the Garden of Eden, you discover that God created Adam and Eve in 4004 BC. These are records of true historical events. Perhaps God created everything six thousand years ago but made everything *look* much older. Or maybe the archaeologists just got it wrong."

"But what about Noah's great flood? How could waters cover the whole earth?"

"I've heard of people finding seashells on mountaintops."

Sean gave up. He'd picked the wrong person to confess to. Bennie's fresh Brooklyn Tabernacle faith buoyed him, bulletproofed him against doubts.

Sean felt a rising sense of dread. He'd pinned all his hopes on entering TBI's mission aviation program. What if Dean Winters found out he'd told people he was an atheist? They would never let him in the program.

They pulled the cake out. It looked risen and their cookery confidence soared. But when they smeared the chocolate frosting on, the cake ripped, so they waited until it cooled, gobbed frosting into the rips, then frosted the whole thing.

Bennie had begged little candles from one of the girls in Meacham's class but he forgot matches. They stuck nineteen candles in the cake and used the gas burner to set a twisted piece of paper ablaze for lighting the candles (a forbidden act). Sean doused the flaming paper in the sink, then threw it in the wastebasket. Now to get the cake back to the room without anybody seeing it. They carried it up the back stairs to Sean and Fulton's room with all nineteen candles blazing.

"Surprise!"

Fulton jumped up. "H-how did y'all know it was my birthday? T-thanks, you guys; y'all are great friends." The aroma of freshly baked cake filled the room.

They invited a couple of other guys in and betwixt them all they consumed the whole cake, washing it down with Pepsi. They'd forgotten forks. And napkins. But no matter—the birthday party came off a smashing success.

A couple weeks later Sean and Bennie were again deposited on the black railing in the quad where they sat in the humid wind talking about Dr. Meacham's John and Acts class. "He doesn't believe the Gospels tell conflicting stories," Sean said. "But did Jesus feed five thousand or was it four thousand? Are these two different versions? And the Sermon on the Mount—one gospel says it happened on the mountainside, another, on the plain. One or two sermons? And how did Matthew *know* what Jesus said? Was he taking it down with a tape recorder or something? Or did he discuss it with the other disciples and agree on what to write down? Or did they write down what other people remembered?"

Bennie urged Sean to trust God's word. "Sean, you and I need to do a study about the *differences* among the four Gospels, to see how they reconcile."

"I dunno, Bennie. I've heard about books on the "harmony of the Gospels but I've kind of given up on harmonizing them."

"But we can do it together. It'll be fun."

"Well, I guess. Maybe Fulton can join us."

They jumped off the railing, walked back into the dorm and pitched their idea to Fulton. But he, a recent convert from Mormonism, demurred. "A-Ah guess ah'm not interested in criticizing the Bible. Ah just want to learn more about Jesus." He was at TBI drinking from a firehose, soaking everything in. And they'd elected him president of next year's Sophomore class. Sean was jealous. But he asked himself, *How can Fulton be so certain of his faith when I feel my own faith slipping away?*

Chapter 16

Soon TBI's spring semester ended and Sean rode home to California with three of the flyboys, driving straight through in Dan's tiny Renault, grabbing food at truck stops. Lots of aviation talk. Dan smiled as he enunciated the formula for flying success: "Low and slow and lots of bottom rudder" (actually, a prescription for disaster).

Over fifty hours later, they rolled up in front of Sean's Santa Ana home. He extracted himself circus-clown-like from the back seat and stretched his numb legs—he could hardly walk. His mother embraced him, cried on him, said she was so proud of him. Sean guessed it was partly because she didn't have Edwin anymore. He teared up himself. He looked around at his familiar house but imagined it more barren, more rundown now. *Does my mother have enough money to live?* he wondered.

His beloved 1950 Chevy was still sitting in the driveway so that same day he jumped in and drove solo around Orange County. Entering downtown Santa Ana he felt like a visitor in his native town. Nothing had changed but everything seemed different with Dad gone. Perhaps it was he who had changed. He drove past his grandparents' home on Spurgeon Street (he would stop in later), then drove by his old high school.

He passed thousands of acres of orange groves, irrigated beet fields stretching out around the huge sugar beet factory near Costa Mesa, irrigated truck farms with Asian women in pointed hats stooping over the pepper and tomato plants. After living in "The East" Sean realized he'd grown up here in a desert kept alive only by sucking waters from the surrounding states.

Driving toward the beach he passed the Quonset-shaped blimp hangars that rose from the tarmac like huge, rounded mountains. He grew sad, remembering that his father, who had been a construction carpenter, had worked on each of the 200-foot-high wooden girders in the mammoth buildings. He remembered the air shows they had watched. The day grew bright but summer-smoggy. *Southern California doesn't have "weather,"* he thought—*no snow, tornadoes, hurricanes, not even many thunderstorms—just smog.* Only eleven or twelve inches of rainfall per year, doubly welcome when it came because it washed the smog away.

Sean had not discussed his atheism with his mother, so when the family drove to Calvary Church the next Sunday Sean felt he should go along. Besides, he was eager to see some of his old friends. Neither Kathleen nor her parents appeared, but Lonnie Thomas was happy to see him. "Kathleen's still living down in Costa Mesa; don't see her much here at church." Lonnie knew nothing more. But he said, "Sean, some of us are getting together at my house Friday night. Wanna come?"

After Sean arrived at the party, he noticed a girl wearing a tight sweater and short skirt with a great sheaf of blond hair that fell to her shoulders. She walked in with a waddle, sat down, then crossed her legs. Sean noticed. When they met at the food table she introduced herself. "Hi. I'm Betty O'Shea. Just graduated from Garden Grove High School and I'm hoping to go to Cal State Fullerton, that new school over in Brea." Girls didn't usually flirt with Sean but Betty, a teeny bit overweight and well-endowed, batted her long eyelashes. When she showed up at church the next week, Sean overcame his shyness and asked Betty to go out with him for dinner and then to Hollywood to see *The Fantasticks.*

That Saturday they drove to the elite Musso & Frank Grill, a restaurant frequented by Humphrey Bogart, Greta Garbo and John Steinbeck. Sean felt out of his element with the maître d' leaning over their table the whole time like a wind-blown palm tree. They received the wine list and because Sean ordered none Betty did not either. Torrey Bible demanded no-alcohol—even when you were home for the summer. But Betty loved the fancy restaurant and *Fantasticks* was a fine play—on the drive home they sang snatches of "Try to Remember." Soon they arrived back at her second-floor apartment in Garden Grove where she roomed with Gracie, whose husband was a Marine away in Vietnam. When they parted at the door Betty said, "I never know how to thank a guy." On the next few dates she found out.

When they returned from the next date she invited him in. After a few dates they fell into a pattern. They would go to the beach or maybe a concert, then come back to her apartment where she would fix Pepsis and a snack.

Sean would sit down on the couch and she would sit on her knees facing him. When they ran out of words, they graduated to embracing. Sean slouched and she leaned into him. He tasted her moist lips; their kisses lasted longer and longer. Then she opened her mouth.

Their embraces reduced the need to talk much. Sean never met Betty's father, met her mother only once. *We never talk about commitment*—he thought—*about the future, even about what our relationship means. Why do I find it difficult to pray with her or read the Bible together?*

After dating several weeks, they were sitting in Sean's car outside her apartment when he turned to her and said, "I love you."

Betty said, "I love you too, Sweetheart." They embraced.

As Sean drove back to Santa Ana, he told himself, *I'm not sure I love her.* But he knew that intimacy should only come with love. He wanted the intimacy so he tried to generate the love. He'd never dated a girl like this—a girl with her doors wide open.

He wrestled with a simple dilemma. She magnetized him. And yet he knew, even with all his religious doubts, that intimacy without any true soul connection was only cheap lust. And yet . . .

One evening, after about an hour of sitting on the couch kissing and inhaling her perfume, he felt his hand drift up under her skirt, stopping only when it ran into her petti pants. Then he slipped his hand under her sweater and up her back.

Feeling her warm skin, he touched her bra strap and discovered that two of the three hooks were unhooked. He did not take his hand away.

She excused herself.

When she returned, Sean said, "Your zipper's down."

She ignored him.

Inflamed, Sean wondered, *Doesn't Betty have any boundaries?* He'd never been with a girl whose moral dikes leaked. He assumed that a woman gave sex to a man because the man wanted it, pushed for it, that the woman would never push for it herself. But Betty seemed to welcome each escalation.

A fateful moment—he'd never been alone in a house with a girl. Sean glanced toward the bedroom door. Her roommate Gracie was at her parents' house. Did Betty arrange this? Aroused, they clutched each other urgently. She melted plaint in his arms.

Betty had dropped into Sean's life from outer space for his enjoyment, he thought. They never talked about their deepening relationship, about their desires and dreams. Their dexterous hands moved more fluidly than their tongues.

In that moment Sean's neo-cortex, his reasoning brain, searched for a rationale to press the accelerator. TBI prohibited sexual intercourse before marriage, a view held by fundamentalists everywhere. But Sean reasoned, *Any sin can be forgiven—I can always repent later. I'm already in a sexual relationship; we just haven't reached intercourse yet.* He knew physical affection should link to love and he wasn't sure he loved her. What was love, anyway? Not sure, but he knew he wasn't there yet. Although his emotions were screaming "I want her," he knew he did not want to spend the rest of his life with her.

Like many young men, Sean assumed he was in control of his emotions. But in truth, he struggled with pornography. His high school friends joked about "dirty magazines" and one day they gave him one. He threw the *Playboy* into a sidewalk waste can but as he turned away, the skin on the cover gripped him. He picked it out of the trash and stared at the cover. He smelled the binding, fingered the slick pages, then found an isolated park bench and sat down. There followed an intense session as he slowly paged through the color photos of almost-naked women in various poses. When he returned home, he hid the magazine under his mattress and brought it out late that night, illuminating the seductive pages with his guilty flashlight. He tried to accept his friends' opinion that "it was no big deal." One day, in a spasm of repentance, he pulled out the magazine and threw it into the backyard trash incinerator. But the images would remain with him all his life. And he was not successful in avoiding further furtive sessions with pornography, a practice that made him feel guilty and weak-willed.

He felt close to Betty, very close. The clock said 3 a.m. She pulled him in and he didn't hold back.

But at that moment, struggling heroically against his own emotions, Sean said, "Betty; we've had a great night but it's time I went home."

She frowned, searched his eyes, then reluctantly released her embrace, lowered her legs to the floor and stood up.

When she walked him to the door she said, "Sean, thanks for a wonderful evening." As they embraced and kissed goodbye she smiled, leaned backwards to look at him and pressed her thighs against him.

On the next date, Sean told her, "I think the only way our friendship can last is if we break it off awhile, take a pause." He felt too cowardly to tell her he needed to break it off completely.

Betty grew silent, then—"I've been thinking too that we should break it off a little."

True? Sean wondered. *Is she just saving face? Worried about our deepening involvement? Falling out of love? Wanting to move on? At least she's making it easy for me.*

A month later, Sean asked Betty to go with him to a jazz club for dinner and music. She answered the door wearing a short, tight dress with her blond hair piled up on her head. "I decided to go mod," she said. When she walked up the stairs into the club, her skirt rode up against her thighs.

The evening was OK. The dinner was OK, with the smell of the food mixing with cigarette smoke. Sean realized that mostly Negroes patronized the place. They stayed for the show, watching a lusty, buxom white woman who quivered when she said, "I just got back from a run in Vegas; I'm not cheap but I'm inexpensive." That night, Sean understood even better what Pastor Carter preached about—"Keep thyself separated from the world."

It was an OK date. They talked. When Sean took her home, he longed to kiss her goodnight but she turned and walked in. That was their last date.

It was late August when Betty appeared at Sean's house in tears, hair disheveled in the light rain. "I need to talk."

"Betty; come in." He hadn't seen her in a while.

"Can we go somewhere?"

"Do you want to just drive around?"

"No—can't we go someplace where we can talk?"

They drove up to Hillcrest Park in Anaheim and parked where they always used to park. Sean wondered what was on her mind.

The warm rain dripped on the car roof and ran down the windows. Sean smelled the moistness on Betty's clothes. "What's wrong, Betty?"

Tearing up, she said, "Sean; I can't stop."

Sean guessed what she meant. She was already dating somebody else—and she'd slept with him.

He'd always assumed girls were reluctant partners in sexual activity. But now he realized Betty had ramped up the couch sessions, not just for his sake but for her own. She escalated because she wanted to, not because he was leading her on. His responses had inflamed Betty and now her desires had pushed her into a new, unholy relationship.

"Betty, it's hard for any of us to stop. I care what happens to you, care about your life. I trust your life will work out well."

He said nothing else, didn't tell her he was sorry. He didn't even consider that he'd disappointed his God—he was telling himself he didn't believe in God.

After that, sexual control became harder for Sean. He knew he'd transgressed TBI's standards and even his own standards. Even if they hadn't reached a full sexual relationship, he would fantasize about Betty the rest of his life.

And he wondered about Kathy. Kathy would never behave like Betty, would she?

Sean’s Second Year

Chapter 17

HEADS TURNED AT TBI that fall when Harold Bledsoe arrived on campus to become one of the men's deans.

Born to wealthy Bostonian parents, Bledsoe had grown up in historic Plymouth Congregational Church, a gray stone edifice that honored its Pilgrim founders. Plymouth was big on social gospel, moral uplift, not so big on sin or the cross. As a teenager in the church, Bledsoe bundled lots of undisciplined energy into his lithe body, sculptured by lifting weights several times a week. Plymouth's pastor, Rev. Emerson Bodie, took Harold on as his special project and confirmed him at age thirteen—a ritual more like a tribal rite of passage than an affirmation of historic Christian doctrine. Bodie told him, "Harold; you'll go far; God has his hand on you."

Starting his senior year in high school, Harold told Rev. Bodie, "I want to help young people like you've helped me." But really, he wanted something else—to get away, see the world.

"Harold, you want to help people and you like athletics. Why don't you major in counseling and coaching? I'll write you a college reference letter."

So, Bledsoe applied to Stanford (as far away from Boston as he could get), got accepted and in the fall of 1948 drove solo to the West Coast. He loved breathing in the smell of leather upholstery in his black 1946 Cadillac convertible, a graduation present from his folks. With its three hundred forty-six cubic inch L-head V-8 engine, hydromatic transmission, fat bullet fenders and a spotlight, it turned heads when he passed.

He rolled through broad Midwestern spaces, traversed the prairies and the dry rolling plains that ramped up to the Rockies, pilgrimaged across the barren Mojave Desert then entered California and drove north. He drove across the Golden Gate Bridge to survey San Francisco Bay, the shining jewel of the Pacific Coast. He felt on top of the world—anything was possible.

After his arrival at Stanford, he met his roommate Jerry who warned him, "If you're a freshman, you can't park a car on campus."

"They can't take my car away. I'll talk to the dean."

So he told the dean, "Say, I need a car to take my disabled aunt to the grocery store a couple times a week." The dean bought it—no one found out that his only aunt lived three thousand miles away—so Bledsoe got a permit to park on campus.

Stanford hit Bledsoe like a shotgun blast. The war years lay just behind and the pedagogues knew that education held the key to bringing peace to the world (ignoring the fact that educated Germans had just presided over the killing of six million Jews). But Stanford's entering freshman class planned for crazy—minoring in academics and majoring in fun, their tanned bodies soaking up the easy living in the coppery California sun. A college degree guaranteed a job, so they studied whatever they wanted to. Harold inhaled this West Coast world, a world where established customs, morality, traditional ideas, hung in a state of suspended animation. He signed up for ballroom dancing (for his phy ed major), English, modern sexuality and a film class. He studied casually, striving for the gentleman's C. He wasn't sure he wanted a degree but he liked the ethos of Stanford and had no alternate plans. Besides, college would keep him out of the draft.

He loved hanging out and smoking with the other jocks in his genteel, testosterone-fueled fraternity. The guys would go to restaurants, beach-comb, body surf. His parents footed the bill, so he used their money to drive his friends down along the old *El Camino Real* to where they hung out at Dinah's Shack or Rickey's Swiss Chalet, savoring the juicy burgers and fries.

And the California girls! They'd flung off the strict morality of their forebearers, along with miscellaneous articles of clothing. He wondered if they'd invented the saying, "Girls just wanna' have fun." He loved their impossibly long legs, painted toenails, slim, tanned bodies and abbreviated two-piece swimsuits.

The beautiful Stanford girls loved Bledsoe's Boston accent (he said *Californier* instead of *California*) and they invited him to beach bonfires and drive-in movies. They relished riding in his black Cadillac convertible with its wheel skirts and white sidewalls, the wicked wind blowing through their hair.

In a word, Bledsoe became a chick magnet. He chased the girls and they chased him. He enjoyed an early liaison with a willing Mexican girl he'd met in film class. He told his roommate, "I never knew any Mexicans growing up in Plymouth, Massachusetts. I love her accent, brown skin, black hair and eyes. But I'm not really serious."

Then came Bledsoe's senior year at Stanford. By that time, his most exciting evening activity was reading *Stag* magazine. He didn't broadcast his literary interests, rationalizing that it was private, harmless and anyway, lots of other guys in the dorm read it.

Since he'd just turned twenty-one he decided to celebrate with a drive down the coast to historic San Juan Capistrano. He was sitting in the Mission Grill sipping a Margarita and basking in the joy of life when a couple girls in two-piece bathing suits approached his table. They appeared to be in their late teens—California-tanned, long blond hair, hazel eyes, looking for adventure.

"Hi; are these seats taken?"

"Nope. Are you guys in college?"

"Yeah; we're both freshmen at San Diego State. We're tenting down on the beach; wanna join us?"

"That's kind of dangerous, isn't it?"

They smiled. "Well, we could use a man to protect us."

In a flash he accepted. They jumped into his black Cadillac and he drove them down to the beach.

The evening started out splashing about in the cold waves and continued with bonfire-roasted hot dogs on a stick washed down with beer. The girls joked with him, putting their arms around his neck, rubbing his back. He read the cues. *Do they want what I think they want?* he wondered.

The sky darkened, the moon rose, the fire died down. More beer, mixed with the taste of the sea-salted breeze.

"Do you have a girlfriend?"

"Well, no . . . I've got several friends but no girlfriend."

"I'll bet you have one and you're just not telling us."

"No, really; I don't have one for the moment."

It was fall and the sinking sun meant the air was cool even with the fire, so the girls proposed that they retire. Their two-person tent accommodated three that night and ended up in communal conjugation. It seemed that the girls were looking for a *manage de trois* with the next reasonable male they could find.

The next day Bledsoe drove the several hours back up to Palo Alto bleary-eyed, sleep-deprived, his head still spinning. He, a child of privilege, didn't agonize over the encounter; indeed, he didn't agonize over anything—he just followed his emotions and animal desires. From the heady atmosphere of the broad sea-smell vistas along the California beaches, the high morality of his old Plymouth church seemed childish and outdated.

The same week as the *manage de trois* Bledsoe found Judy, a Stanford coed from Santa Barbara. She told him her father was doing well as a realtor in the booming post-war economy of coastal California. More serious than most girls, she was looking for more than a one-night stand.

Judy and Harold began going out almost every day, and sometimes all-nighting in a motel. Theoretically, Stanford protected their young women—they had to sign out of their hall and back in. But some desk girls sluffed off and the rest were corruptible. One weekend they drove down to Los Angeles—Grauman's Chinese Theatre, Pathway of the Stars, an alcohol-fueled party for two at Malibu Beach and a night drive along beautiful Mulholland Drive overlooking L.A. with all its bright winking lights. With all the parking and embracing, the drive took a long time.

By graduation, they had been dating several months. They married, rented an apartment near the university and lived happily for a time. He started working in a counseling clinic, she, in a senior care center.

Harold's life had lots of breadth but no depth and soon he grew restless. It's a lie that marriage extinguishes a man's lust—he still possessed a roving eye and many opportunities. His proud, secretive spirit made him disconcertingly quiet, confiding nothing to Judy.

After a couple of years and twice that many affairs, Judy gave up. She told Harold, "I want a divorce," and kicked him out of the apartment.

"What? You can't kick me out. What about your promises?"

"What about them? I haven't noticed you have your marriage vows pasted to the dashboard of that sex magnet of a car you drive."

"I can't believe you're serious, Judy. I didn't see this coming. Can't we think this over awhile?"

But she'd already thought it over; she told him to pack his bags and leave. Bledsoe, blind to his own selfish promiscuity, got angry that Judy was betraying him, breaking her marriage vows. He saw no problem in holding women to a higher moral standard than himself—he lived in an echo chamber where the only moral rules he heard were his own.

Chapter 18

AFTER THE DIVORCE HAROLD Bledsoe decided to travel back to his Boston roots where he received a joyous reception. His mother never questioned his choices. "Harold; why don't you move into your old room? You can take your time healing from your disappointments."

He walked into his bedroom, untouched since he'd left for college—family pictures, overstuffed chair, writing desk, body-building posters, the familiar smell—all the same. He took advantage of his willing parents—hibernated, paid no rent, didn't help with household tasks, borrowed their car when his was in the shop. Such is the logic of the single man.

Divorce had shaken him. Thinking back to his high moral training at Plymouth Congregational, he resolved to straighten out his life by reducing his alcohol consumption, stopping smoking and even avoiding dating.

He worked a few odd jobs—restaurants, construction. Even though he didn't see the point of attending, he felt guilty about staying away from church. But what could the church give him? Plymouth's teachings provided thin porridge for his thirsting heart. He felt condemned and uncomfortable with Plymouth's high moral standards. How could anyone live up to them? His parents didn't pressure him but he realized how much his life diverged from theirs.

Two years had passed when he told his father, "I'm going to apply for some high school teaching jobs."

"Great idea, Harold. You can use your counseling degree, your coaching minor," his father said.

Bledsoe knew he needed to move out but didn't want to go back to California and face the debris he'd littered on those shores. He stumbled upon an ad mentioning that Cleveland's Cuyahoga High School needed a coach and guidance counselor, so that summer he applied, then drove out for an interview. Cuyahoga High was housed in one of those massive

L-shaped brick buildings built in the 1920s with a tall brick chimney on one of the gable ends and a flagpole on the other. He walked the halls imbibing the institutional smell of wax and old wood, talked to teachers and staff, then interviewed with the principal and superintendent.

The superintendent queried him about the two-year gap after his Palo Alto counseling job.

"Well, I was recovering from a nasty divorce."

But beyond that speed bump, he wowed them with his personality, good looks and articulate answers. They hired him on the spot and that fall he started coaching and counseling at Cuyahoga.

His first year went great—the bronzed Odysseus awed everyone. Divorce encouraged Bledsoe to make some moral amends, amends he was proud of—he stopped smoking and cut back on his drinking but the giant of lust still loomed. A couple of times he'd visited Roxy's Burlesque Theater on 9th Street ("peek-a-boo burlesque at its best"). He filled his mind with the girls on the stage, reasoning that enjoying burlesque didn't hurt anyone.

One day in early fall of his second year, he found himself in his office behind closed doors, listening for two hours to one of his counselees who oozed pain and struggle. "Mr. Bledsoe, all my dad does is yell at me," Beth said. "I have no friends. I'm afraid to talk to boys. I'm a bad student. I don't think people like me." He gave her a sympathetic hug and she responded. He smelled her perfume, felt her warm skin.

"Why don't you think people like you? I think you're a nice girl."

Beth looked up and smiled. "I don't know. I hope I can keep meeting with you, Mr. Bledsoe." She gave him a warmer hug, then left.

Being in an unfamiliar city far from home, still wounded from his divorce, Bledsoe desperately needed human touch and here was a young girl that idolized him. After a few sessions they began furtive meetings after school. *She has no one and she needs me,* he reasoned. *What harm can it do if no one finds out?*

If he wanted something, he pursued it. Not Beth's need but his own selfishness impelled him to continue seeing her. She came to him as a fragile, vulnerable flower struggling to bloom. Desperate, she found in him a harbor for her soul. He became more attached, more afraid of being found out.

What am I doing? he thought. *She's fifteen years old.* He knew if the school discovered their liaison, he would not only lose this job; no other school would hire him. *But,* he rationalized, *Beth needs me. I'm the only one that can reach her, help her. I mustn't fail her.* He congratulated himself on his compassion, his skill in dealing with Beth's anxieties. He employed his neocortex, not so much for logical thinking but for rationalizing the things his little rat brain really wanted. He could not admit that his meetings with Beth fueled his own lust and jeopardized his job.

One day Bledsoe exited the Harp Bar on Lake Erie's waterfront where he had consumed a great ribeye and, exercising great discipline, drunk only two glasses of Coors. Aimlessly walking the sidewalk and inhaling the Lake Erie breeze, he felt no joy, no strength to rise above his dismal life. The sky was neither light nor dark but hesitating in between. The disappeared sun still lanced with gold the stratus clouds that hung low over the lake. He felt like an open fuse box ready to explode at any minute.

Singing reached him from a small church door—"What a Friend We Have in Jesus," a song he remembered from his Boston church Sunday school. Bored, depressed and with no evening plans, he walked in on impulse and sat at the back. Except for a wedding he'd attended, this was his first time inside a church in Cleveland.

He stayed—tethered there by inertia, boredom and nostalgia. The ceiling fans washed the warm air over the congregation as they sang. Then came the sermon. He learned many new words he'd never heard back at Plymouth Congregational—words such as eternal security (once saved, always saved), inerrancy (no mistakes in the Bible), separation (standing apart from a dangerous, sinful world). Pastor O.I. Runnell was not giving suggestions or someone's opinions. He quoted the Bible, preaching like he believed it. The congregation ate it up. Bledsoe had enjoyed a well-churched childhood but this sermon seemed to come from a different planet—new vocabulary, new theology, Bible-smart preaching.

The sermon sounded familiar, yet somehow different. Bledsoe remembered the Beatitudes of his childhood and the Sermon on the Mount. He knew the basics of Jesus's life—the disciples, the crucifixion story. But they were Mother Goose stories to him—interesting, but divorced from any historical, geographical or cultural context. Plymouth hadn't emphasized miracles, not even the Resurrection. Like so many modernist churches, Plymouth tried to extract Jesus's moral and social teachings from the gospel narrative, squeezing the moral juice from the gospel fruit and discarding the pulp—pulp such as sin, Jesus's physical resurrection or anything supernatural. Bledsoe's thin Bible knowledge shocked him.

He could not know this church had begun as part of a movement opposed to modernist churches like Plymouth Congregational. The great fundamentalist movement of the 1920s spawned thousands of churches like these—independent, non-affiliated, the pastors trained with a couple years at a Bible institute or maybe just a few correspondence courses. But what the pastors lacked in education they made up in zeal. Committed, earnest men. The gospel had rescued their lives from futility; now they wanted to share it with others.

Plymouth answered all my questions except the most important one, he thought. *How do I conquer the evil in myself? I've bought the lies I heard in my frat house—"Sex is like taking a drink of water. Women want it as bad as you do. If it feels good, do it."* These mind-voices still tutored him but he was growing weary, tired of his selfish choices that had strewn wounded women in his wake. Incredibly, this was the first time he thought about how *they* might be affected, how *they* might be faring right now. For the first time he wondered if his selfish desires had damaged *their* own best interests.

Bledsoe's life was spinning out of control and he felt guilty about more things than just "below the belt" issues. He was drinking more now and even smoking again. He had cheated on college exams, ignored his best college friend when he fell into alcoholism. He hadn't even done much to support the food collection efforts at Stanford. Guilt and regret overwhelmed him. Weary he was, and fearful. Life's certainties disappeared. He felt like a ship's captain without compass, chart or rudder. Life just wasn't worth living. *Am I suicidal?* he asked himself.

Good News Community Church seduced him. A mostly blue-collar congregation with a few college students, twenty-somethings earnestly seeking God. The preaching and Bible studies drew him in and nurtured his thirsty soul. Here he found a lighthouse that blinded his own flickering candle and drew him mothlike toward the light.

How ironic, he thought. Here was a church the opposite of Plymouth Congregational—an uneducated pastor, even anti-intellectual, who preached hell, condemnation and naïve certainty. Legalistic, narrow, even bigoted. Criticizing the sexual habits and entertainments of modern America. *So why am I paying attention?*

This night, Pastor Runnell preached, "Nothing you can do will gain your own salvation." *How could that be?* he wondered. *That sounds so hopeless.* He shifted on the hard bench. "But Christ can do it all for you; his death has freed you. You can't out-sin his grace. You must turn to him."

The messages seared Bledsoe's shriveled soul. He didn't remember hearing about sin and moral failure at Plymouth or what you did about it if you should fail. Plymouth proclaimed positivity—speak positive, act positive, think positive. But those childhood truths weren't durable enough for the twists and turns in his own life. He walked home fearing his life was out of control.

Something kept clawing Bledsoe back to GNCC like a grappling hook. But he would just sit there dejected. He reflected across the blurred landscapes of his life, realized he needed forgiveness, needed restoration. He began to despair trying to direct his own life.

GNCC evening services always included an "altar call," an extended plea for people to come down front, get right with God, "accept Christ" publicly. Plymouth Congregational's Pastor Bodie had warned Bledsoe about these kinds of churches—too fiery, strident, dogmatic. But somehow, he couldn't walk out. He thought, *Of course God knows my past, knows it better than I do. Can God forgive me?* He sat glued to his seat, skeptical, unconsciously pumping his right leg pumping up and down, a nervous habit he'd acquired in junior high school. The invitation seemed too good to be true.

The next Sunday evening, Bledsoe walked back into the church, miserable. *Why am I here?* he asked himself. This was the kind of church his parents tolerated with superior smiles, the kind his friends made jokes about. But Bledsoe felt desperate, powerless to face himself, paralyzed by his own selfishness, longing for something better.

Brother Runnell preached passionately. "There's nothing you can do. 'Nothing in my hands I bring; only to the cross of Christ I cling.' Embrace the cross; accept the gift. God loves you and God calls you. God does not judge you for your past. He offers you grace and total forgiveness today."

Bledsoe felt the net tightening, squeezing his breath away. He felt captured by Jesus's words but captured even more by Jesus's actions. H*e loves me,* he thought; *he died for me.*

Abruptly, Harold Bledsoe got up, walked down and grasped the altar rail with sweaty, penitentiary hands.

As he knelt, Pastor Runnell came over, laid a hand on his shoulder and prayed for him. He teared up and poured out his soul, longing for the transcendent to break in upon his failed life. Pastor Runnell told him, "Christ will come into your life and cleanse you, give you a new heart."

"I would like to believe that but I don't want to live like a hypocrite, just denying that I've done some pretty wretched things in my life."

"Harold, God knows all about your past life. God doesn't approve of it but Christ died for you, died to erase all these mistakes and bring you back to God."

Now, Bledsoe saw how alcohol and sexual liaisons had failed to medicate his sick soul. *I've not only damaged the women I linked up with,* he realized, *but I've also offended God.*

The bright light of Jesus's message illuminated the vanity and temporality of his life. That night he gave up and, in the only way he knew, embraced God's Christ.

Walking home Bledsoe looked up at the paling stars, tiny sparks caught in the tree branches. The world seemed different; he seemed different. Much later, he sat in his Cleveland apartment chewing on what happened. He truly believed his conversion but didn't know what to do next. He took a drink of iced tea and a bite out of the ham sandwich he'd made to quiet his rumbling stomach. He passed up the bottle of Coors.

Although he knew God forgave him, his past continued to haunt him. He grew concerned about his California women of a few years ago. He still had some telephone numbers. *Why do I keep these?* he wondered. *Will they still work?*

All at once he picked up the phone and called Anne long-distance. His voice trembled. "Anne, I just wanted to call and tell you how sorry I am for how I treated you. I didn't respect you, didn't consider your feelings. I'm going to a good church now, trying to change. Would you forgive me?"

Silence. Then, "Why did you wait four years to tell me this? Harold, do you think one telephone call can make it right between us? Do you want to get together again? How would that work?"

"No, Anne, I know we can't get together again, I just wanted to tell you I'm sorry."

"You've got a bad conscience? I've moved on, tried to make a life for myself. This is more about you than me, isn't it?"

"No, listen, I'm just hoping you would forgive me for violating your trust, then walking away."

"Well, thanks, I guess. I hope things work out for you."

"And for you too, Anne."

He called others, those whose numbers he could find. A few thanked him with tears; others just seemed puzzled.

The next week Bledsoe walked down the hall at Cuyahoga High. He knew he was in too deep with Beth, knew he must break it off. He couldn't trust himself—continuing to contact her endangered him and endangered her also.

He called her into his office. "Beth, you must find another counselor. I feel bad that I did not, cannot help you. I'm afraid I've just harmed you. We need to stop meeting but I hope we can say hello in the halls."

Beth blanched, her jaw dropped, then she broke into tears. She hadn't seen this coming. She needed him, wanted him, the only still point in her chaotic world. "But you're the only person who understands me, the only person who cares about me. I don't have anybody else."

"Beth, you'll find others. You are a wonderful person and deserve good friends. I'm your friend; it's just that we can't be seeing each other anymore."

At last, she walked out with her head down, disconsolate. She'd just lost her beacon, the only person she'd ever trusted.

It was in the spring of his third year at Cuyahoga when the principal called him in. "Bad news. One of our students got pregnant by a senior classmate, then dropped out of school. This morning her mother called sobbing, said that last night she jumped in front of a fast-moving Baltimore & Ohio freight train down at Whiskey Island crossing."

"Oh no. What's her name?"

"Beth Jackson."

Bledsoe walked out of the principal's office in shock, his stomach roiling. Over the next week, he grieved over what he knew was his part in Beth's death. He hadn't even shared his new Christian convictions with her. Plus, he still worried that people would find out about their liaison.

After another year Bledsoe grew weary of his job and began looking for a change. Sitting in his office, he saw an ad in the TBI Monthly. (Pastor Runnell had subscribed for him.) Bledsoe had heard of Torrey Bible Institute—one of the GNCC people was studying by correspondence with TBI and preparing for overseas missionary service. The short ad read: "Dean of men wanted at Torrey Bible Institute for fall, 1960. Must be Bible-believing and embrace the fundamentals of the faith. Starts in September. Respond with your resume."

This is a great opportunity to get to where God wants me, he thought. *High moral ground, a safe place to work and grow. A way to get away from my memories of Beth.* Would this be the place where he could conquer his demons? He picked up his pen and wrote for an application.

When he received the form from TBI, some of the questions surprised him, questions on detailed doctrinal beliefs. And then, are you married? *No.* Were you ever married? Bledsoe hesitated. *I dare not bare my backside to TBI,* he thought. He knew if he answered truthfully his chances of success would be something like a baby guppy in a shark tank. If he put *Yes*, it might sink him—they would want to know about his wife and family. And he would have to reveal his divorce. Unlikely TBI would ever find out about it, though. He wrote *No.*

The detailed questions about his sexual history shocked him. Have you ever engaged in sexual intercourse? He pumped his nervous leg, pondered the question, then wrote *No. I've just turned myself into a virgin,* he thought.

When Bledsoe finished the three-page questionnaire he felt guilty. He'd already confessed his past sins, felt God's love and forgiveness. But now he'd just lied on a questionnaire. As he licked the envelope, he tried not to think about it. I just need to get there; then I can work on my life's problems. They don't need to know all about my past. Besides, God has already forgiven me. But he could not know the deep consequences of his little lies.

Beth's death still tortured him, made him afraid that his earlier relationship with her would become public. So he resigned from Cuyahoga High School and moved home, hoping his TBI application would lead to an interview and a job. He was correct on both counts.

Chapter 19

September 1960. Back at Torrey Bible Institute that fall, Sean was running to class, late as usual, his shoes scraping the rough tile floors as he rounded the corner and plunged down the stairs. Later, swinging by the P.O.'s on the slim chance of a letter, he remembered the bright vision of Kathy Wilberforce at the luau two summers before and wished she would at least write. He twirled the combination on his box, leaned down, peered into the empty box and turned away, disappointed.

Then, across the large room, contradicting everything he knew and believed, he saw a vision. Blinking, he tried to clear his head—was it wish-fulfillment or was it real? There, at the other end of the line of P.O. boxes, appearing like an avatar, stood Kathleen Wilberforce.

"Kathy—is it you?" He ran over. "What are you doing here?"

She flinched, then raised her eyes. "Hello, Sean . . ." Her visage seemed darker, transformed from the high school girl Sean had known. Was she ill?

"Kathy, why did you come without telling me? Are you OK?"

She shriveled under the barrage of questions. "I don't know . . . I don't want to talk about it [spoken hesitantly, her eyes cast to the floor]. Sean, I'm sorry I didn't let you know . . . I dropped out of Biola last November, moved back to the apartment in Costa Mesa, then went to work again at the Jolly Roger down in Balboa."

"But what are you doing here? Why didn't you write me?

"I made a quick decision. I needed to get away, far away, from California but I didn't want to quit school and this was the only place I could think of."

"Well, it's sure great to see you." And then Sean thought about Reggie—sophisticated, fast-track, confident, outgoing. Kathleen had worn Reggie's varsity sweater. He knew Reggie was dating someone else now but didn't know if Kathy was still interested in him. "How's Reggie?"

"Oh, I don't know; he is well, I guess," Kathleen said, her eyes focused on something distant in time and space. "You heard we broke up. We are not dating or anything now."

She was polite but her heart seemed shut up like an insect in amber and her answers oblique. *I don't dare think she's come to TBI because of me,* Sean thought. *Is she running away from something?*

"I don't understand, but I'm glad you've come, Kathy. It's so great seeing you. You're one of the few people I know here from Southern California. I hope we have some classes together, hope we can see each other."

"Yes . . . I hope I did the right thing in coming. But after Reginald and I broke up, I just lost interest in dating. I hope you understand. It would be nice to talk sometimes, though."

"Kathy, you've changed. That really puts me off. If you broke up with Reggie, we should start dating again here. Why did you come back east if you weren't interested in seeing me?"

"Oh, Sean. Please don't ask me any more questions." Her eyes grew moist as she wheeled around and disappeared, ghostlike, up the stairs toward the Cromwell Hall classrooms. Stung, Sean felt his threadbare hopes waver, then fall headlong into the breach that had opened between them.

Kathleen Wilberforce arrived at TBI as a troubled woman on the run. She'd lied on her application and hid from TBI her liaison with Reggie, reasoning that it was only one time, that she had broken off with him, that the question was too personal and that TBI had no business asking these things. She tried to dedicate herself to her classes. Visited the Hargreaves prayer room often. Tried to feel joy. But to no avail. She would walk across the campus in fear, feeling like a traitor, fearing someone would discover her deception, fearing Sean would show an interest in her and above all, knowing she could never find forgiveness, never recover from her great sin.

The days passed and Sean hardly saw Kathleen but one Wednesday evening he happened to walk by the Muslim Prayer Band room. There she was—all tan-sweatered, full-skirted, wearing brown flats. She didn't see him staring.

Why did she choose Muslim? The most admired mission field was Africa and northern Africa was Muslim—hard-core, resistant. Maybe she joined Muslim Prayer Band for the challenge. For his part, Sean didn't attend a prayer band. He found them boring and anyway, he didn't understand how prayer worked and didn't believe in it anymore.

One cold, rainy morning that October, Sean jerked awake; then yelled over at Fulton, who was still sleeping, "We're late for devotions; you gotta get up." He jumped up, threw on shirt and pants, spitting on his hand to smooth his cowlick. They left their dorm room and joined several guys running down the Norbert Hall stairs.

As they jogged along, Sean's thoughts drifted to the previous summer with Betty. He realized he hardly knew Betty, except physically. He'd told her he loved her, tried to talk himself into loving her but realized it was only because he wanted to take more liberties. Kathy seemed so different from Betty—more complex, more substantive. Why had Kathy come? Was she running away from Reggie? *Anyway, I'm glad they broke up.*

Chapter 20

At the first men's devotions of the fall semester, Dean A. Franklin Puckett introduced Harold Bledsoe, the new men's dean. Sean McIntosh stared at the dashing Bledsoe—bouncing on his heels, full of brio, seeming to refract an alien light. He didn't look very deanish; he seemed an iridescent circle among rectangles.

After Bledsoe got settled in his tenth-floor office, Dean Puckett assigned him campus block patrol. Sean had heard the rumors. TBI couples would walk the city block that circled the campus—traversing the cracked and broken sidewalk along the chain-link-fenced parking lot, then turning back toward the women's dorm. The deans warned students not to linger in the recessed doorways of Moody-Sankey Auditorium. The rule was—keep walking. Bledsoe would cruise around in his big black Cadillac convertible with the top down heedless of the weather, shining his spotlight into the recesses, flushing out couples.

Bledsoe also flushed people out of Moody-Sankey's balcony, one of TBI's best hiding places. At random times he would burst in, shine his big flashlight and surprise couples in the act. He wouldn't take down names, just kick them out the door with a warning. Sean fantasized about the balcony; he had no girlfriend, but the prohibitions made the dark balcony attractive.

Bledsoe's portfolio was dean of men but several times Sean saw him chatting up the women students. He supposed they loved his California stories, loved his black convertible. On the nights when the deans spread out to sit at student tables in the dining hall, he would often end up at the same table as Kathleen Wilberforce. His casual style, so different from the other deans, seemed to rivet her attention. *Something new to worry about,* Sean thought.

The next day Sean arrived at Moody-Sankey for mandatory chapel and initialed his name on the sign-in sheet. Often President Clearson spoke, or a visiting Bible teacher. But today it was Harold Bledsoe.

Sean saw Katheen signing in alongside another girl he didn't know. They walked in a different door but Sean saw where she sat— attentive, serious, beatific, her big blue eyes focused on the podium.

President Clearson introduced the new dean. He said that Bledsoe was born in Boston, then attended Stanford University where he did a B.A. in counseling with a coaching minor. He came to faith, Clearson explained, while teaching at Cuyahoga High School in Cleveland. Wearing a sports coat and light brown slacks, Bledsoe gave a touching testimony about his dissolute life at Stanford, his teaching days in Cleveland and his powerful conversion, ending his talk with a call for Christian commitment.

After the service Kathleen and her friend turned to walk out. Sean saw how Bledsoe's sermon had touched people—Kathleen was blowing her nose and dabbing her eyes with her handkerchief. He overheard her and her friends enthusing over the new dean so he walked away angry and didn't try to talk to her.

Two weeks into the semester, Dean Harold Bledsoe elevatored up to his Cromwell Hall office, sat, and rocked back in his desk chair. Unseen, Dean Darla Dickenson observed him from a distance. He was inhaling the smell of his office, sighing in satisfaction. Dickenson saw an eligible bachelor in his thirties who wore dark brown pants and a gold watch. He seemed a bronzed god—over six feet tall with a Caesar-like nose, wavy dark hair and ears that pressed against his temples. When he turned his head toward her, she disappeared into her own office.

Bledsoe grew popular with the students but not so much with the deans, especially Dickenson. Only an office partition separated her from Bledsoe and she thought he took up too much space, said she could smell his cologne. But despite herself Dickenson admired his self-confidence, his relaxed, joking manner and especially, his Roman physique. But these very qualities also fueled her dislike for him—he, with his black convertible and casual attitude. The little rat part of her brain grew jealous of the attention he paid to the TBI girls. She'd heard his conversion story and knew he wasn't reared in a fundamentalist church. To her he was like the Wandering Jew—no origin, no identity—an enigma.

Bledsoe smiled a lot. At TBI, smiling was mandatory—it was thought to radiate a "good testimony" to the world. *Some people smile out of habit,*

Dickenson thought, *some out of obligation, some because they see the ironies of life and some because they're happy. Why does Bledsoe smile? Is his air-brushed image genuine or is he hiding something?*

Dickenson walked over to Dean Puckett's office and whispered, "I don't think Bledsoe is very TBI-esque. He's too friendly with the girls. When he drives around the block, he shines his spotlight up at Hargreaves Hall and the girls open their windows and wave. I'm afraid he's not a good role model for the boys, either. TBI forms serious, mission-driven men and women, not clowns."

"Darla, we need to give him some time to settle in, not judge him so soon."

"Not judge him? I wish you could see him chatting up the girls."

Puckett said nothing.

Dickenson's suspicions were not unfounded. Harold Bledsoe brought with him a tangled background and closely guarded secrets.

Chapter 21

Sean McIntosh grew tired of earning ninety-nine cents an hour working TBI maintenance, so he was happy when Mrs. Thomas in Student Affairs told him, "We have a factory job at a dollar twenty-five an hour. You can go over and apply." So in September of his second year Sean ate early lunch in the dining hall, then exited the arch and walked toward the "L" to go for his job interview.

Disappearing down the "L" stairs at State Street, he heard the roar and clacking of the approaching train and broke into a trot. After a ten-minute ride he got off, climbed the stairs to ground level, then turned west, walking away from the office skyscrapers toward the industrial section. The vast city with its tired old brick factory buildings depressed him. His mother had suffered from a saturnine spirit; he wondered if that explained why he sometimes felt depressed. Or did he just have fading, flagging faith?

He stopped in front of an ancient brick building with dead-eyed windows (for a Californian, all Chicago buildings seemed ancient) and a brownstone-linteled door. He entered and walked into the musty hall.

He found the manager sitting at his desk in a high-ceilinged room with blinds drawn over tall windows. "Hi, I'm Sean McIntosh. Mrs. Thomas at TBI's Student Affairs sent me to apply for your open position."

Mr. Allen looked up, then shoved a small form across the table. "You can write down your Social Security number here." That was it—no application, no job interview; he was hired. TBI students enjoyed a good reputation.

Sean grasped a splintery banister as he followed the manager up a flight of uneven wooden stairs to a large room dominated by a huge, roaring machine. Overhead, cobwebs hung from sleepy wooden beams.

Mr. Allen called over to Tom, the floor guy. "This is Sean. Put him on the can line." Then he walked out.

Tom yelled at Sean, "Put on eight cans at a time. Just make sure you keep up." Tom didn't say much else; you couldn't hear over the roar of the machine anyway. Standing on a rough pine-board floor, Sean stuck his fingers into eight empty cans and placed them on the roller belt that disappeared into the beating heart of the machine. As they moved, he picked up eight more cans. Easy to get the hang of it but you had to pay attention. After the machine squirted pie filling into the cans, they marched out the other end capped and sealed. After two weeks Sean figured out what "pie filling" was—a processed mixture of fruits for pouring into pie crusts before baking. Sometimes Sean would dip his finger into the mix for a taste.

Nobody seemed to care where the product came from or where it was going. He felt like Oliver Twist in the Dickens novel— solitary, alone amidst a multitude of mute minions performing mindless work in a bleak, industrialized world.

After Sean had been working a week, Tom rolled a cart in with an enormous tub of hot pie filling. He yelled, "Come over and grab a handle." Sean heaved to hoist the tub to the enormous vat but faltered halfway up. Several gallons of pie filling spilled out across the floor.

"Yikes. Sorry. I guess I should a used two hands."

"Hey. You gotta watch what you're doin.' This stuff is hot." That was the last time Sean helped with tub-lifting. Back to putting cans on the conveyer belt.

After two hours work he got a fifteen-minute break. Walking into the break room he saw another guy sitting at a table. Sean didn't know what to say to him and soon the guy got up and left. Sean pulled a Mars candy bar out of his pocket along with a textbook he was reading.

His thoughts drifted to Kathy. He felt happy she'd come to TBI but wondered about her hermetic demeanor and despaired of getting close to her. He'd mentioned about getting the job in a pie filling plant. She said she'd started working in TBI's dining room.

He tried to concentrate on his textbook but someone had thrown an old *Playboy* on the table and the cover drew him in. He glanced over his shoulder at the door, then opened the magazine. A world of partially clad women magnetized him, so much so that he almost forgot to go back to work. He returned to the production room feeling weak-willed and guilty. *Wait a minute,* he thought. *If I'm an atheist, there's nothing to feel guilty about, certainly not* Playboy. But he couldn't unsee the pictures. *Pornography is scab-scratching,* he thought. *It feels good, but you want to keep scratching even after it turns bloody.*

At 5 p.m. Sean placed his last eight cans on the belt. Without a word, the shift manager shut down the huge machine and walked out. Sean descended the steps and exited into the city that still belched smoke from its hundreds of stacks, raining down Chicago freckles on his head and shirt. Chicago—harsh, impersonal, businesslike, building industry to build capital. Compassionless city, God-forsaken. He walked alone for ten minutes, then joined the crowds squeezing into the "L" train. At Chicago Avenue he exited and walked west.

Entering TBI's arch, he stepped into a saner, gentler world. His friends were here, and staff and faculty who may not know his name but still counted him as one of their own. Few people guessed his faith foundation was crumbling.

During the three months he worked at the pie-filling factory, all he learned was how to put cans on a conveyer belt, eight cans at a time, four hours a day—numbing movements that freed him to explore the great inscape of his troubled mind. He would look out the dirty window to glimpse the dead, wax-paper sky and dream of summer days with J-3 Cubs ascending and descending over grassy airstrips. He thought back to flight camp, still tasting the bitter failure. Would TBI accept him for flight camp this summer? It was the only reason he was staying there.

Chapter 22

The next Monday Sean left his dorm room and headed down the hall for chapel. Because TBI stood tall as a fundamentalist breeding ground, chapel drew internationally known speakers—Olford, Redpath, Barnhouse. (When Donald Grey Barnhouse spoke, he bellowed, being used to preaching before microphones came along.) These speakers were supposed to deepen student faith but also to model good preaching for TBI's aspiring pastors. Scheduled to give the sermon that day was the famous G. Victor McGraw.

Darrell Reardon had told Sean, "G. Victor McGraw broadcasts a syndicated radio program across the nation. He's spoken several times at Torrey Church and Dr. Clearson studied under him at Dallas Seminary. He drinks from the Source." Sean couldn't wait to hear him.

TBI housed speakers on Norbert Hall's sixth floor but Sean was surprised when he walked into the elevator and almost bumped into a scowling G. Victor McGraw. Sean stood statuesque, feeling like Moses gazing at the burning bush. But this "bush" didn't say anything, except: "I'm going to first floor," spoken as if someone put sand in his toothpaste. Full-suited, fat-necked, gray-haired, untalkative, he exuded the demeanor of a man of God. He didn't look at Sean as they descended but when they exited the elevator, he broke wind.

Sean had loved to listen to McGraw's radio messages—"Dear friends, all people on the topside of God's earth need salvation . . ." In his TBI chapel talk, he seemed the epitome of charm and grace. *Which man is the real G. Victor McGraw?* Sean wondered.

He had another celebrity encounter that fall. Jack Parker served as the popular radio pastor of Los Angeles' redoubtable Church of the Open Door—the church Kathleen attended when she was at Biola. Parker spoke internationally at conferences and was almost as well-known as McGraw.

On the way to chapel, Sean stopped by Smith Hall bathroom and walked up to a urinal, being careful to leave an empty one between himself and the next guy. Out of the corner of his eye he saw—Jack Parker.

He'd shriveled before G. Victor McGraw but resolved to do better with Parker. He still believed that if he could find the right pastor or theologian, he could silence his biggest doubts, answer his most urgent questions and regain his faith. He decided to risk it.

"Dr. Parker, I've got a question. Is this a bad time?"

Dr. Parker glanced up frowning, then focused on Sean. (Both men continued to pee.)

"I was wondering, if God knows the destiny of all people even before they're born, why do we worry about saving people?"

Dr. Parker finished and zipped up. "We cannot know whom God has predestined but our testimony to them may be part of God's plan." Then he washed his hands and walked out.

As he left Sean thought, *I really botched it. Hmmm. How can anybody believe people are predestined anyway, that they have no choice in salvation? How would you even "sell" this doctrine to your friends?* Fundamentalists were always on the alert for sales tips; evangelization was important. He'd failed many times trying to sell fundamentalism to others and now had no desire to even try.

He walked over to chapel, initialed the sign-in sheet, entered the large auditorium and took his seat next to Connie who wore skirts about one inch shorter than average. Like all men he felt a catholic attraction to girls—generic, not specific. He could smell her perfume, perfume like his sister wore, and when she slouched, he could see her knees. "Hi, Connie. You won't believe who I just bumped into in the bathroom—Jack Parker. I wonder what he'll say today." *If it gets boring,* he thought, *I can keep awake by looking sideways at Connie's knees.*

It wasn't just Parker's preaching about predestination that troubled Sean; it was the doctrine of eternal security (once God "saves" you, you never lose your salvation). These arcane doctrines formed the center of fundamentalist teaching and even rose to a test of one's faith. Good sermon but it left Sean with even more questions.

Dr. Meacham, instructor for the John and Acts class, was a fresh DMin graduate from Dallas Theological Seminary and a crisp lecturer. He told the students he was organizing a class debate on John 15—*Resolved: John 15 teaches that a person can lose their salvation.* The argument hinged on seeing Christ as the vine and his followers the branches. Branches yielding no fruit were "broken off" and thrown into the fire.

Did that mean a person could fall away, lose salvation? Sean wondered. When Meacham asked for volunteer debaters, Shawn thought, *If Meacham suspects I'm an atheist, I'll get kicked out of TBI immediately—no graduation, no aviation. Maybe I'll enter the debate for the extra credit but I'll take the opposition side.* He raised his hand and took the "Opposed" position, along with Jenny, a girl he didn't know. Two other students took the "Support" position. They had to meet in Meacham's office. Meacham explained, "You don't have to hold the position you're arguing but you have to try to present it with great conviction."

Sean and Jenny spent hours in preparation—consulting commentaries, seeking cross-references. The night before the great debate he lay tossing on his bed, grinding his teeth—had he prepared enough? He knew the opposing side was just as strong as his side but you can't pee down both legs of your pants—you must stake out a strong position and defend it. On the day of the debate he felt his hands clammy as he obsessed about arguing for a position he did not believe in.

Each of the four students presented their case. Sean and Jenny emphasized God's sovereignty to choose and his faithfulness to keep the branches safe, that true believers had "eternal security." Their opponents emphasized the plain-language meaning of the text—clearly, the branches could be broken off and burned, so a person could lose his salvation. Then the class voted. When five students voted for the "Opposed" side and thirty "Support," Meacham expressed frustration that so many students questioned eternal security.

Sean felt disappointed they hadn't won but he guessed why. Even here in a TBI classroom, he'd failed in defending eternal security—because he didn't even believe it himself. He wondered what Kathy thought about eternal security. He thought a lot about Kathy but his sexual dream-fantasies centered on Betty. Over the next few weeks, he grew quieter and more troubled.

Late one night Sean sat alone, gazing out the window of Norbert prayer room, trying hard not to pray. *Why am I in a prayer room?* he asked himself. *I don't even believe God exists—I'm like a Nazi in a synagogue.* He smelled the humid carpet and a chill gripped him—was the radiator working? *I guess you don't ever become a perfect atheist; you just work harder and harder at it. Am I working hard enough?* He slammed his fist down on the table. *Damn it—tonight I'll burn some bridges.*

He walked in stocking feet down the hall to fetch the steel wastebasket from his dorm room along with some towels, a paper bag, a jar of water and a book of matches he'd picked up from a restaurant. And his Bible. Propping a chair under the knob of the closed prayer room door, his hands trembled as he picked the Bible up and opened to the inscription on the fly-leaf—"For you, Son, on your twelfth birthday. God bless you. Love, Mom." This black leather Scofield Bible symbolized his fundamentalist Christian life. But tonight he was leaving it all behind. Why couldn't he just throw it away? No, he had to do something more, something to make a clean break with his past.

His heart stopped as he heard footsteps outside, probably someone going to the bathroom. Grasping his Bible by the spine, he struck a match and held it under the hanging pages. When they curled and blazed into flame, he dropped the burning mass into the wastebasket. He stuffed some towels in the crack under the door. Coughing, he ran over and opened the window, hoping no one would smell the smoke. It seemed to him that the acrid smell, along with his childhood faith was pouring out the window and disappearing into thin air. He felt the loss but at the same time felt empowered by his action.

When the smoke died down, he poured in the jar of water, heard the steam hiss and then sat a long time in one of the wooden chairs, trembling. In his desperation he'd done the deed, committed the sacrilege, put into action his atheism—the boldest thing he'd ever done. And he'd done it in this sacred place of prayer. Henceforth his "Christian faith" would only be an act.

He scooped out the sodden mass and put it in the paper bag, trying to wipe the condemning wet ashes from his hands. Opening the prayer room door and looking both ways down the hall, he walked down to the men's bathroom and stuffed the bag deep into the trash can. Just then he looked up at the mirror and saw a bulky form walk in and enter one of the stalls. Dean Winters! He must be on overnight duty this week. Sean panicked. He quickly washed the stains off his hands, hoping no lingering smoke smell would betray him, hoping Winters wouldn't notice the soggy, burnt mass in the trash can. Then he crept back to his dorm room, threw himself on his bed exhausted and said out-loud, "I'll never believe in God again."

That same week, Kathleen Wilberforce swung by the P.O.'s to see if her mother had written. But she found only a small, folded note with the name "Kathy" on it.

> Hello, Kathy,
>
> I'm here on business and came by the institute this morning to see you but you weren't in. All I can think of is you. I'm tortured, lamenting our breakup, still hopeful we can work something out. Staying at the Ambassador here on State Street.
>
> Can we meet for a 6:00 p.m. dinner tomorrow evening here at the hotel? I'm in meetings all day but you can leave a phone message at the hotel and I'll come by to pick you up. Or grab a cab and come over and I'll meet you here. I long to hear from you, long to talk to you.
>
> Love,
> Reggie Radcliffe

Kathleen's knees buckled, then she shut her eyes and shivered. Reginald—here in Chicago. Why had he contacted her? What should she do? There was no one she could go to for advice.

Chapter 23

THE SAME DAY KATHY received Reggie's note, Sean visited the notorious Cook County Hospital. TBI required each student to do "Practical Christian Work" (PCW) and Sean and four other students were assigned to the hospital. They walked to State Street and disappeared down the concrete stairs to the "L." A besotted man lay face up on the station platform, still as stone, his flaccid skin outlining his bones like a too-large coat on a fasting man. Heedless of the chilly day, he lay insensible when two flies crawled over his scalp. Sean felt revulsion and a little guilt stepping around him.

A rising roar and bright light signaled the "L"'s arrival. They boarded the great integrator, filled with people of all social classes, colors and races wanting to get somewhere fast. Sean swayed, holding onto the strap. Not much talking—people stared straight ahead or read the paper. You couldn't talk much anyway over the thunder of the train.

All at once they burst into daylight and rose onto elevated tracks where Sean had a bird's eye view of the heads of pedestrians, the tops of cars and buses and beyond, the windows of the office buildings that framed people working at their desks.

Soon the PCW group disembarked, descended the steel steps and headed toward the hospital, inhaling the diesel exhaust from the buses, keeping their heads down to protect their faces.

A forlorn young woman walked toward them crying as she carried some dirt and a small plant in the chalice of her cupped hands, looking like a poster child for the human condition. Thin and slightly built, she wore open sandals and only a light windbreaker against the cold. One of the girls in the group asked her, "What's wrong?"

"God just gave me this gift, the most precious gift in the world—the Tree of Life." She held up the small plant cradled in her dirty hands. "And now it's dying." She raised her bulging, frog-like eyes to her. "I don't know where to plant it, how to water it, how to care for it. The world's so cruel and I am so sick. If this plant dies, I die with it, the whole world dies. Please help me."

Sean stood speechless. Tanya put her arm around the bedraggled girl's bony shoulders then turned to whisper to Sean, "She smells of alcohol." The whole group sympathized but they needed to hurry to get to their hospital assignment, so they prayed for her, sat her on a bench hunched and shivering, then walked away. Sean glanced back over his shoulder at her pitiful form, her hands still clutching the Tree of Life.

Cook County Hospital's Beaux Arts façade featured sweet cherubs and rampant roaring lions anchored by fluted Ionic columns, beauty reminiscent of a magnificent woman, but past her prime. Known as "Chicago's Ellis Island," Cook County embraced all who came, all who otherwise could not afford medical care.

They entered the huge doors and walked across the cracked floor tiles. "Look at those sagging doors," Sean said to Tanya, "and the paint peeling from the walls." Bleak, unwashed windows looked out on the careless city.

TBI's Practical Christian Work director had given no orientation—only told them to walk the halls and talk to people. The rooms smelled of urine and rubbing alcohol and overflowed with beds. IV feeds hung down from hooks; oxygen tubes protruded from patients' noses. A woman moaned and thrashed about. One old man raised his head to cry out while a young boy kept calling "nurse, nurse." Patients lay on gurneys lining the hallways. One wore a body cast, steel rods protruding out of his shins to hold broken bones in place. Harried nurses passed from one patient to the other, their voices echoing through the vast building.

The PCW director had told them, "Just submerge yourself; do more than get your feet wet. Figure it out yourself. Let God guide you."

Sean walked slowly through the painful corridors, still consumed with thoughts of his Bible-burning. He wondered, *Why am I here? These desperate people, some terminally ill, have no one to talk to. What to say? I have enough trouble talking to people I know. I don't think I have anything to offer them, certainly not any spiritual hope.*

Somehow he got separated from the others and found himself at a cul de sac in front of locked doors. Then an orderly walked up to a keypad. "Here; I'll punch you in." Sean wondered (too late) where the other TBI students were. The doors slammed behind him and he entered purgatory.

Perhaps the hospital staff imagined that these naïve Bible Institute students could distract the patients and relieve the orderlies for a few minutes.

A Negro girl about twelve years old sat at a table and looked up at him. "They say I killed my two kittens. But I loved my little kittens. I don't know . . . They just ate something and died. I took their little bodies out and buried them in the back yard but our dog dug them up and was eating them just as Daddy got home . . . He whupped me. Mommy said she's coming back this afternoon to pick me up. I don't like it here." Tremulous, sobbing, she paused coloring in her book and turned to look at her beat-up, dark-faced, doll. "Abigail says Daddy can't come home anymore because he drinks too much." Then turning back to Sean, "I love my mommy and daddy. They're coming to get me." When Sean tried to touch her, she recoiled.

Raising up from his chair, a shriveled man mistook Sean for his son. "So good to see you, Roger. They treat me terrible here; I'm so glad you're taking me home."

A heavy-set woman lay on her bed, just staring up at Sean. He froze. *What should I do? he wondered. Read the Bible? Pray? Try to engage her in conversation?*

Then the woman yelled, "Turkey, turkey, turkey." Was she anticipating Thanksgiving?

Another man whispered, "My daughter brought me here with a bad fever. They're discharging me tomorrow. Some of these people are crazy."

Another: "God will send fire to consume the whole world. Most of these people are lost souls but I'm saved by the blood of the lamb."

A middle-aged woman smiled at Sean, then whispered, "I'm a virgin; I've kept myself for Christ but one of the doctors tried to rape me. I screamed and he ran away. Everybody woke up. Nobody believes me but God protected me."

A nurse walked up. "We keep the dangerous people in a different ward. Most of these folks just need medication—they're not a threat to anybody. Not much we can do. Nobody ever visits them, not even their relatives." She punched Sean out of the lockup.

Walking into the men's bathroom, Sean stared at the urinal, trying to control his urge to vomit. He'd just paid a visit to the last refuge of the damned. He wanted to show compassion but instead, he felt revulsion. The piety of the mentally ill shocked him. *How could Christianity be true if crazy people believe it?* he wondered. Where was God in the lives of these troubled people? The sick and injured, bereft of grace, cut off from the love of family and from God. Who cares about these people? *Do I even care?*

His own lack of compassion, his emotional weakness, guilted him. *Kathy would flourish here,* he thought. *She harbors a huge heart that embraces all kinds of hurt people.* But he vowed to himself—*I'll never come back here again.*

Shaken, he joined the other TBI students in the entry hall. Some of them enthused about their conversations; others remained silent. *A visit to Cook County Hospital gives your faith a reality check,* Sean thought. *I think I'm just fated to unbelief.*

Meanwhile, Kathleen was in the Hargreaves prayer room reading and rereading Reggie's letter, She was breathing fast and felt her heart pulse her throat. Crumpling the note, she threw it in the trash basket—then pulled it out and smoothed it on her desk. Reread it. *How dare he come here? I did nothing to lead him on!* What should she do? She had nobody to talk to. She'd gotten closer to him than to any other boy. *Does that mean I am chained to Reginald for life? Could I ever forgive him, ever love him?*

Finally, she walked to the Hargreaves Hall telephone, not to call Reggie but to call Sean's dorm. She respected him and trusted him to help her make this decision. He'd just returned from Cook County when the call came in.

"Sean, Reginald is at the Ambassador Hotel and wants to meet with me." Here, she read the letter to Sean. "I just don't know what to do. I've prayed and prayed about it but feel like I'm not getting any answers."

"Kathy, why would you want to see Reggie? I thought you broke up and that was the end of it. Do you still have feelings for him?"

A pause. Then, "No, I don't wish to see him but I feel so many things were just left hanging between us, I wonder if I have an obligation to at least talk with him. Maybe he'll apologize."

"Kathy, he's toxic. And if you go see him, he might suck you in again. I'm going over to tell him to leave you alone."

"Oh, Sean, please don't do that. You can't . . . Reginald might do something. Promise me you won't go." Sean promised and she hung up.

But Sean wasn't convinced Kathy could resist Reggie. *I promised her I wouldn't try to see him but I guess I could call him.* He walked down to the phone booth in Norbert Hall lobby. Reggie was not in, so he called him again about 10 p.m. that evening.

"Hello, Reggie, this is Sean McIntosh."

"Hey, Sean. How are you, anyway? Great to hear your voice. It's been a long time. How are things at Torrey Bible?"

"Listen, Reggie. Kathy told me about your note to her. She's upset. You need to leave her alone and not contact her."

"Oh, I just want to talk to her. I need to explain some things to her."

"You would upset her more. It would be better if you just left."

"Well, I'm not leaving town until I see Kathy. I bet I can get her to meet with me."

"Reggie, leave her alone."

Reggie hung up.

After she'd talked by phone with Sean, Kathy walked back to her dorm room troubled. Of course Reginald would assume she would come for dinner, would be waiting for her, even if she had not confirmed. Something inside her drove her to Reggie. She tried to forget him but still felt tied to him. *He's the father of my child,* she thought. *Maybe I owe Reggie one last meeting. Maybe he's looking for a way to apologize.* She feared he had lost any spiritual impulses, assuming he'd ever had any. Maybe she could even share her growing faith with him. She fell into a restless sleep.

TBI told their women never to walk the Chicago streets alone but there was no one else she could ask to go with her, not even her roommate. So late afternoon the next day, Kathy snuck out the back gate and into the street.

The sun was just setting but the streets were filled with people coming home from work and she felt safe walking. She found the Ambassador and walked through the lobby to the restaurant. Flowered wallpaper, crystal chandeliers, Persian rugs. Reginald was already living his best life.

As she expected Reginald had arrived early. Resplendent in his blue blazer, cufflinked white shirt, Windsor-knotted tie and pressed, dark slacks, he rose to greet her. "Kathy! I'm so glad you came." He gave her a warm hug that Kathleen did not reciprocate. She said nothing as she slid into the booth opposite him.

After they ordered ice teas, Reggie began the conversation. "Kathy, I know we had some hard times. We moved too fast. I tried to move on but I just couldn't forget you. It's not too late. Let's do a reset and start over. We can begin with the attraction we both felt a year ago."

Kathleen had not seen Reggie since the day she'd told him about her pregnancy. As usual, Reggie did most of the talking. "I had a small business problem here to fix for my new company, used it as an excuse to fly back.

I just had to come to Chicago to meet you, to renew our relationship, put the past behind us so we can move on together. Sean called me, warned me not to see you." (Here, he smiled.) She noticed he made no apologies. No mention of her pregnancy and miscarriage. It was as if the miscarriage was a relief for him, clearing the way for their future together.

"I've missed you so much; thought about you every day. I knew I could not go on without talking to you, mending the past, planning a future for us together."

Kathleen was a woman, he a man. She felt the old attraction rising in her—physical, animal. He always exuded confidence, acting already like a worldly success. *No wonder my mother liked him,* she thought.

"Kathy, I have a few days here on business, so I hope we can meet several times. Go to Grant Park, the Natural History Museum. I want to take you over to Dorney Park to ride the roller coaster. We can have a great time, get reacquainted, catch up on our lives."

She realized he had no understanding of the chaos he had caused in her life, the confusion, and then the devastating loss. This was the old Reggie—blithe, unempathetic, accustomed to getting what he wanted.

Kathleen knew her chances of attracting another man had diminished. She "belonged" to Reginald. And yet she could not conceive of a happy life with him.

"Reginald; I just don't know. I need some time to think, to pray." (Here he wrinkled his brow). She teared up, rose abruptly, then ran out of the hotel without eating.

For Kathleen, her decision had to be based on her faith, based on her desire to please God. Back in her dorm room she prayed earnestly, pouring out her heart to God, pleading for forgiveness, for wisdom as she faced this crossroads.

An unexpected result of her seeing Reginald again—she began to contrast Sean with Reginald. She had been horrified Sean had offered to see Reggie but she was impressed he had called him. When Reggie called her the next day she was ready. "Reginald, please never contact me again."

Chapter 24

Before Sean knew it, the calendar said November. He'd turned nineteen that past spring and he told Fulton, "Wow; this is the first time I can vote in the national elections."

"K-Kennedy's a Catholic," Fulton said. "Don't ya'll know Catholics follow the Pope? They w-worship the Virgin and believe you get s-saved by your good works, Anyway, Kennedy's a *D-Democrat*" (pronounced like a curse word).

"Well, my parents didn't talk politics much; although I know Dad voted Republican. The last presidential election, Mom told me she used to go to the polls to cancel out Dad's vote but with him gone, I wonder if she'll even vote this year."

Fulton consulted his silver pocket watch. "The deans moved a TV into Norbert Hall lounge so people can watch the K-Kennedy–Nixon debates. Let's go watch it." So that evening Sean and Fulton entered the stuffy, packed-out lounge and stood leaning against the wall.

Most fundamentalists distrusted Democrats because they held liberal views on sex and marriage and supported the United Nations, an entity that would create a one-world government headed by the anti-Christ himself. In the debate, both candidates showed strong preparation but John Kennedy's Boston accent charmed his audience with well-turned phrases.

After the debates all the people Sean talked to said they would vote for Richard Nixon—a card-carrying Quaker and a Republican. Sean told Fulton, "Nixon comes from Yorba Linda, just a few miles from my home. John Kennedy comes from the East. But he's charismatic, inspiring, young and a great debater. I'm voting for Kennedy."

"K-Kennedy? I don't see how you can vote for Kennedy."

Maybe voting for Kennedy would be part of Sean's little rebellion against fundamentalism. But he felt torn; he knew no one else who was voting Democrat. He wondered who atheists voted for.

In chapel service the day before election day, Dr. Clearson told the students, "If Kennedy gets elected, he'll honor the Pope more than our nation. And he'll put little Catholic idols in the White House on the fireplace mantel. Scripture says, 'Thou shalt have no other gods before me.' Exodus 20:3."

Sean considered this. He doubted Kennedy would let the Pope overwhelm his loyalty to America. But he couldn't sleep that night. Idols on the White House mantel. Gossip about this frightening possibility spread across TBI like a virus.

On November 8 Sean walked into the polling booth and voted for Richard Nixon.

The week after elections Wesley Stuart spoke in chapel, a man who had spent twenty years as an undercover missionary to Muslims in Arabia. His fervor and personal sacrifices gained him huge respect from the students. Sean noticed that Kathleen Wilberforce paid careful attention. What was it with Kathy, anyway? She seemed even more troubled, even more distant. He had dropped a note in her P.O. but she'd ignored it.

That evening Wesley Stuart walked into the dining hall. Scowling, head lowered, he seemed heedless of his surroundings. *But who wouldn't seem strange after evangelizing undercover twenty years in Arabia?* Sean thought.

Then he walked over and sat down next to Sean. Sean supposed the administrators sprinkled the missionaries around the dining hall like garden seed, hoping that something they said would take root in the heart of a student.

Sean didn't say anything. After all, this man had just addressed the whole student body. And what do you say to a saint? Stuart had chosen the most challenging mission of all—Muslims. Sean felt radioactive, a toxic unbeliever in the presence of a holy man. He felt Stuart's eyes burn straight through him. Could he perceive that he was an atheist?

Stuart fiercely chewed his roast beef (a special dinner that night) and reached for the serving bowl to spoon out a dollop of mashed potatoes. The pressure was building in his chest. *We can't just sit here,* he thought. *Someone's got to say something.*

"Brother Stuart, how many converts have you made during your twenty years of work?"

Stuart wrinkled his black brows and stared at Sean. "None. God's work and calling doesn't depend upon numbers; you just must be faithful. Young man, what is God calling you to?" He stabbed a small potato and thrust it whole into his mouth.

Sean froze. "Overseas, sir." He lowered his head. Neither spoke again the whole meal. He thought, *This is not a guy you'd like to party with.*

After dessert, Sean was getting up to leave when Stuart addressed him. "Are you going to the mission field?"

Sean gulped a weak, hypocritical reply. "The Lord willing, Sir."

"Of course the Lord is willing [furrowed brow, insistent]. Get your training and get out there." Sean got up and stumbled away.

A few days later, Sean and Aaron sat at a Sweet Shop table over bowls of ice cream (Aaron's treat; Sean never carried extra money to spend). Sean had told no one, not even Aaron, about his great Bible-burning desecration. They gazed out at the quad, talking aviation.

"One of the flyboys told me TBI just bought three new Cessna 150 trainers," Sean said, "all metal wings, tricycle landing gear, one hundred horsepower and instrument-equipped—what a change from the J-3s we flew in flight camp."

"Wow, flying an airplane with a heater. I wonder if they'll use those for flight camp next fall. I hope we can both go back."

"I don't know. I wonder if failing the first time around reduces our chances."

They stared out the window. "Look, Sean; there goes Greg Weiman. I can't wait until I go to Mexico with him on his Spread the Light Mission. Greg's an apostle, a modern-day Joshua, who will lead a victorious assault on Mexico. He's organizing students to pray for the world and for Mexico. He has no money; all he receives he plows into Spread the Light mission and wears his pajamas under his clothes to give him more time for prayer in the mornings.

"Greg tells his Spread the Light people, 'If you don't eat your apple, carry it apple out of the dining hall for Diana.'" Sean had seen Greg's fiancée on campus—plastic-rimmed glasses, Goodwill clothes, buttoned sweater over a nondescript busy-patterned dress and scuffed Oxford shoes. She wore no makeup and usually pulled her long hair into a loose ponytail, radiating unadorned spiritual beauty. The perfect missionary stereotype.

She'd graduated from TBI in May and worked no paying job— how she subsisted was a mystery.

"What does she eat besides apples?" Sean asked Aaron.

"She lives over at Clark Street Rescue Mission, helps the staff there, I guess." Sean checked and it was true. Each morning she would get up to serve coffee, juice and sweet rolls to disheveled, left-behind men, men beaten down and hopeless, the cast-off detritus of the capitalist industrial machine, men vomited up on modernity's shores and left vacant-eyed and wandering. Aaron described how Diana spread her light over them as an angel of sanity and normality, evoking memories of better times. She would circulate, pour coffee and talk with the men. *She probably eats all her meals there,* Sean thought.

"Greg and Diana are dedicated to Spread the Light mission. You should go with us to Mexico."

"Oh, I don't know, Aaron. I don't have the money."

"No, really; you should go—see Mexico City, speak a little Spanish. Greg will help you raise the money."

Mexico. Sean had grown up in California but had never even set foot in Tijuana. However he felt himself an implausible recruit, considering his conversion to atheism. Asking anybody for money for a mission trip felt hypocritical. And he'd burned his own Bible.

"At least come to one of the planning meetings," Aaron said. So the next evening they went to listen to Weiman giving a talk to prospective STL'ers. He waxed fiery-eyed about changing the world through literature distribution. When he said *literature,* the word pulsated like Holy Writ. *Literature*—evoking Spirit-hurled missiles that would pierce the guilty heart of the lost. *Literature*—the God-given tool to evangelize the world.

He also talked about self-discipline, strict sexual control, spoke about his own sexual immorality and how God delivered him from it. Strict control of thoughts and actions. Don't yield to temptation. Sean knew that "temptation" was a placeholder for masturbating. He resonated with the challenge of this high morality but knew he could never achieve it.

"If you need clothes," Greg said, "get them from another STL member; don't buy them. And don't go to restaurants." Sean was pretty good at this. Unlike some other students, Sean rarely went downtown to Pizzeria Uno, rarely ate out. He tried to shun the lascivious vending machines near the campus post office. But the dining hall rarely served ice cream, so he would occasionally drop a quarter on an ice cream sandwich, hoping no STL person would see him.

A week later, Greg called an all-night prayer meeting in Norbert Hall lounge for the STL men and Aaron persuaded Sean to go along. Greg told them to fast all day. (Fasting wasn't core fundamentalism but Greg was all for it.) So everybody arrived hungry. Fifteen or twenty guys sat in the dark-paneled room listening to Greg, then broke up into smaller groups to pray for revival at TBI (Greg considered the school in a deficient spiritual state) and to pray against disingenuity, backsliding. Prayers also went up for the trip to Mexico, for support funds, for open hearts and minds in Mexico.

As the long hours passed, Sean couldn't pray and grew bored and restless. He looked across at Langston Brooks, Greg's right-hand man (the guys called him "Super Glue"). His dark forehead glistened as he struggled mightily in prayer. A huge, zealous Negro, he shouldered life as a cross to bear, never smiled, never entertained any religious doubts. In all humility he considered himself (and the other STL'ers) as works of holiness.

When they stepped outside for a break, Aaron removed his red Queen Dairy bill cap, tousled his sandy-colored hair and then told Sean a tale about Langston. "When TBI accepted him, the dean told him, 'You know you can't date white girls.' Last month during another all-night prayer meeting, some guys coaxed a pony up to Langston's second-floor dorm room and pushed it in. I don't know how they ever forced it up the stairs, or maybe they put it on the elevator. Langston got back in the early morning to a smelly room and found the pony restless, stamping, head stretched out the open window, looking down into the quad. The fire department had to tranquilize it to get it out. Langston considered this just another cross to bear on his pilgrimage in holiness."

After the meeting, Sean gave in and told Aaron he would go on the Mexico trip.

TBI didn't charge tuition but Sean needed money to pay his room and board and he needed money for the long trips home to California and back. He'd saved about eleven hundred dollars during high school, packing oranges at the Sunkist Packing House. He grew concerned Greg would discover he was an atheist, so one night after an STL meeting, he went up to Greg and gave five hundred dollars for STL.

Greg seemed grateful but he told him his donation didn't count toward "prayed-in money." "Prayed in" meant you asked God for the money and you couldn't mention it to any friends or relatives. Sean wasn't sure God heard the prayers of atheists and departure loomed in just three weeks.

After his big donation, Greg told him, "Let's go to the prayer room and ask God to give you the money you need." Sean wondered if Greg was motivated by Sean's huge gift or perhaps he felt obligated to add his major league prayers to Sean's. At any rate, they went to the prayer room and found it unoccupied.

STL guys prayed on their knees, head on the floor. So Greg and Sean knelt. "You go first," Greg said.

Sean hesitated—before his atheist experiment, his prayer life could be summarized as, "Dear God, what have you done for me *lately*?" He felt embarrassed. Was it wrong to pray to a God you didn't believe in? But he started, "Dear Lord, thank you for Spread the Light and the great literature mission to Mexico. Lord, please send in the money I need for this trip." He wondered if God heard the prayers of an atheist.

Then Greg prayed a mighty prayer, with much crying out, moaning, sweating and tearful petitions. "*Move*, Lord, Mighty God, *move*. You know Sean's heart, his passion, his holy desire to go on this, your mission. Vindicate him, Lord, show him your mighty power by bringing in what he needs from your vast storehouse of treasures . . ." And such like, deploying the full panoply of power and protection. If heaven had gates and windows, Greg forced them all open that night.

After a long hour they walked out. *Greg trusts my purpose and passion more than I do*, Sean thought. *If the money doesn't come in though, Greg will have proof that I'm not supposed to go.*

In the morning he swung past the P.O.'s and peered into the small box. Last week his mom had again airmailed him some homemade cookies, along with a letter of encouragement: "So proud of you . . . happy you're at TBI. Miss you."

Sean asked himself, *Is Mom being honest with me—is she doing as well as she says?*

But no letters today and no money for Mexico. Now Christmas was almost here and the day of departure for the Mexico trip loomed. *Apparently, God doesn't want me to go*, he thought. *Or he doesn't care. Or doesn't exist.* Sean ground his teeth and felt his stomach knot. He told Aaron, "I'm not sure I can go; I don't have the 'prayed-in' money."

The next week he peeked through the tiny P.O. box window to see a solitary letter. He twirled the brass knob, pulled the letter out and was disappointed when he saw the Amarillo, Texas address. A letter from his Uncle Jack who was not born again. It read, "Hello, Sean. Hope the weather's not too cold in Chicago. Use the enclosed to take friends to a restaurant and have a great time." Attached was a check for fifty dollars. This was a huge amount of money to Sean but, more importantly, he could count this unsolicited money as "prayed-in." He was going to Mexico.

That evening Sean walked over, knocked on Greg's door and turned over the money. He'd cleared the last hurdle for his trip. He'd violated Uncle Jack's purpose for the money but he hoped he would understand. Of course this letter was just a coincidence—or was it? If God existed, how could he ever forgive him for burning his childhood Bible? He'd told no one, but what if Greg somehow found out?

Chapter 25

Down the Norbert dorm hallway from Sean lived Joseph Dvorak. Joseph—a below-average student, unlucky in love, confident and loud—sucked Sean out of his introspective shell like a vacuum cleaner. Sean rejoiced that Joseph treated him like a regular person, one of the boys—a new experience for him. One day in November Joseph met him in the hall. "Sean, you wanna come to my house for Thanksgiving dinner?"

"I dunno, Joseph. Are you sure your mom wants me?"

"Sure. She loves having people in. Besides, I want to show you my car."

So on Thanksgiving morning they walked down to the garage where Joseph kept his old 1947 green Dodge pickup that he'd inherited when his dad and mom had separated. By the time they drove away the day had turned colder. Sean cranked down his window and felt the frigid air rush in as he stared at the passing city, but he had little time to absorb the industrial sounds and smells before they'd exited the city and were speeding through fields of snow-glazed corn stubble.

Joseph Dvorak worried about everything and today he worried aloud, raising his voice above the roar of the engine. "I don't know if I can make it to the end of the semester . . . don't know if I can pass Meacham's class . . . I'm not sure what I'll do when I get out of TBI . . . don't know if my girlfriend wants to break our engagement . . ."

Sean didn't know what to say but he remembered a quote, *What's friendship when all's done but the giving and taking of wounds?* So he spoke more out of hope than certainty: "Joseph; you'll be fine. God has a plan for your life." Joseph hadn't yet heard about Sean's atheism. Joseph's scowl turned into a smile.

It had snowed all night, making the roads slippery and forcing Joseph to reduce speed. The truck needed gas so they pulled into a truck stop for coffee and a fill-up. Besides noticing that gas was thirty cents a gallon, Sean saw that the place was populated mostly by truck drivers—solitary, untethered men, bleary-eyed from long hours over the road.

They sat at the counter next to a talkative trucker, "Bud," who looked like he'd just walked out of a Marlboro ad. He wore two days growth and a black bill cap that read "True Outlaw Country."

"You guys students?" He put down his cigarette.

"Torrey Bible Institute," Joseph said. "We're on break; just stopped a minute to get some gas and coffee."

Bud's smile widened. "Well, watch out for them lounge lizards."

"What?"

"Short-skirted, big-breasted lounge lizards. Them skags hang around these truck stops and talk to truckers who got them new sleeper cabs. Course they'll pick up anybody." Bud spoke as a worldly-wise traveler who was eager to pass on valuable counsel to naïve teenage boys.

"OK; we'll watch out." Sean smiled as he noticed a young woman walking past behind them. They paid and drove away.

When they reached the small town, Joseph turned down Center Street and drove almost to the railroad tracks. "That's our house there, on the right." They pulled in the drive, grabbed their overnight bags and jumped out.

"Are you sure your mother knows I'm coming?"

"Of course." Joseph's home appeared a modest bungalow with an old flat-tired car slumbering alongside. "That's my baby," Joseph said, peeling back the tarp to reveal his black 1945 MG TA. "I just need the time and money to work on it." Sean stared with envy.

Joseph's Czech mother dominated the Thanksgiving meal with its wonderful, homey smells flowing out of her tiny kitchen. They sat down and Mrs. Dvorak asked Joseph to offer a prayer of thanks. After a couple months of institutional food, the bounty overwhelmed Sean—a perfectly browned turkey, heaps of mashed potatoes and gravy (Sean's own mother rarely made gravy), cloven slices of cranberry jelly, candied sweet potatoes. Mrs. Dvorak kept saying to him, "Sean, eat." Music to Sean's ears—he served himself two extra helpings. After dinner he inhaled a big piece of pumpkin chiffon pie topped with two scoops of vanilla ice cream. Then she said, "Sean, do you want another piece?" *I must have died and gone to heaven,* Sean thought.

They spent two wonderful days in the Dvorak home, where Sean slept up in the dormer bedroom. Joseph became a true friend, a friendship that would last more than fifty years.

On the trip back, the guys talked about their future. "I'm studying for the ministry or maybe missions, Joseph said. "But I'm worried about Emelia; I'm afraid she's going to break our engagement." Sean tried to reassure him.

After they got back to TBI late Friday afternoon, Joseph asked Sean, "Wanna walk over to Michigan Avenue and pass out gospel pamphlets?" Fundamentalists felt a holy obligation to tell others the Good News of the gospel and this meant passing out pamphlets. Sean reluctantly agreed and they set out, walking east.

Michigan Avenue. Broad sidewalks and steel-posted streetlights with their four-clustered hanging globes. Sean leaned against the frost-silvered stone wall of one of the upscale department stores and stared into a cold display window filled with plastic mannequins clothed with the latest fashions. Up and down Michigan Avenue strolled the Beautiful People—women hatted and high-heeled, displaying sequined sheath dresses, fur wraps and sheer hose; men wearing black wingtip shoes and double-breasted dark suits with handkerchiefs in the breast pockets. Most wore Fedoras or stiff-brimmed, creased-crown Hombergs.

"You know, Joseph, I've never bought anything, never even walked into one of these stores." Like most students, Sean came from a modest background. The Depression still lingered in his parents' minds and dictated frugality. Besides, TBI's ethos encouraged marshalling energy and resources for Christian evangelism and mission. Sean felt like an alien among the Beautiful People of Michigan Avenue. And what could an atheist offer people anyway?

Joseph gave a passing man a pamphlet and said, "God loves you."

The man replied, "I doubt it."

I know how you feel, Sean murmured to himself.

Joseph told the man, "Don't doubt God. Our god is a consuming fire." The man jumped back and stalked off into the distance. Joseph attributed this to the power of God.

Walking back along Chestnut Street the sharp winter winds blowing off Lake Michigan pierced their clothing. They passed a brown-skinned man—sandals, baggy pants, wrinkled shirt, ripped sweater—and handed him a pamphlet. "*No leo Inglés*," he said.

"I don't think he speaks English," Sean said. He tried to talk to him in his broken Spanish. "Jose" ended up inviting the guys up to his apartment. Joseph opted to walk back to TBI but Sean climbed upstairs with Jose to a tiny third-floor room where Jose showed him his Spanish Bible, which they read together. Jose mumbled a prayer, then crossed himself and Sean left, promising to return.

One night a couple weeks later the Norbert Hall guys heard fire sirens, so they poured down the stairs and ran out into the street.

"This one's close." Joseph was running next to Sean, breathing in the sharp air as they ran toward the blaze.

"Sean—That's Jose's apartment building!"

As firemen stood on the hook and ladder truck spraying the upper floors, the water was misting down and freezing on the sidewalks. Sean strained to see Jose's apartment window—there it was, with smoke pouring out of it. Surely he'd gotten out by now. The flames consumed the wood-frame building, lifting smoke high into the sky. When the heat drove Sean back, he talked to a couple of firemen. "We don't know much; whole building's destroyed, though."

The firemen controlled the blaze and the spectators straggled away. The guys walked back to TBI leaving behind the collapsed, charcoaled rafters, their embers still glowing. Sean was worried. "I hope Jose's safe; surely he got out in time."

The next morning Sean sat in Norbert lounge scanning a small article in the *Chicago Tribune*. One person died in the Chestnut fire, it said, name of Jose Torres. Sean shivered—Jose! He turned to Joseph: "The dear man, far from family and his native home, trying to survive alone in the city, perished in the fire. I wonder what his Catholic faith did for him." *And what did fundamentalism do for me? Who am I kidding? And I can't go to Mexico as an atheist.* He dropped a note in the P.O. to Greg with a single line: "I'm sorry; I can't go to Mexico." Greg was busy; he never got around to asking Sean why.

Chapter 26

TBI's SPRING SEMESTER STARTED and Sean sat daydreaming in Spanish class, thinking about his "kitchen agreement" with Bennie Delarosa to study the Gospels. But, he thought, *Just because I need a god, just because my life would make more sense with a god doesn't mean a god exists. The world wasn't designed to please me.*

Sean hadn't realized how hard it was to be a good atheist. He worked seriously at it, tried to believe that nobody was home in the universe. He memorized Stephen Crane's words:

> A man said to the universe:
> "Sir I exist!"
> "However," replied the universe,
> "The fact has not created in me
> A sense of obligation."

While Señorita Clara waxed eloquent on the subjunctive case (*fuera, estuviera, hubiera . . .*), he was thinking, *Am I truly alone in the universe? How cowardly of Christians, to invent a "god" to comfort them. How brave to face the universe alone—without gods, without meaning, without any reason for hope—alone!* This terrified him; his respect for atheists grew.

He felt isolated, unprepared to explain his atheism to anyone. How does an atheist live? Sean didn't know any other atheists, except Sam Clancy in high school. Sam appeared well-adjusted but they hadn't talked much about how you do atheism. Good atheists needed an encouraging, supportive community but Sean had no access to fellow unbelievers. So he read books like Bertrand Russell's *Why I am not a Christian* or Freud's *The Future of an Illusion.* Their bleak pessimism troubled him, gave him cold comfort on this cold January day.

That evening the quiet prayer room drew him—a place to think without distraction. He looked out across the street where sleet sliced through the rays from a solitary streetlight that illuminated a sign on a door with peeling paint: "Olivet Holiness Mission: Spreading God's Love." Trash covered the dirty sidewalk. A scrawny cat disappeared around the corner. Nothing else. Was this church Negro? Independent? He'd never seen anyone enter its doors. Ironic—an illuminated word of hope hanging over a lifeless building, a cruel sign offering a false promise. The derelict mission saddened him. If faith moved mountains, why did this mission lie neglected?

Sean teared up. *My life is just a string of failures. Maybe I made a mistake coming to TBI. Maybe I should have just stayed home.* His low mood shrunk his past victories and bloated his defeats.

Faith, optimism, even life itself, seemed so futile. He considered that people of faith have such small effect on the world. What good was faith, anyway? This metropolis of industry and high finance made faith irrelevant. The wind rose now and the sleet increased, obscuring the church sign. Sean rose in the center of the small room and started walking in slow circles.

Bennie and he still remembered their pact to read the Gospels but Sean read with more urgency because for him it seemed a matter of life or death. One evening the next week Sean walked over to the TBI library and sat down in a remote corner. He'd read the Gospels casually but now for the first time he buried himself in them like a wood tick, comparing the four gospel stories and looking for inconsistencies and errors. He found quite a few.

Miss Wu worked the library at night. The swish of her slit-up-the-leg dress broke the silence as she walked by, wafting a faint perfume, casting her all-seeing eye on him. She pounced. "You need to check out a book?"

Sean jerked awake. "No; I'm just studying." She smiled a tight smile and walked on.

Sean remembered the familiar Jesus stories he'd learned as soon as he could walk and talk. He knew Jesus was God—a magic, larger-than-life Mother Goose character. But today he discovered something else—Jesus was human. Strange—Sean's teachers had emphasized Jesus as *God.* Had that blinded him to Jesus the *man*? This man one could admire, love, long to pursue. Something sacred shimmered on the pages and he devoured the words like candy, loving even the smell of the binding. *But it's too good to be true,* he thought.

Miss Wu may question me, stuck here for so many hours. So he returned to his dorm room and lay on his top bunk bed, vacantly gazing out the window. He felt mixed up—and worried. An atheist should avoid reading the Gospels, he mused. They mess with your atheism.

The next day he sat in the library again. Miss Wu came by frowning as he shifted on his hard library seat. If no mind existed, no volition, no design, how did all the world come to be? And where did humans come from? Sean was vaguely familiar with the idea of evolution (although it wasn't mentioned at TBI) but did he have enough faith in it, enough courage to embrace this "theory of everything" as a god-replacement? He pulled a Snickers bar out of his bag, inhaled the sweet smell of chocolate, then stuffed the whole thing in his mouth—Miss Wu prohibited eating in the library.

Am I an atheist because I'm mad at God? he wondered. Atheists don't disbelieve in God; they believe God doesn't *exist*. How can I get mad at somebody who doesn't exist? He got up to go to the bathroom, then came back to a chair in a different part of the library.

He felt troubled going to class. What if Mr. Meacham found out he was an atheist? Or worse, Dean Winters? They would kick him out and no flight training for him.

But as the weeks passed, Sean felt less interest in finding mistakes in the Gospels and more interest in exploring the man Jesus. Despite the stories' familiarity, he felt like he was meeting someone new—a powerful human being, rooted in a specific time, place and culture, but authoritative and loving. The warmth of this bright light blinded him but it clarified his thinking.

Sure, Sean thought. *Many Christians are hypocrites, egotists, troubled people. But I know many Christians who live a good life. I can't deny their honesty, their friendships, how they face problems, make decisions. And, what about love? Without transcendent values, love is just lust and social bonding, isn't it? It's got to mean more. What about right and wrong? Where does "rightness" come from if not from God?*

Another Miss Wu epiphany. As she glided past him he felt like a trespasser. Could she sniff out his heresy from afar, discern the smell of an unbeliever?

Am I just playing at atheism? he asked himself. He needed an atheist mentor, a tutor. He knew he made decisions with incomplete knowledge but with a certain faith and trust—choosing a college, for instance or planning a missionary career. How did atheists make decisions?

And what about aviation? He still longed to fulfill his one, bright dream, his only passion. He asked himself, *How can I be an atheist missionary pilot? Who would accept me? Maybe I should just become an airline pilot. Triple the pay, less risky and no faith in God needed.*

He sensed a presence. Maria was strolling down a far row, a vision of beauty in her beige sweater and red skirt, studying the books in the stacks. Even his deep existential angst failed to weaken his magnetic attraction to any female form. He decided not to go over and talk to her, though.

Talk about not fitting in. My friends don't understand my atheism. Even if TBI people have doubts (and I suspect many of them do), they rarely voice them. TBI's classes aren't designed for debate and discussion; they're places to build doctrines like toy castles—block by block until you're done. Boring.

Sean never discussed his atheism with Maria or Kathy. *Does Kathy ever have doubts?* he wondered She seemed a great woman of faith, dedicated, unquestioning. And yet, could faith even *exist* without doubt? *Has she ever faced the questions I've faced? I would like to talk with her but that would be risky. Why does she keep her distance? She doesn't seem stuck up; it's more like she carries a deep, unhealed wound. What happened to her?*

Chapter 27

SEAN HAD TOLD THE student employment office he was sick of his factory job, so for the spring they found him work downtown at an insurance company on the 25th floor of the Tribune Tower. This job would be different. But in fact he had no idea how different.

On his first day of work Sean ate early lunch then walked out through TBI's arch toward downtown. A group of about ten guys who worked at the Federal Reserve Bank streamed past him, talking and yelling as they jogged across the intersections, ignoring traffic lights, zigzagging between stopped cars, hopping over hoods. When they left work that afternoon, the bank guards would turn their pockets inside out looking for pennies.

Sean turned left on Illinois Street then walked down Michigan Avenue toward the Chicago River. The giant Tribune Tower shrunk him into insignificance. Built in 1925, the 36-story steel-and-concrete monolith soared 462 feet high above its glass façade entryway. A revolving door opened into the lobby.

Exiting the elevator he found the huge First Chicago Insurance office suite where the hiring manager waited. "The bulk of our staff works here," he said, "but you'll work in the smaller office down the hall." They walked in to see the office supervisor sitting at a large desk inside his glassed-in corner cubicle. He wore a dark business suit with white shirt and tie. His umbrella hung on a wooden coat stand. "Sean, this is Mr. Merton. He'll introduce you to the others."

Sean shook Mr. Merton's hand, who pointed and said, "This is Duane; he's our junior underwriter. Marion and Myra are our office assistants." They all nodded and smiled. Mr. Merton never smiled. "Myra here will give you a stack of policies to file. The red-tagged folders are active; the others are expired." Then he walked back into his glass cage.

Myra helped Sean learn how to organize the dog-eared folders hanging in the file drawers. He liked Myra immediately. Bombastic and friendly, she lit up the office. He began organizing the bills, receipts and records of sprinkler damage that Myra had strewn helter-skelter across his desk. *These wrinkled folders wouldn't inspire much customer confidence,* he thought.

Mr. Merton kept a clean and organized space. The few times he emerged from his office he would lean against a desk and deliver pep talks to his minions—"If we get these insurance claims wrapped up, it'll put a real feather in our cap."

Privately, Duane told Sean, "He means a feather in *his* cap."

Duane, tall and darker-skinned and smelling of cologne and tobacco, slicked his black hair back with a careless hand. When he smoked he sucked in his cheeks, his languid eyelids drooping over a clenched smile that revealed confident teeth.

He loved to flirt with Marion, a slightly built Catholic girl who would toss her blond hair and blink her big blue eyes. She always looked cute in her see-through blouse and tight skirt. Duane confided to Sean, "I like Marion but she's Catholic and I'm Lutheran, so I don't know how we could get together."

One day, Mr. Merton called in sick and put Duane in charge. That would be the day the inmates took over the asylum.

Duane opened his desk drawer and pulled out a bottle. "Myra, get some plastic cups in that cupboard over there. Could you pour?" Sean had never tasted alcohol and TBI prohibited students from drinking but the pressure of the social occasion pressed him to take a sip. He coughed as the unfamiliar liquid slid down his throat. Duane laughed, sitting relaxed with his feet on the desk, cigarette hanging from his lower lip. Marion came over and sat on his lap. Duane pretended to ignore her but Sean could see he loved it. Sean tried concentrating on his filing, but in vain.

Then Myra went crazy. Dear, bubbly Myra, not quite obese but pleasantly plump. Long dark hair, black eyes, plenty of lipstick and red fingernail polish and a loud, sultry voice, she radiated Eau de Toilette and always brought her fun with her.

Myra told Duane, "Put some music on your radio." She stepped up on her chair, then onto the desk, revealing her red high heels, plump legs and sheer hose. She flung her arms above her head, swayed her hips, twirled her short dress and sang a lusty song, her gold bracelets and Star of David earrings swinging in time. Marion and Duane sang and clapped. Sean eyes riveted on Myra.

Then the big boss from the main office walked in.

Silence, hung heads, as all returned to work, tails between legs. No one lost their job but the next day, Mr. Merton walked into his tiny cubicle, hung up his black overcoat, scarf and umbrella and called his troops to attention. "People, I'm surprised at this behavior. It casts a shadow on my leadership. You embarrassed me in front of my own boss." He droned on—lack of maturity and professionalism, black marks, etc. Plainly, the big boss had reamed him out and charged him with castigating his staff. *It was still so worth it,* Sean thought to himself. Almost for the first time in his life, he felt comfortable with what he knew to be "worldly" people.

With her behavior, could Myra be an observant Jew? Sean didn't think so. And Duane—suave, worldly wise, sophisticated—did "Lutheran" mean he was born again? And were Catholic girls allowed to sit on Lutheran men's laps? Sean's childhood formation made him critical of people, even churchgoers, outside of fundamentalism. He didn't think Marion or Duane were real Christians. And how could he share his Christian faith with them if he no longer believed it himself? His atheism was getting more complicated and he was running a risk of getting kicked out of TBI. His dread intensified.

Chapter 28

"LET'S GO OVER TO Lincoln Park," Dave Sanders said to Sean. Over the next weeks Sean would meet several times with Dave who lived on Norbert Hall's fourth floor. A former Navy man, he had invited Sean to read together the devotional meditations from *His*, the magazine of Intervarsity Christian Fellowship. IVCF had chapters on many secular campuses but some TBI teachers considered the organization too liberal for TBI, too ecumenical. Sean was puzzled by Dave's attention but trusted his warm friendship.

Spring arrived, the snow disappeared and the mornings still felt crisp but not frigid. Today, the breeze banished the Chicago haze and the few trees along LaSalle Street displayed a mist of green. David and Sean walked past Elm-LaSalle Church and a few minutes later paused in front of the dreaming, sun-warmed bulk of Torrey Church. "This church is historical," Dave said. "R.A. Torrey himself used to be the minister."

They entered the park. With its sculptured lawns and gardens and a small lake where you could rent rowboats, it looked like a Renoir masterpiece.

As they sat on the bench by the lake, Sean marveled how Dave Sanders had come out of nowhere. Why had he singled him out? He never felt like Dave's "project," never felt manipulated. Dave became a true friend, a rare star in Sean's universe. Other of Sean's friends cooled toward him when they learned of Sean's atheist project but Dave warmed. He was a few years older than Sean, spiritually mature, calm, kind. When they prayed together Sean listened, then mumbled a few words. His atheism made prayer difficult.

Junior high and high school had been friend-deserts for Sean. But here, Dave appeared so personable, caring, encouraging. Patient as a saint, he did not judge Sean's beliefs, was not put off by his criticism of TBI. A piercing light shone into Sean's despair, a light sharpened by Dave's bright lens of compassion. His experience with IVCF opened a whole new world for Sean— classical music, contacts with international students, and well-reasoned Christian ideas. And the *His* magazine articles spoke directly to Sean's questions. They revealed to him a different way of being Christian—more tolerant, more generous, more grace-ful.

On the opposite side of the lake irises stood in rows with their tight, thrusting buds. As the guys watched a child launch a tiny paper boat on the lake, the brisk breeze blew up ominous clouds that obscured the sun. "We'd better make a run for the bus," Dave yelled, Then the heavens opened and rain fell in buckets, scrubbing the park walkways clean of dirt and trash. They ran across a soggy lawn with their shoes squelching in the sticky slush, then walked and ran to the bus stop, pants spackled waist-high with water and mud.

As their friendship grew, Sean confessed his atheism to Dave "Come on, Sean. I don't believe it. You're just having a few struggles. I can't explain all the contradictions in the Bible but Jesus has the ring of truth. There's lots of evidence for his resurrection. Why don't you talk to Pastor Reynolds at Torrey Church? I'm sure he'll answer your questions, encourage you, pray with you."

Sean had heard the redoubtable Alistair Reynolds preach many times. His Oxford accent guaranteed inspiring sermons. The next week Sean decided he'd try it so he called for an appointment, then trudged the mile down to the storied Torrey Church and sat down in Reynolds' office. "He'll be with you in a few minutes," the secretary said.

After he'd waited thirty minutes, he began having second thoughts. Why talk to Reynolds? He realized he didn't need Reynolds' help—what could Reynolds do for him? When the secretary disappeared for a minute, Sean snuck out.

On the walk back he thought, *Christian faith—so much hypocrisy, so many unanswered questions.* But he knew now how hard atheism was, how hard to be consistent, hard to live without a transcendent moral foundation. Further, he'd discovered the man Jesus in the Gospels and this man fascinated him. And Dave Sanders attracted him like a magnet.

When Sean walked out of Torrey Church, he was still an atheist but twenty minutes later when he walked through TBI's arch, he again counted himself as a Jesus-follower. He remembered the lines of an anonymous poem he'd memorized from his English class: "Whoso draws neigh to God one step through doubtings dim, God will advance a mile in blazing light to him."

He still had doubts but he determined to draw near. He realized it wasn't his strong faith that drew him, wasn't his reasoning—it was the initiative of a pursuing, hounding God incarnated in the Jesus of the Gospels—and in David Sanders.

He found Bennie and told him, "I'm giving up on atheism." Bennie rolled his eyes so hard they hurt. "Duh. It's about time. Welcome back to God. I'm sure he's relieved and grateful."

The sarcasm was lost on Sean. He felt jubilant, reintegrated into the great community of faith. He still had questions (inerrancy, evolution, God's judgment, Old Testament violence) but somehow all these seemed less important now. He never again considered abandoning faith.

Looking back on his dalliance with atheism Sean felt embarrassed. Even some of the teachers had heard about it. Had he just been trying to get people's attention? Was he angry at God? Punishing God by denying his existence? His doubts reminded him of the story of the rabbi who confided to his fellow rabbi that he was sleeping with his neighbor's wife. "Why would you do such a thing?" asked his friend. To which the rabbi replied, "I'm angry with my God." *As if I could punish God by violating his commands,* Sean thought. *Did I have genuine doubts? Or maybe I just couldn't understand my personal problems.*

He wondered where his "reconversion" came from. His gospel readings helped him discover the human Jesus. Studies with Dave provided him new insights into the Bible. But more important, they gave him a compassionate friend. Dave's non-judgmental, patient spirit and frankly, his love, won him over.

Chapter 29

March came, the days brightened and the weather turned warmer and windy, the trees dragging their leaves like nets. Sean walked across the quad and up to his English class. He loved some of the poetry they were reading but would never admit this to his friends. And Christian Education class. Mr. Getsch's lectures fascinated him—he taught them how to teach, how to get organized, how to start a file drawer. Or maybe Sean just enjoyed sitting next to Linda Fuller from Manchester-by-the-Sea.

Slightly built, Linda's shoulder-length chestnut hair framed her hazel eyes. Usually she wore a white blouse, black flats and a straight, pleated skirt that hung just to her knees—casual but not sloppy.

Fascinating, exotic Linda. *Fuller*—he loved the name; it sounded English. Sean marveled at her self-confidence and he loved her New England accent. She said *cah* for car; *sneakahs* for tennis shoes and referred to Sean's home state as *Californier.* "Yes, my hometown was founded in 1645, just after the Pilgrims . . . Mother belongs to the Daughtahs of the American Revolution." Imagine growing up, not in Santa Ana but in Manchester-by-the-Sea!

Linda complained about how Darla Dickenson shadowed the lives of the Hargreaves Hall girls like a darkening eclipse. "She's always calling someone in over something. She cares about us but she tries to control . . ." Possessing the metabolism of a hummingbird, Linda never harbored an unspoken thought, never finished a sentence and never provided segues. But Sean, usually at a loss for something to say, loved the way her words filled his awkward silences.

"Last week my roommate asked Dickenson if French kissing was a sin." Linda said as she opened her textbook and binder. "She needs to get married. That'll solve all her problems."

Sean blushed; he wasn't used to such frank talk. He assumed most girls weren't interested in French kissing. Then he thought of Betty. Maybe some girls were like Betty, even TBI girls.

"What did Dickenson say to her?" He knew that Dickenson was long on law, short on grace. She lived a disciplined life, defending her moral barricades so tenaciously that no man ever dared breach them.

"Oh; Dickenson said it was a sin." Linda chattered on, stopping only when Dr. Getsch's opening prayer drowned her out.

It was 1961 and many colleges, secular or parochial, enforced firm rules. *In loco parentis* meant locking the girls up, tracking their movements, curfews, no alcohol, segregation of the sexes. But fundamentalist schools more so—they endeavored to shield them from the attacks of a post-WWII culture that threatened to overwhelm their moral defenses.

Linda, beautiful Massachusetts Linda. A few days after their conversation, Sean asked her to go with him to Lincoln Park. Walking up LaSalle Street, Sean realized they would miss TBI's dinner, so they stopped at a little restaurant for sandwiches. "I wish my parents would come visit," Linda said, "but they won't leave my baby brother and can't very well bring him . . . Oh, look. A couple CPD cars stopped at that apartment. I wonder what . . . I'm glad they're . . . My dad got stopped by a policeman once." Linda burbled on about her classes, her roommate, her church and family back home. Sean searched for a verbal handhold to vault himself into her monologue.

Then they reached Lincoln Park, a beautiful summer gathering place—gardens, little lakes, curving walkways, manicured lawns, trees misted green with their tiny new leaves. Along the border of the park, elite residential buildings towered overhead.

They sat down on a bench to watch the ducks swim around in one of the little pools rippled by the brisk March wind, their reflections moving with them across the water. In the trees above, sparrows rose in random gusts. Linda slouched down and her dress drifted a couple of inches above her knees. Sean pretended not to notice. Linda pretended she didn't notice that he pretended not to notice but as she gazed at the ducks she wriggled her dress back down.

She wore a thin chain with a cross that nestled between her breasts like a golden river cascading down a mountain vale. "Where'd you get that cross pendant?" He longed to grasp it.

"Oh; I got that in the TBI bookstore. They've got all kinds of . . . Oh look, a squirrel." She looked, fascinated, as the animal scurried up a maple tree. "Our dog at home loves to chase squirrels down cellar . . . Isn't this lake beautiful? Look at those ducks . . . I wonder if there's a bubbler nearby. I'm thirsty . . ."

Linda talked like she was strewing potato chips on the table—Sean didn't know which to pick up first. Was she nervous, having to comment on everything? Regardless, her idle babble reassured him. After careful thought, he reached over and took her hand.

She stopped talking and stared again at the ducks. Embarrassed, he released her hand. After a while they stood up and started walking. Linda stared ahead. "Holding hands is like being on an elevator, you know. I'm scared of elevators. You start going up slowly but then you go higher and faster. It's hard to stop."

Sounds exciting, Sean thought. But her objections confirmed that girls didn't welcome his advances. Betty must have been an anomaly. It was getting chilly so they walked over to the "L," rode it south to get off at Chicago Avenue then walked the short distance back to TBI.

As they reached the school Sean glanced at the façade of Moody-Sankey Auditorium. D.L. Moody was a great nineteenth-century evangelist. His partner, Ira B. Sankey, was a gospel singer and hymnwriter. Sean thought about the dozens of huge brass organ pipes that lined the front of the auditorium. He fantasized about taking Linda up into the dark balcony but he lacked the courage.

They walked into Hargreaves lounge, a sterile space as formal as a king's reception room. Sean figured it was designed to guard couples' morality. The rule was "three feet on the floor."

"The afternoons are growing warmer and the park has so much green grass," Linda said as she sat down. I wonder about our lawn at home. Oh; did you hear about the spring banquet? I suppose Dickenson will check the girl's dress lengths as usual."

Sean said nothing. Was she hinting he should take her to the banquet? Linda seemed so different from Kathy. Linda viewed life like a tourist, staring out the bus window at a foreign country. In contrast, Kathy faced life as a thoughtful pilgrim and was able to shed light on topics like politics or theology. Linda was immediate, practical. Kathy was more of a visionary, encouraging Sean's passion for overseas mission. *Will I ever get close to Kathy?* Sean asked himself. He enjoyed being with Linda, took her out a couple more times but sensed their relationship wasn't going anywhere.

One day Sean was leaving Getsch's class when Aaron Byler walked up to him with a face the color of putty.

"Aaron, what's wrong? Are you sick?"

"I might have to leave TBI."

"What? You can't do that. I thought we were trying again for flight camp this summer."

"They might kick me out for cheating."

"Cheating? When did you cheat?"

"At the beginning of the fall I copied some answers from another guy's test in theology class."

"How did they find out about it?

"They didn't. I felt guilty for several months; then I went and told Dean Winters."

"Winters? He's tough. He's the dean that threatened to block me from getting into the flight program."

"Well, the deans talked about it and are deciding whether I have to leave the institute."

"That's unfair since you confessed. Isn't there any way you can stay?"

"I'll just have to wait to see what they decide."

Sean watched Aaron walk away. The news pierced him—how could they kick Aaron out? He had confessed, said he was sorry. *No good deed goes unpunished, I guess. TBI sets high standards but they don't demonstrate much grace.*

What if they discovered Maria and he had gone to that frat party? And to the movies? What if the deans find out he'd told someone he was an atheist? He wondered if he should confess like Aaron did. *They might kick me out of TBI even before flight camp. Of course they'd kick me out. I'll never tell them anything.*

He remembered cheating in fifth grade. He hadn't dotted the "i" in "America" on a spelling test but when he got it marked wrong he added the dot inside a word on the line above and returned the test to the teacher. (She didn't buy it.) He never told anyone else, never felt guilty. Thinking back, he'd never felt guilty about anything. He felt a little guilty about his Betty summer but it was her fault too, he reasoned.

Chapter 30

HAROLD BLEDSOE GRATED ON Darla Dickenson like fingernails on a blackboard. At the deans' weekly consultation, French kissing came up. She cleared her throat and flashed a stiletto stare straight through Bledsoe. "I talk to the girls but you never talk to the boys. Why don't you support me? And the couples don't just walk around the block; they linger in the alcoves. That's your responsibility."

Ah yes, lingering. Couples should never linger anywhere—alcoves, the dark balcony of Moody-Sankey Auditorium—anywhere. Too much temptation.

He replied, "If they're still there the second time I circle the block, then I flush 'em out. Besides, some of 'em are engaged."

"They shouldn't be engaged while at TBI," Dickenson replied. "Engaged couples take more liberties and they're a bad influence on the other students." She couldn't deny surging sexual desire but she determined to hack at it like a noxious weed. Five years earlier, Dickenson's fiancé had dumped her for a younger woman. Now she retailed her bitterness to men in general, especially young, eligible men. Bledsoe presented a perfect target. "The parents trust us with their sons and daughters. What if that were *your* daughter in the alcove?"

"I don't have any children but please cut the young people some slack, give them some opportunities to get to know each other." The other deans remained silent while Bledsoe and Dickenson slugged it out.

Bledsoe just got here, Dickenson thought. *Why does he dare challenge me? I hate him.*

But to Dickenson's great surprise, as they exited into the warm, windy March day, Bledsoe turned to her and asked, "Will you go out to dinner with me?"

Dickenson started. She was several years older than him. What was he thinking? Did Bledsoe enjoy their sparring matches? Did he admire her maturity or did her formality attract him? She wouldn't admit it to herself but his invitation flattered her. She accepted.

When she saw Sean the next week, Kathleen dropped her bomb. "Sean, Bledsoe is taking Dickenson out; he told me yesterday. I know; I am just as shocked as you are. But please, Sean, please do not tell anyone."

"What? Why would Bledsoe take Dickenson out? And anyway, why did he tell *you*?"

She didn't answer but Sean knew she often talked with Bledsoe. Why did Bledsoe take Kathy into his confidence? Was Kathy jealous about Bledsoe dating Dickenson?

That Saturday evening Darla Dickenson spent more time on her face and dress than usual and even sprayed on some *Unforgettable*. She stared in the mirror and saw a proper, thirty-something woman staring back. Her image questioned her—Are you still the same woman you were? Still attractive? What do you want from this date? She tucked in her blouse and walked out onto the street.

Bledsoe had suggested Fanny's in Evanston, beyond the reach of any curious TBI students. Dickenson had refused his offer of a ride. She rode the express "L" north to Evanston, then walked a few blocks to Fanny's. She hadn't gone on a date in years. She felt curious, excited, but tried to quiet her doubts about his motives.

He drove up to the restaurant, parked his convertible, then entered and picked out a table. With its Italian cuisine, Fanny's sparkled like a little jewel.

As she entered she spotted him in a corner booth staring at the menu. She walked over, sat down and they made small talk. Both (for different reasons) knew this was a high-stakes meeting. She shifted in her chair. He nervously pumped his right leg under the table, giving the impression he moved to some invisible beat. They placed their orders, then ignored the maître d' hovering over them.

"I'm eagah that you and I are on the same page here," Bledsoe said. "I'm the new guy on the block; you've been here a long time. Students need some room for experimenting, need some grace. I have trouble with some of the harsh punishments." He eyed Dickenson, trying to gauge her reaction.

"I'm charged with a great responsibility for the girls," Dickenson said. "Many of them come from small towns, sheltered backgrounds. The men's deans need to clamp down on the boys. It's not fair the girls must obey the rules and the boys can do whatever they want; I expect you to enforce the rules with the boys." The voice of authority. She outranked Bledsoe and wasn't shy in reminding him of that. He didn't intimidate her—nobody intimidated her.

"But the students need to find Christian partners, need some space for dating. If we're too strict they'll just do things behind our backs. They need to know we're on their side. And they need to explore the city more, get more comfortable with what they'll face in adult life."

"Too much freedom," Dickenson said, "and we'll lose them to the world; their moral fences will collapse." Her sturdy Midwestern values stiffened her.

"Well, at least I hope we trust each other, see each other's point of view."

Why does he just want to talk about TBI rules? This isn't a date; it's a business meeting, Dickenson thought. She tried to change the subject. "How was your time in Cleveland at Cuyahoga High School? Did you enjoy the city on Lake Erie?"

"It was OK; lots of discipline problems though. Different races of people. Here at TBI, of course, the students are more mature, less crazy."

Bledsoe oozed courteousness but he didn't seem interested in *her*, didn't ask any personal questions. She looked down at her lap. He offered to drive her home but she declined.

When they met again at another restaurant the following week, the conversation followed much the same lines. She told him, "I must be getting back." She rose and walked out the door without ordering dessert.

Stung, she vowed to punish Bledsoe for playing with her affections. When he asked her out again, she refused. The next day at the office she dug out his TBI application papers, then called his Cleveland pastor, O.I. Runnell. Because Runnell assumed Bledsoe had told the truth on his application, he told Dickenson some things. She found out what she wanted.

She stopped talking to Bledsoe, avoided him, nurtured a rising anger. The next week she pounced with a typed note through the P.O.'s:

> Dean Harold Bledsoe,
>
> You have hurt me deeply, betrayed me. I know you lied on your job application—you were divorced before you came to TBI. If you embarrass me again, I'll reveal this to the president and he'll fire you. Don't cross me.
>
> Darla Dickenson

Chapter 31

LOUD BOOMS SHATTERED THE night. Sean and Fulton woke with their hearts thumping. "I've heard gunshots across Chestnut Street before but this sounds a lot closer, like in the quad." Sean said.

They ran across to the stairway window, open because of the warm night, and looked down into the quad. One guy ran up to them. "I saw flashes and a couple guys running toward the chain-link fence."

Another boom-*boom*. Then a car on Wells Avenue started up and sped off but the night was too dark to see well. "I-Is someone shootin' off firecrackers?" Fulton asked no one in particular. "Sounds like gun shots, though. W-what's goin' on?"

The booming stopped. They saw Dean Winters wearing his double-breasted greatcoat over his bathrobe and slippers, limping across the quad. A police car with red emergency lights and dying siren wheeled through the Wells Street gate and into the parking lot.

The policemen picked up some remains of firecrackers, then looked up at Norbert Hall. Sean and Fulton pulled their heads back in.

After fifteen minutes the police left. Winters limped back toward Norbert Hall. "Gimme a break," Sean said to Fulton. I read that Chicago had 331 homicides last year. The cops can't be worried about a few firecrackers."

The next morning, rain dripped off umbrellas as people formed little knots in the quad.

"I wonder who set off all the firecrackers?"

"I'll bet the girls heard the booms too."

"Are they sure they were firecrackers? What if they were gunshots?"

"How will the deans find out who did it?"

"Do you think someone at TBI did it or was it an outsider? Why would an outsider do it?"

Maria emerged from Hargreaves Hall, walked into the quad, then saw Sean.

"Someone shot out Dickenson's tires last night."

"What? Who told you?"

"Dickenson lives in an apartment down Chestnut Street but at night she parks her car in the quad for security. When she came on campus this morning she discovered the shot-out tires and told the girl at the Hargreaves check-in desk."

"She's kind of paranoid. Maybe someone just let the air out."

"She said she saw the bullet holes."

"Wow, I wonder who did it. I know some people don't like her but no TBI person would do this. So they *were* gunshots. This is more serious than a few firecrackers."

That night Dean A. Franklin Puckett called a general meeting of the Norbert Hall men in one of the larger Cromwell classrooms. The guys entered in twos and threes and found seats. They knew why they were there—Puckett and Winters wanted to know who lit the firecrackers but shooting out Dickenson's tires was more serious. They were determined to find out who did it.

Dean Puckett, brow furrowed over a face as serious as a Puritan preacher, addressed the hundred or so guys. "Men [he always addressed them as 'men'], we're gathered for a serious reason [wheezing]. We're going to ask each of you two questions and we want you to answer as honestly as you can.

"The first question: Do you have or have you had firecrackers in your dorm room?

"Second question: Do you have or have you had a gun in your room?"

He began in the front row, moving left to right, asking each guy the same two questions. Almost everyone answered *No, No.* A couple of the guys answered *Yes, No.* But no one answered *Yes* to the second question.

Until they got to Dan Hardy and Earl Downton. They both answered *Yes, Yes.*

A murmur spread around the room. Then it got quiet. The deans went on questioning the other guys but no one else said *yes.*

The meeting broke up when Dan and Earl exited with Dean Puckett. "This is serious," Sean said to Fulton. What did they do? Will they kick them out of the aviation program?"

"A-ah don't know but they're in deep trouble."

After the deans' meeting, a bunch of guys gathered in Sean and Fulton's dorm room.

"What will Puckett do to them?"

"Do you think they shot out Dickenson's tires?"

"Will Dan and Earl get kicked out of the flight program?"

Then Dan and Earl walked in and the room got quiet.

Sean asked Earl, "What happened with Puckett? What did he ask you?"

"Well, he was unhappy; said we weren't setting a good example. Asked if we knew that firecrackers and guns were prohibited in the dorm rooms. We both said yes. He said he needed to confiscate the guns. Then he asked if we'd done the firecrackers.

Earl said, "I told Puckett I did some of 'em; pitched a couple of cherry bombs out of the window down into the quad." Puckett asked who else threw firecrackers. We gave him a couple names—they won't get in too much trouble." Dan added that he worried the guys would call him a snitch.

"Puckett asked about the shots and Dickenson's tires. I told him we didn't know anything. I have a .22 rifle and Dan here has a .380 pistol but our guns are always cased and locked.

"The Dean walked us back to our rooms, confiscated our guns, said we couldn't leave campus for three days until they checked with the police. We're not worried because we never used our guns."

As Sean left the meeting, he bumped into Aaron. "Sean, they're going to kick me out over the cheating thing. I have to leave Saturday."

"No, I can't believe it. It seems so hypocritical. Think of all the guys who cheat and never confess. I'm so sorry, Aaron."

"Well, I'm going home. I'll try to get training at Smoketown Airport. More expensive but after a year or so maybe I can apply to a mission as a pilot."

The two guys parted reluctantly, promising to write. Sean didn't see Aaron again for a long time.

The next morning the police reported the caliber of bullet that punctured Dickenson's tires—9 mm. Sean told Fulton, "So Dan and Earl are off the hook for the tire damage but they'll still get disciplined for the firecrackers and for possessing guns on campus. I wonder, why the firecrackers and shooting on the same night? Do Dan and Earl know about the shooting and just aren't telling? Dickenson is unpopular with some people but I don't know anybody who hated her. If Dan and Earl are telling the truth, who did it?"

Dean Bledsoe was off on assignment, so Puckett and Winters met in the deans' conference room. Darla Dickenson walked in. "May I join you? I'm the victim of the attack and anyway, I've got important news."

Puckett said, "We're agreed Earl and Dan broke TBI rules. We need to confine them to campus for having firecrackers and guns. I told them we would return their guns at the end of the semester but they must take them home."

"But what about my shot-out tires?" Dickenson demanded.

"We recovered some cartridges. Earl and Dan's guns couldn't have done this," Winters said, "they're the wrong caliber."

Then Dickenson dropped her bomb. "One of my students told me that Harold Bledsoe showed her roommate his glove-box pistol—for his protection in the big city, he said."

The room got quiet. Could this be true? Puckett knew Dickenson disliked Bledsoe.

When Bledsoe returned to campus the next day, Puckett told him about the gunshots. He denied having a gun and when he let Puckett search his car, he found nothing.

The weekend passed quietly but on Monday an enraged Dickenson powered into Puckett's office. "Someone broke my windshield last night. Let that sink in—shot tires and now a broken windshield. It's true someone hates me—and I know who he is."

Puckett's face darkened. He was used to Darla's histrionics but this latest incident would force him to do something.

"Bledsoe's the darling of Hargreaves Hall," Dickenson continued, "And he's eroding my authority with the girls. I *know* he shot out my tires—and broke my windshield. Who else could have done it? He hates me."

She still resented her secret "dates" with him, how he'd tricked her. One of the most embarrassing episodes of her life. She remembered what she'd learned from Bledsoe's Cleveland pastor and how she could use this to ruin Bledsoe. She didn't consider herself a vengeful person, she told herself, but Bledsoe was dangerous for TBI and no one saw this as clearly as she did.

In truth, Dickenson served as a valuable dean at TBI but she was also a disappointed, unhappy woman and somewhat paranoid. One day when she'd fallen ill, she told Ma Hutchins, "My tea looked so green and even before I added sugar it tasted sweet. It made my stomach sick all night. I think someone put antifreeze in it!" When Puckett heard about it he briefly lamented that they used such a stingy dose. Then he scolded himself, reprimanding his mind demons.

The next day, Bledsoe went missing.

Chapter 32

Puckett parked his car, crossed the quad and elevatored up to his office humming to himself. He'd tapped Bledsoe for devotions that morning but noticed he hadn't yet arrived. Bledsoe drove his black convertible to campus five days a week and always parked in the same place—inside the quad's chain-link fence. Puckett told Winters, "Go check the parking lot."

Winters came back. "No car."

"Really? Maybe he's sick; I'll call his apartment."

No answer. Puckett searched Bledsoe's office. It looked normal, as if he were coming in today. He ruffled among the papers on his desk. Nothing unusual. He checked the main Cromwell desk to see if Bledsoe had called in. Nothing.

Puckett gave the 7:30 a.m. devotions himself, explaining to the gathered men that Bledsoe was sick. Now he was back up sitting in his big office chair, thinking hard. *If he suffered an accident last night,* Puckett thought, *someone would have called us by now.*

The Deans conferenced. "I don't even have his landlord's number," Winters said. "And they don't keep track of people, I'll bet, except when the rent comes due."

Puckett—always calm, always the reconciler, always wheezing: "I doubt he's left. He probably just had an emergency. He'll show up or phone in . . ." (He interrupted himself with a long coughing spell.)

"I dunno. I'm afraid something's happened."

"We don't want to alarm the students. We don't know any relative or anyone to contact. He lives alone in his apartment up beyond Torrey Church. If he doesn't show up by tomorrow morning, I'll drive up there."

Darla Dickenson sat smugly, saying nothing.

That same morning Sean walked across the quad toward Cromwell Hall, pulling his jacket around him against the brisk wind then took the stairs down to the dining hall.

Kathleen Wilberforce's roommate Joan ran over and told him, "Kathleen didn't come home last night—I just told Dickenson over there at the deans' table. Maybe I shouldn't have told her."

After breakfast Dickenson called Joan in and wrung out of her that Kathleen had been secretly meeting Bledsoe at restaurants off campus. *I knew it,* Dickenson thought. *No coincidence they've both gone missing.*

After Joan left, Dickenson walked over to Puckett's office, noticing his pained face as she sat down. "I never trusted that man. He hid the gun somewhere, broke my windshield, took off to avoid questioning and now he's kidnapped Kathleen."

"What are you talking about? Kathleen who?"

"Kathleen Wilberforce—that girl who just transferred in last fall. Her roommate, Joan Bauer, told me Kathleen left last night and never came back."

Puckett urged caution. "Perhaps she's at a relative's house. Did you talk to the night desk girl over at Hargreaves? Did Kathleen sign out?"

"Nine p.m., but she never signed back in. I doubt she's with a relative. I'll bet anything Bledsoe snatched her."

"We shouldn't jump to conclusions."

Then Dickenson dropped her grenade. "Really? Well, her roommate told me Kathleen's been secretly meeting with Bledsoe!" She flounced out without elaborating.

Puckett flinched, then sat stunned. He wondered what they had missed when they hired Bledsoe. What secrets was he hiding?

By lunchtime there was still no word about Bledsoe or Kathleen. Dickenson didn't want to call Kathleen's parents—it would terrify them and the scandal wouldn't look good for the school. She walked over to Hargreaves to interview Kathleen's roommate again.

"Kathleen didn't say anything," Joan said. "She wasn't here when I went to sleep at 9:30 but that wasn't strange—she often stays out until curfew and doesn't tell me where she is. But this morning, no Kathleen."

Dickenson pressed her. "What did Kathleen and Bledsoe talk about?"

"Not much [a lie]. Of course, all the girls thought him nice and friendly—and Kathleen likes his car. Sometimes he would drive by Hargreaves and we'd wave at him when he flashed his spotlight up at our windows."

After lunch Joan walked into Dickenson's office and told her she'd found a note from Bledsoe among Kathleen's things. "The note isn't much," she said, "but I thought I should show you." Trembling, she handed it to Dickenson. It was brief:

> Kathy, trust in God. If he's the guy for you, the Lord will bring him to you. "Commit thy way unto the Lord, trust also in him and he shall bring it to pass." Psa. 37:5
>
> Praying for you,
> Harold Bledsoe

"I wonder where Kathleen is." Joan broke down sobbing.

Dickenson pondered the note, reading between the lines. Was Bledsoe *counseling* Kathleen? That violated TBI's policy. Men counseled men; women counseled women. She folded the note and filed it in her "Bledsoe" file that she guarded like an ammo clip to use later.

Dickenson and Joan went up to search through Kathleen's things. Besides the note, they found little. Most of her clothes remained, and her schoolbooks. "She even completed today's assignments," Joan said.

Fear seized Dickenson's chaste heart. "Did she talk to any of the other girls? She must have made a snap decision to leave." Vile, sinful city of Chicago—anything could have happened; she could be anywhere, could be hurt or dead. Running off with Bledsoe seemed the lesser of several horrific alternatives. What if he'd forced her? Now she *must* call Kathleen's parents—but what would she tell them?

She checked Kathleen's registration data. Ben and Jane Wilberforce lived in Anaheim, California, near Disneyland. So far away. Two hours time difference—it was morning there. *Will they take the next plane and come back?* she wondered. She called.

The babysitter picked up. "Oh; the Wilberforces aren't home. Is anything wrong?"

"Please, this is Dean Dickenson from TBI. Just have them call me as soon as they arrive."

An hour later, a concerned Ben Wilberforce called back during his lunch hour. Dickenson asked him if they'd heard from Kathleen.

"No. What's wrong?"

"I regret to say Kathleen left her residence hall Monday night at 9 p.m. and we haven't seen her since. Would you know where she might have gone? Her sign-out says, 'Out with friends.'"

Silence. Dickenson could hear his heavy breathing. "O dear Lord. No, she hasn't called. We've heard nothing . . . She has no Chicago relatives. She has a cousin in Iowa and an uncle who teaches at Southern Illinois University."

"Were you aware of anything troubling her?

"Well, there was but I thought she'd gotten that worked out." He dared not tell Dickenson about Kathleen's pregnancy.

Dickenson didn't say anything about Bledsoe's disappearance. "Can you telephone the uncle and cousin to see if she's there?"

"We'll call them right away. Did you notify the Chicago police?"

Dickenson hesitated . . . "Not yet. But we'll call them now. Maybe she was just upset and took off to a relative or friend's house for a couple of days. I'll call you as soon as I learn anything."

Dickenson walked into Puckett's office. "I called Kathleen's parents—they haven't heard from her." And then, "I found a note from Bledsoe to Kathleen in her dorm room."

Puckett paled. "O dear God . . ."

Kathleen had been swallowed up as if by a vast ocean, sunk out of sight without a trace. Her empty place at TBI ached like the soreness of a pulled tooth. People were asking about her.

Puckett made up his mind. Bledsoe could take care of himself but they were responsible for Kathleen. He called the Chicago police and reported Kathleen missing. He could almost hear the officer shrug: "Look, people disappear all the time. We can't track everybody. Maybe she overnighted with a friend, forgot to call in, was embarrassed to come back today. Maybe she's lyin' in an emergency room somewhere. Did you call her parents in California?"

"Yes—they haven't heard from her. Can't you please put out a bulletin on her?"

"We don't raise alarms unless they're missing forty-eight hours or more. Why don't you give it a few hours? If she still hasn't shown up by tonight, call us back."

Puckett frowned. Was he panicking too soon? He hated to entertain Dickenson's dark possibility—that Kathleen had left with Bledsoe.

Late that evening Puckett again called the Chicago police. He said nothing about Bledsoe. They took information and said they would put out a missing person report.

On Thursday morning Dean Puckett decided to check out Bledsoe's apartment. He knew he lived up beyond Torrey Church, and the address led him to the Gold Coast. He parked in front of the Patterson-McCormick building ("built in 1891," the sign said), an old mansion broken up into individual suites. Puckett found it surprising that Bledsoe lived in such a high-end apartment. Family money, maybe. The doorman stood mute in front of the locked main door. Puckett told him he needed to see Harold Bledsoe.

"Call your party; they'll buzz you in," the doorman answered. Puckett called on the intercom but no answer. Then he buzzed a couple other numbers on the directory but nobody answered.

"Look; I've got to check out his room—he hasn't reported for work for two days—I'm worried."

Not even a glimmer of compassion. "Here's the number of the manager; call him from that payphone over there. I can't let you into the apartment without permission from the occupant or the police."

Puckett now faced a dilemma. Should he get the police involved? He'd wanted to keep this whole affair secret if he could. Five years before, a distraught TBI girl had jumped out of the ninth-floor window of Hargreaves Hall and her suicide made all the Chicago papers. Many people considered the school hypocritical, judgmental, closed-minded—TBI didn't need another embarrassment. If Bledsoe's disappearance got out, the critics' fires would just flame higher. And since the police knew about Kathleen's disappearance, they would link the two.

Puckett saw no alternative—he called the police, then waited an hour until a tall officer pulled up at the apartment complex and got out—blue shirt and black pants, badge, pistol at belt. "We had trouble getting a search warrant on such flimsy reasons," he said. After arguing with the officer, the doorman let them pass and they elevatored up to the third floor. The hall with its richly carpeted hallways, chandeliers and brass appointments smelled of a faint floral scent. They rang the doorbell. Rang again. No answer. The policeman used the manager's skeleton key to let himself in. "All the furniture's still here, pictures still on the walls, dishes still in the cupboards." But the bedroom closet was bare. Bledsoe had taken off.

"Can you put the word out to your officers? He's single, lower thirties, about six-foot two."

"We're swamped right now, can't put out a search unless we think there's been foul play. People leave their apartments all the time. Maybe he just decided to cash his paycheck and take a joyride. I'll check the local hospitals and emergency rooms, though. Any relatives in Chicago?"

"Not that I know of; he's from Boston."

Puckett drove back, parked and walked up to Dickenson's office. "Bledsoe's gone; cleaned his clothes out of his closet."

"I told you so," Dickenson said. "He didn't want to face the music about the shot tires, the broken windshield. And he's kidnapped Kathleen."

"We can't jump to conclusions, Darla. Something might have happened to him."

"Yes; something did—he was scared he'd be caught and now he's taken off with one of our students."

Now, everyone knew about the double disappearance. The campus roiled, rife with multiple rumors. Bledsoe shot out Dickenson's tires and ran away. Kathleen ran off with Bledsoe. He had coerced Kathleen to go with him. They were driving to Massachusetts, they were holed up in Chicago, they were flying to Mexico . . .

Tiny details now loomed large. People thought they remembered conversations between the two. Dickenson pursued all these rumors. She knocked at the dorm mother's door, who said, "I've talked to her a couple of times. She mentioned a nasty breakup a couple of years ago but I thought she was over it. She attended chapel faithfully, broke curfew once, never gave me any other trouble."

Dickenson sat in her office, stewing. For the second time, she called Cleveland. "Pastor Runnell, I need to talk to you again. Harold Bledsoe has disappeared from Torrey Bible Institute, along with one of our woman students. We're worried about the safety of the girl."

Because Bledsoe was missing and suspected of running off with a TBI coed, Runnell felt forced to give out more information. "Miss Dickenson, Bledsoe is a man of many secrets. He hasn't always been single." Dickenson knew this and probed Runnell further.

Bledsoe was popular here," Runnell told her, "but he got into some trouble with a Cuyahoga High School coed—they never proved anything."

Dickenson pressed him but he wouldn't give more information. When Runnell hung up, he felt guilty betraying Bledsoe's trust. But he rationalized that he must give the information because a TBI girl was involved.

Dickenson's phone call gave her the truth—Bledsoe had lied on his TBI job application. He married in California, then divorced. He'd tried to seduce a high school girl. *I opposed hiring him from the beginning,* she thought, *Now I know I was right and Kathleen is in danger.* She frowned into her office mirror, squinting molelike through her pince nez. "He destroyed my car because he hates me," she said to the mirror. "I know he's run off with Kathleen. I should have told Puckett right away what I knew about him."

Kathleen's parents called the Chicago police themselves and the police came knocking on Dickenson's door, then Puckett's. The police hadn't yet linked Kathleen's disappearance to Bledsoe's. The deans kept quiet about Dickenson's new information, fearing for TBI's reputation. But she threatened to tell the police what she knew.

Kathleen's parents didn't know Bledsoe had gone missing. Dickenson told Kathleen's roommate to stay mute, so when Kathleen's mother called her dorm room and spoke to Joan, she said nothing about Bledsoe. Kathleen's father called Puckett again, said he was flying back to Chicago to help search. He demanded answers—answers Puckett didn't have. But he knew they couldn't keep the dual disappearance a secret much longer—the whole campus knew it and soon all of Chicago would know.

Chapter 33

Early Saturday, Ben Wilberforce called Puckett at home. "Kathleen's arrived here safely. We're so relieved. She came out with Dean Bledsoe; he just dropped her off last night."

Puckett sighed and picked up the phone to notify the president. Then he called CPD to let them know Kathleen was safe with her family, and that Bledsoe was also safe.

Then he called Dickenson, dreading the conversation.

"Darla, Ben Wilberforce just called me to say Kathleen is safe with them in California."

"What? Did she travel alone?"

"Her father said she drove out with Harold Bledsoe."

"I told you so. How terrible. Who knows what happened to her on the trip. I never trusted that man."

That night they announced at dinner that Kathleen was found and also that Bledsoe was safe (no details).

On Monday evening Kathleen telephoned long-distance to Norbert Hall and asked the desk guy to go call Sean down. Sean came down the stairs, smelled the pizza the desk guy was eating and picked up the phone in the little booth.

"Hello?

"Hello, Sean. I just needed to call you."

"Kathy? Where are you? Why didn't you let me know where you were going? I'm so glad you're safe. You just disappeared and no one knew where you'd gone. I worried a lot. Then the Deans announced you were safe but no details." His voice betrayed his worry and his sincere care for her welfare. He looked around to see if anybody was listening.

A pause, and then, "Oh, Sean; I'm so sorry I didn't tell you . . ." She caught her breath. "I'm home with my parents. Did the Dean say anything else?" She wondered how much to tell him.

"No one knew where you were but I was scared. Why did you leave so fast?"

"Sean, there are some things about me you don't know. I struggled with so much going on, so much to sort out. I just needed to work on some things."

"Kathy, I'm happy you're OK but I've got lots of questions. Will you come back to TBI?" He didn't mention his greatest fear—Bledsoe. Joan had told Sean about their secret restaurant meetings. He feared for Kathy—even grew worried Bledsoe would woo Kathy away.

"I don't know how long I need away," she said vaguely, "don't even know if TBI will let me back in."

Another week passed. Then on a Wednesday, Kathleen stepped out of an O'Hare airport limo with suitcase in hand, walked through TBI's arch, rode the elevator up to the tenth floor and knocked on Darla Dickenson's door.

Dickenson's head jerked up like a meercat at the sound of Kathleen's voice—the lost bird is returned. "Hello, Kathleen." She offered her a seat, poured her a cup of hot tea, folded her carefully tended white hands and waited. Kathleen inhaled the strong aroma, took a quick sip, then raised her head.

"Some things in my past weighed on my mind, made me depressed, desperate," she said vaguely. "I left unfinished business in California but had no money and no way to get there. I didn't know what to do.

"I turned to Dean Bledsoe for counsel." (She used his formal title to distance herself from him.) "He was so understanding. Then the gunshots happened. Dean Bledsoe felt like they would blame him, so he decided to make a clean break with TBI. He didn't want to crawl back home as a failure to Massachusetts, so he decided to go back to California. He knew it would make him look guilty but he didn't care."

Kathleen was bursting inside and she knew she'd be severely questioned. She had surprised herself telling the dean so much but she thought, *It's my only hope of readmission.* Dickenson just sat mute, her eyes blinking, looking at her. Kathleen didn't know much she hated Bledsoe.

"He knew I wanted to talk to my parents, how desperate I was to get back. He told me he would drive me to California. At first I said no but after a while I didn't see any other solution. I trusted him. I had no money and felt ashamed to ask my parents. So I grabbed a few things, signed out of Hargreaves, took a taxi and met him at his apartment. I now see how stupid that was but I felt desperate. I'm so sorry."

Dickenson thought, *She ran away with Bledsoe of her own will and he somehow played the innocent victim. I pity her.* Dickenson resented how Bledsoe had misled her, resented he'd deceived her, resented that Kathleen seemed so close to him. She squinted at Kathleen through her pince-nez, then cast her eyes down, adjusting her inbox papers so Kathleen could not see her anger or sense her jealousy.

"He dropped me at my parent's house," Kathleen said as she took another sip of tea and shifted in her chair. "It felt so good to go home. I acted like a little girl who needed her mommy and daddy. I talked to my parents a long time, poured out my heart. They tried to understand. I talked to a couple of friends, felt like I was working some things out." Kathleen was deliberately opaque.

"I still wanted to return to TBI—the classes, the teachers, my friends. So after a few days my parents bought me a ticket to fly back and here I am, asking forgiveness and promising to stay." She averted her eyes and waited.

Dickenson fixed her eyes on Kathleen after this incredible story, bereft of crucial details. Kathleen and Bledsoe had gone beyond a counseling relationship. She wondered what had drawn her back to California and what dark stain she longed to erase. Why had her parents allowed her to return to TBI? Dickenson had her eyes over all her girls and tried to learn everything about them but Kathleen was a mystery. She ruminated on Bledsoe and Kathleen. Also, she'd seen Sean and Kathleen together—had Sean drawn her back to TBI?

"Did Dean Bledsoe do anything to you during the trip? Where is he now?"

"No; he didn't do anything." (She didn't tell her he tried.) "I don't know where he is. He just dropped me off and disappeared into Los Angeles. I think he found some friends to stay with."

Dickenson wanted to ask if they'd become intimate but refrained. "Kathleen; I'm so glad you're safe," Dickenson said genuinely. "It took a lot of courage to return here, courage to come to see me. You have a bright future. God can meet you where you are and guide you forward. I must meet with the deans and president to discuss your situation; I'm sure you understand. Please stay on campus and we'll let you know our decision."

She didn't give Kathleen a hug—Dickenson wasn't a hugger. She shook her hand and wished her well. Then she phoned Kathleen's parents to report her safe arrival and to verify her story. She wondered how the institute could just ignore this. Kathleen had broken rules, provoked chaos on campus, forced TBI to hang out their dirty laundry for all Chicago to see, stained the reputation of the school. Dickenson blamed Bledsoe but Kathleen was complicit.

What to do? If they dismissed Kathleen now, she reasoned, she might lose her way, sink into greater despondency. Many students and faculty would see dismissing her as evidence the institute was too harsh. Dickenson remembered how some Chicagoans had slandered TBI when that girl had jumped out a Hargreaves Hall window five years ago, remembered how some Pennsylvania alumni had criticized TBI over expelling Aaron Byler for cheating. She wondered if they'd been too hard on Aaron, wondered if it had discouraged others from coming forward to confess their faults. But that was the TBI way—a high standard of purity and harsh discipline for those who violated the code. *Will Puckett plead for mercy in Kathleen's case?* she wondered. *He might.*

Chapter 34

KATHLEEN LEFT DICKENSON'S OFFICE and, amid surprised stares and whispers, walked across the quad into Hargreaves Hall and signed in just as if she'd been gone a half hour or so. When she arrived at her room Joan wasn't in, so Kathleen put her few things away, flopped down and lay with her eyes open. She worried about all she'd told Dickenson—would she tell other people her secrets? Probably not. But the hardest part lay ahead.

When Joan returned to her dorm room she flinched, then ran over and embraced Kathleen. She urged her to tell all but she said, "Joan, I am sorry; I can't talk now." She dropped her stuff, wheeled around and left the room.

One person on campus knew her better than the deans, better than her roommate. He knew her parents, knew her pre-TBI history, her pre-TBI boyfriends. She determined to talk to him. She trusted him, felt grateful for his friendship and listening ear, felt growing affection for him. But now she couldn't predict his reaction.

Most of the students were still in afternoon classes when Kathleen walked over to the campus post office and dropped a note addressed to Sean's P.O. box. It was the only way she knew to contact him without raising questions. She hoped Sean, like most students, would check his P.O. before dinner.

She surprised herself when she realized that Sean's opinion mattered the most. She entertained no idea that he would even talk to her, much less forgive her. A cloud hung over her head. She regretted she had turned a frigid shoulder to him. He seemed patient, seemed as if he was trying to understand but she had never opened up to him.

She felt drawn to the Hargreaves prayer room. It held a couple of chairs that sat next to a table with an open Bible lit by the window's light. She knelt on the floor facing the Bible.

She knew God forgave her for her liaison with Reggie, for running away from TBI—now she asked God to help her *feel* forgiven. Thanked God for taking her safely to California and back. Thanked him for the courage to confront Reginald. Thanked him for Sean's understanding ear. Prayed for Mr. Bledsoe who seemed so lost. Prayed that the deans would allow her to stay at TBI. Praying, she felt a tremendous release. She returned to her room and fell on her bed like a rag doll.

Sean walked out of his afternoon Isaiah and Romans class and jogged with Fulton across the quad toward the dining hall. Neither had heard the news. As usual they swung by the P.O.'s to check for mail. Sometimes there was a school memo; many days, nothing. "As usual, a-ah didn't get anything," Fulton said.

Sean leaned over and peered into his mailbox to see a flowered envelope. No stamp. Puzzled, he pulled it out, smelled lavender and recognized Kathleen's handwriting. How could that be? She'd fled to California two weeks ago—he'd talked to her by phone. He'd prayed for Kathy every day, beating back his darkest fears.

He turned to Fulton. "I've gotta go." He walked over to Cromwell Hall, ascended the stairs, sat down in an empty classroom and took a deep breath as he opened the letter.

> Dear Sean,
>
> I am back at TBI. I am so sorry I just disappeared without letting anyone know. It wasn't fair to you, worrying you like that. But I felt desperate.
>
> And now I am scared—scared I'll lose my friends, scared I can't face the criticism, scared Dean Dickenson will dismiss me from TBI. I so want to stay; I am ready to apply myself and work hard.
>
> And scared what you will think, Sean. We've known each other since high school. We have dated a few times. I'm sorry I wasn't friendlier; many things were weighing on me.
>
> I must talk to you, explain things, tell you why I returned and what happened.
>
> Please forgive me. Please come to Hargreaves this evening and ring for me.
>
> Kathy

Kathy was back! And she wanted to talk to him. *Has she talked to anyone else?* he wondered.

Looking around the vast dining hall at dinner, he didn't see Kathy but he saw Joan. He walked over and whispered to her about Kathy's note.

"You and I need to talk," Sean said. "But I need to find Kathy now."

Right after dinner Sean hurried up to his dorm room to clean up a little, waited until it was getting dark, then walked over to Hargreaves Hall with his heart thumping in his throat and asked the attendant to ring for Kathleen.

No answer. "Please ring again," Sean asked.

A couple minutes passed. "She just answered; says she'll be down."

It took fifteen minutes. Sean waited mannequin-like, hands in pockets, talking to no one.

The elevator doors opened and Kathleen walked out. Red-eyed but beautiful, her new pastel summer dress boasted a narrow "crumb-catcher" band low around the hips. She wore a pearl choker necklace, with her shoulder-length hair curved back from her ears. She smiled and walked toward him, a picture of beauty and grace.

"O Sean! I am so glad to see you. Thank you for meeting me. This afternoon seemed so strange. I haven't talked to anyone; they just stare. I feel radioactive."

"Kathy, I don't blame them. I don't understand why you left or why you came back. But I'm happy you're here. Are you staying, I hope?"

"It's up to the deans or maybe even the president. Dean Dickenson said she would let me know soon."

"Don't let them kick you out; that's not fair. You've got to insist they give you another chance."

"I don't know how many chances they give. I'll just have to wait and see."

Sean pondered a hundred questions but he didn't know what Kathy wanted to talk about or even if she wanted to talk. She'd taken the initiative; he'd wait to hear what she said.

"Sean, I don't want to sit in the dorm lounge; it's too public. Can we walk?"

They exited the arch and walked north along the sidewalk in the falling darkness. When they rounded the corner of Moody-Sankey Auditorium they noticed a couple Torrey students cocooned in the huge, recessed doorway, embracing. *Who patrols these streets now that Bledsoe is gone?* Sean wondered.

"I'm sorry I could not let you know where I was going or even that I left," Kathy said. "I felt so mixed up and despondent so I traveled to California and stayed with my folks."

"Wow; you left two weeks ago."

"Yes; I left with Dean Bledsoe."

Sean felt a knife rip his heart. Bledsoe. So it was true. "I can't believe it. Why did you run off with Bledsoe? Were you dating him or what?"

"Not exactly . . . He knew he wasn't supposed to but Dean Bledsoe was counseling me about some of my issues. We would meet for lunches over on Michigan Avenue—sometimes Joan would walk over with me. It was a fancy restaurant, so we didn't expect any TBI people walking in. I considered him more like a father, I guess, but I knew I shouldn't have met with him. Usually Joan came along but sometimes I met him alone.

"I was convinced he cared about me and I needed someone to talk to other than just friends. Dean Bledsoe always had a caring, listening ear and we would talk for two hours or more.

"I gradually told him all my problems, told him I loved TBI but I just needed to get some things straightened out, told him that I was getting more frantic, that I was thinking about leaving TBI. I just couldn't talk about this to Dean Dickenson, couldn't trust her. I knew I couldn't talk to you about it and I just felt Harold would understand."

Harold! Sean grimaced. They must have been close. *Why is Kathy telling me this; am I her best friend on campus? We do go back a few years; maybe she thinks I'll understand. Does Kathy know how much I care for her? How distressed I felt when she disappeared? What's her real relationship with Bledsoe?*

"Harold told me Dean Dickenson didn't like him, did not trust him, had opposed hiring him. Said Dickenson ran some background checks and found out some things. She threatened to tell the president if Harold ever crossed her.

"He told me that people at TBI accused him of shooting out Dickenson's tires. He admitted he disliked her—saw her as prudish, legalistic, critical; said he feared her feminine fury in deans' meetings; said he wasn't surprised she had enemies. But he denied damaging her car.

"He explained he carried a gun in his car 'for protection.' I couldn't understand how he felt the need for protection but I guess he was used to carrying. After someone shot out Dickenson's tires he knew they would blame him so he got rid of the gun. But he feared Dickenson's wrath and was fed up with TBI's no-alcohol, no-dancing, no-movie policies. He no longer did much of that but resented the restrictions. Anyway, when someone smashed Dickenson's windshield, Harold said he knew that she would try to pin it on him, so he was forced to leave, quickly. He was running scared, I guess."

Stunned by these revelations, Sean grew silent. Now they were walking down Chestnut, the darker side of the block with few streetlights. They moved over for a drunk guy toppling by wearing a dirty shirt, shoes with flapping soles and eyes looking dustbowl flat, hustling any passerby for a buck—the kind of guy destiny has a serious grudge against, one of thousands of men representing the effluvium cast up on the shores of every large city. Sean felt a brief sadness for him but they carefully avoided engaging him.

"I listened to Harold's story," Kathy continued. "Dickenson's anger shocked me. She crippled Harold; I felt sorry for him. When he said he was driving to California my heart leapt because I needed to get home, talk to my parents, straighten out some things.

"I told Harold this and he said, 'Look, Kathy, I've got to leave immediately but you can come with me. We won't tell anyone we're leaving. We'll be gone before they ever miss us.'

"I hesitated. Could I trust him? I thought I could. But if I left like this, how could I ever return? What would my parents and friends think? But I was desperate to settle some things and didn't care what anybody thought. I saw Harold as an older mentor, much more than a dean to me. He'd helped me work through so many things. I knew I had to get home but I couldn't ask my parents to send me money; I felt stuck. So I told him I'd go with him."

"Kathy; that's crazy. It's not like you making a snap decision."

From across Wells Street the dark, silent warehouse windows stared down at them. Not the safest territory, but another couple was walking about twenty paces ahead of them.

Kathy ignored Sean's scolding and continued to pour out her story. "I didn't tell anyone. I just threw some of my things together and tried to hide my suitcase when I signed out. Then I walked out to Chicago Avenue and took a taxi over to Harold's apartment. He told me he was leaving most of his stuff behind. I put my suitcase in the trunk of his convertible and at about 1 a.m. we drove through Chicago, but roundabout, to avoid TBI.

"After we picked up Highway 66 we drove about ten hours straight, stopping only for gas. I drove some on the open roads of Kansas while he slept; then he took over again. We stopped once at a truck stop to sleep an hour or so. He bought a six-pack of beer.

"Harold talked a lot on the trip but not like at the restaurant. He began rambling, talking about himself, lamenting his debauched California life. I told him I didn't need to hear the details. He mused about where he would stay in Los Angeles.

"He worried about getting entangled with his old California friends, the women, his drinking buddies, his pre-conversion friends. Maybe he would end up going back to Massachusetts after all, he said. He seemed distracted, uncertain but then he told me, 'I wanna see if I can reconcile with my ex-wife up in Palo Alto.' I always thought he was a carefree bachelor, at least that's how he acted at TBI. I told him I never knew he'd been divorced."

Sean asked, "What? Divorced? How could he get hired by TBI?"

"By the time we arrived in Amarillo we were both exhausted. He rang the doorbell at the house of some Stanford friends, got them out of bed, and after a little explaining we crashed there for a few hours. About an hour after I went to bed, I heard him knock and whisper 'Kathy!' at my closed door, but I didn't open for him. I had a hard time sleeping after that."

Sean tensed.

"We left in the morning and planned to drive through Albuquerque and on to Flagstaff. He asked me to scoot over next to him but I refused. As the hours passed, I became increasingly uneasy. I felt stuck; I couldn't just get out of the car and start walking across the desert. I'd gotten myself into this pickle with Harold and didn't see a way out.

"Not far out of Albuquerque a tire went flat. Harold stopped, got out his bumper jack and looked for his spare tire. He cursed when he saw it was flat and he had no air pump. We hitched a ride with a guy in a pickup truck (I didn't want to stay in the car alone) and he drove us into the closest little town to repair the two tires. We waited a while for them to fix both—a big nail stuck out of one of them. Then the station guy gave us a ride back to our car. By the time we started out again night had fallen so we got a motel in Albuquerque. Harold suggested we get a room together but I said no. I double-locked my room door that evening and hardly slept.

"On Thursday we traveled eight hours to Flagstaff. I told Harold, 'I know a missionary couple here, friends of my dad's; we can stop there.' I figured if things got too bad with Harold I could throw myself on their good graces. Our hosts were surprised to see me with this guy but I tried to explain why I wanted to return to California, so they put us up for one night. I begged them not to call my parents. I lay down on a cot and fell asleep.

"We started out again early next morning. I helped with the driving for a couple of hours on the open roads. The Mojave Desert sweltered and we put the convertible top down. We entered California through Needles, then finally drove into Anaheim late that same night. Harold dropped me off at my home, met my parents, then drove off toward the vastness of Los Angeles. I felt so relieved."

"Wow, what did your parents say?"

"I hadn't telephoned them I was coming because I thought they'd tell me not to come—they wouldn't want me driving all the way out to California, especially with this older man. They scolded me for leaving TBI without telling anyone, scolded me for driving all that way, scolded me for traveling with Harold. But mainly, they were relieved to see me, happy I was safe."

Sean fixed his eyes on the sidewalk waiting, wondering. Why had Bledsoe gone back to California instead of Massachusetts? Kathy was at least returning to her home state. According to Kathy, Bledsoe was acting the prodigal, returning to his "far country"—the country of his lust and debauchery, the place of bad memories, needy, eager women and a broken ex-wife. Maybe he hoped to link up with one of his old girlfriends. Why did he confide in Kathy? It didn't make sense. And was Kathy telling him the whole story?

He hated to ask but he felt compelled. "Did you and Bledsoe have sex?"

"No. He tried a couple of times. He was desperate for human understanding, human touch. He got emotional, told me, 'Your friendship has been like cool water running over my thirsty heart.' I never responded, though.

"I don't know how he'll live down the rumors and gossip. Come to think of it, I don't know how *I* will ever live them down either . . ." She teared up and looked down at the sidewalk.

They turned the corner, passed Torrey bookstore and walked back through the arch. Sean felt like a priest sitting behind the confessional screen listening to a catalog of sins. But she still hadn't told him what had drawn her back to California. She went to her folks, but why? What did she mean she must "take care of something?" What else happened in California? Why had she come back to TBI? He returned to his dorm room and fell into a fitful sleep.

The next week Kathleen swung by her P.O. just after breakfast. She flinched when she saw a white envelope with the TBI logo staring out at her and her name written on it in pen.

Clutching the unopened letter she ran over to Norbert Hall and asked the guy at the desk to go up and see if Sean was in. In a couple of minutes Sean came down, saw her anxious face and noticed the letter. They walked into the quad and sat down on one of the wrought iron benches. She opened the letter and read out loud, her hands shaking.

> Dear Miss Wilberforce,
>
> After consulting with the president and deans, we have decided to welcome you back to TBI under the following conditions: [Here, Kathy gave a happy scream.]
>
> 1. You are on probation for this coming semester (fall, 1961).
> 2. You may not leave campus without special permission.
> 3. You are to have no contact whatsoever with any of the men's deans.
>
> We all pray you will settle back into your life at TBI. Please see me if you have any questions. God bless you.
>
> Sincerely,
> Darla Dickenson, Dean of Women

Kathy's face filled with joy.

"Kathy, that's wonderful—you're staying. Good for you and good for me." He put his hand on her knee.

Kathy's face colored then she laughed. "Oh, Sean; I'm so happy." They put their heads together and spoke a prayer of gratitude.

Kathleen was thrilled she could stay and thrilled she and Sean were growing closer. But she knew she had to tell more of her past. When should she tell him? How?

Chapter 35

THAT WEEKEND KATHLEEN AND Sean were walking along Lake Michigan hearing the sea gulls screech overhead and watching the wind-wrinkled waves flinging their spray. He smiled, thinking how the guys talked about "taking a girl down to Lake Michigan to watch the submarine races." Sean knew he cared for Kathy deeply despite her many mysteries. How different she was from Betty. More serious, more in touch with herself, more mature.

They entered beautiful Grant Park that stretched for a mile along Lake Michigan's waterfront with its gardens, manicured shrubs and long walkways. They sat on a bench to talk about their classes and to pray together. The deans always cautioned the guys about praying with a girl. Praying opened your heart, brought you closer together. Not with Betty, Sean thought. But with Kathy, yes. Prayer revealed her struggles. He grew to learn her heart, her passions, her commitments. Her prayers seemed genuine. Here was an ungilded girl, transparent, even holy. True, she brooded at times, guarded her silence, as if manacled by a great sadness. But that was changing. Like a flower at dawn, she was turning her face toward the warming sun. And toward him. At times she seemed to teeter on the verge of telling Sean something important.

They walked slowly now and Sean waited. Buckingham Fountain loomed in the distance. "Sean . . . Some things I haven't told you; haven't told anyone at TBI. It's about my dropping out of Biola. This is the hardest part . . ." Sean kept silent, focusing on her face.

"I fought some with my parents, wanted more independence, so I moved into an apartment with my friend Valerie soon after graduation; I helped pay for our apartment working at the Jolly Roger in Balboa. I wasn't saving anything; most of what I earned went into rent and food."

The wind chased a dirty newspaper and a couple of empty paper bags down the sidewalk. Sitting down on a bench near Buckingham fountain, they stared for a long time at the grotesque stone creatures whose mouths spewed water into the pool. A limpid dusk fell and as the sky lost its light, sparkling floodlights colored the fountain.

"You knew I was dating Reginald at the end of high school. I admired him because he was a man on a mission—he knew what he wanted, knew where he was going. And so much confidence. We dated throughout that summer after I graduated. Remember the luau? We were together a lot after that and got increasingly serious . . .

"After our dates he would drive me back home to my Costa Mesa apartment and I started inviting him in. Valerie would stay in her bedroom.

"We talked a lot about college, jobs, friends. Reginald beamed with talk about UCLA, his international business major, his good grades. We would attend Calvary Church sometimes but we didn't pray much together, except before a meal. Didn't discuss our faith much.

"I knew he'd dated several girls but I thought I was the girl he cared for. We became closer and closer. He told me he loved me.

"At first he would kiss me goodnight at the entry door. After a few dates, he would come in and we would sit on the couch together. He would always leave by midnight or so to drive back up to UCLA."

Why is she telling me this? Sean asked himself. *She must be desperate to unload.*

Several couples walked by them, the women holding their skirts against the wind. A few seagulls splashed in the water of the fountain.

"Valerie was at her folks one weekend. The apartment complex was anonymous; none of our neighbors knew or cared what we did. I invited Reginald in, poured a couple of drinks and we sat on the couch as usual, talking a little but mainly embracing. We never talked about setting boundaries—I trusted him to stop before we went too far. But maybe he was expecting *me* to stop; I don't know . . . We both needed each other, I guess. I always believed I could stop whenever I wanted to, never believed Reginald would press me beyond limits, assumed he had high standards. It grew later, after midnight, and yet he lingered. Our passion seemed to gain a life of its own, started to run on autopilot. That night he didn't go home . . ." Kathleen buried her face in her hands and started sobbing. "I committed the worst Bible sin . . ." She dabbed her eyes.

"Next morning he got up, dressed, kissed me goodbye and left for UCLA. We hardly even talked. It didn't seem to affect him that much. But I felt so ashamed. He was at fault as much as I was but I felt violated, dirty.

"He called several times that week but I told him I never wanted to see him again. I never told anyone, except my parents. After that he just kind of moved on. I found out he started dating Maddie soon after. You remember Maddie?"

Sean was still recovering from the shock. "Maddie? Sure. I dated her once, back in high school."

"Sean, I told Dean Dickenson a lot—about my leaving TBI, about Bledsoe and the trip west, about California. But I never told her what I've just told you. There's more to tell but I just can't tell you now."

Sean ground his teeth and squelched a reply. They got up and started walking in silence. *I've already heard way more than I wanted to, The last thing I ever imagined I would hear. Kathy's link-up with Reggie makes me sick.*

On the north end of Grant Park stood the Prudential Building, highest in Chicago in the 1960s, a monument to progress and modernity with its "Top of the Rock" observation deck on the forty-first floor. Sean and Kathy elevatored up and stepped out onto the deck. On this clear evening they could view Grant Park stretching away to the south under the last glow of the sun, sunken now into the vast prairies beyond the city. At night the city softened, slowed down. Lights twinkled on in a thousand buildings, offering promises they could not fulfill.

After another sobbing silence, Kathy dabbed her eyes with a hankie, looking up at Sean with a question in her eyes. Impulsively, Sean put his arm around her shoulders. "Kathy, I'm sorry how it went with you and Reggie. I think I understand your moods a little better now. I'll never tell anyone about what you've told me."

But privately, Sean was trying to control his disappointment and anger. He remembered how he'd vowed to never date any girl who had given in to another guy. But Kathy was caught at a vulnerable time when she was living alone, he reasoned, drawn into a liaison she did not fully want, deceived by a selfish player.

They elevatored down and walked the mile back to TBI, each plumbing the depths of their own thoughts as the sidewalk beat backward under their feet. Somehow, Kathleen felt glad she'd come back to TBI, glad she'd told Sean her great secret. She felt a burden lift from her shoulders and she knew Sean would guard her secret but she feared she'd lost all his respect.

As for Sean, perhaps his dalliance with Betty made him more understanding. Kathy had done a terrible thing but at least she loved Reggie. In contrast, Sean had lied to Betty and to himself when he'd told her he loved her. Should he tell Kathy about Betty? Kathy didn't really know her. He'd already told her they'd dated but never told her how close they'd come to having sex. *Why am I so reluctant to tell her?* he wondered. And what did Kathy mean, "There's still more to tell?" What more could there be? They walked through the arch and Kathy buzzed herself into Hargreaves Hall.

She again sought out the prayer room. Here, Kathleen felt the quietness wash over her; here she felt insulated from the complex world. Her instincts said she should pray, that she needed prayer, that prayer would clarify, calm her, bring her into God's presence. But she prayed nothing, felt nothing; she simply soaked in the thunderous solitude, trying to hear that still, small voice within.

Chapter 36

THE DAY AFTER SPRING semester ended Dan Hardy drove Sean and Kathleen out to O'Hare Airport. As they walked across the tarmac to the boarding stairs of the huge Boeing 707, Sean inhaled the smell of JP-5 fuel as if it were oxygen.

The flight home took almost four hours. As they descended through the warm night into the Los Angeles basin, Sean thrilled again to see the myriad lights winking like shining stars beneath the gigantic wings.

They walked out of the terminal into the warm, smoggy air to where Mr. Wilberforce waited. He embraced them both then drove away toward Santa Ana.

When they pulled to the curb in front of Sean's home, Sean said goodbye to Kathy and her father. Walking in, he acted as if he'd never left, sticking his head in the door. "Hey, Mom, what's for supper?"

He'd always felt close to his mother but felt even closer now after his dad died and after living away the better part of two years.

"Sean!" She ran out to the entryway and smothered him in a hug, her head only reaching up to his heart. "Sean, it's so good to see you. I'm happy you're home for the summer." They both were missing Edwin but neither wished to bring this sadness into the happy conversation of reunion. "It was kind of Mr. Wilberforce to pick you up."

With the confident entitlement of a mother's son, Sean took a bite of a homemade sugar cookie that lay on the kitchen counter. "Yeah. You remember Kathy disappeared from TBI last month. I was amazed to see her come back."

"Maybe she returned to TBI because she was chasing you." His mother laughed. She loved Kathleen but knew little of her troubles. "What do you think of her, Sean?"

Sean could always talk about anything with his mother but now he faltered. "Mom, she's struggled some but she's a great girl. When she first arrived at TBI we hardly talked but since she reappeared, we've become close. I hope we can see each other lots this summer."

"That would be nice, Sean. When do you have to go back to Maple Plain for flight camp?"

"It starts July 10 and runs for two weeks. I don't know what I'll do if I don't get in this time. I feel like I'm pulling on the ripcord of my reserve chute and if it doesn't open, I'm lost."

"Sean, you can't defeat yourself before you even get to flight camp. You just must trust. I know you'll get in if it's God's will."

"Yeah, I guess. But I'm still scared.

"Mom; have you seen Lonnie? He wrote me that he's in business school in Los Angeles. And Dan Hardy told me he'll work this summer for his dad on their Atwood cattle ranch."

"I don't know but I do talk to some of your friends' parents. Roy's still at Wheaton. Arnold and Jill got married last summer; I think they're living up in Washington state now."

Meanwhile, Mr. Wilberforce had barely pulled in the driveway when Kathleen jumped out, ran across the lawn past the tall palm trees with their heads full of wind, ran past the pink roses that clung to the yard fence, and ran toward the welcoming front door. The scent of bougainvillea hovered in the air like a benediction.

Jane Wilberforce opened the door to her and gave her a long hug. "Kathleen; welcome, Sweetheart! I know you've had a rough year but you look so happy now." She'd just seen her daughter a few weeks before but now Kathleen appeared released, more at peace, more content. She'd prayed for her, wept for her, agonized for her. Had she recovered from the trauma of two summers ago?

Soon Kathleen stood by her mother helping to dry dishes. The two seemed much closer now. "Mother, I'm so grateful TBI let me back in. I finished Introduction to the Bible with Dr. Moreau. He is amazing, makes the whole Bible cohere—explains how the Old Testament progresses into the New, what God's great plan for humanity is. I wish I knew what God's great plan is for me."

"Kathleen, you have made a great choice to go back. You'll get your TBI diploma soon, then come home to one of the universities for nurses' training or go to Swedish Covenant there in Chicago to finish up in two years."

"Mother, everything's so opaque. I wish I knew for sure. But I am happy where I am right now."

Jane wondered if any of her happiness had to do with Sean. She asked a question only a mother could get away with. "Are you planning on seeing Sean much this summer?"

"He wants us to spend time together. He's volunteering over at Fullerton Airport at Winging the Word. You know how he loves aviation.

"I'm worried about him, though—afraid he'll get drafted. He's got a ministerial student deferment now but I don't know if that will last long after he graduates. Russia just built the Berlin wall and now they've exploded a hydrogen bomb. I'm afraid the U.S. will stumble into another war."

"Some things we can only pray about," Jane said.

Kathleen changed the subject. "I want to get back to Calvary and see all my friends, see the kids who've come home from college." And then, "Er, Reggie hasn't shown up at Calvary Church anymore has he Mother?"

"No, Sweetheart." She spoke slowly, gently. "I don't know if he's *going* to church; I know he's not at Calvary. I hope he's attending somewhere. I don't know if he's still dating Maddie."

Maddie was one of Kathleen's best friends. She asked herself, *Did Reggie treat Maddie like he treated me?* She wondered if Maddie would still be friendly if she was dating Reggie. Things seemed so confused. She found herself wanting to talk all this through with Sean.

After he arrived home Sean's mind turned to the previous summer and Betty O'Shea. *I didn't sleep with her,* he told himself, *but I told her I loved her, then used her for my own pleasure, never intending any future together. I've confessed this to God, felt his forgiveness; do I have to confess to Betty too?*

He did not know how to find her, although only a year had passed. He heard she was married. He still had her old apartment number in his little black book. He hesitated, then dialed. But the message said "number disconnected" so he called her mother and left a message with Mrs. O'Shea to give to Betty.

The next day, Sean jumped when the phone rang. "Sean? This is Betty. I was surprised to hear you called. Where are you?"

"I'm home; just got here on Saturday." He paused, not knowing what to say. "Betty, can we meet somewhere for half an hour?"

"I guess so. I'm busy with summer school and working at the flower shop but I can meet." They agreed to meet at Mrs. Knott's Chicken Dinner in Knott's Berry Farm for old times' sake.

Willing but not too eager, Sean thought. He wondered how it would go. He truly cared about how she was doing now. The next afternoon Sean drove his Chevy over to Knott's Berry Farm, clenching his teeth, tense about the meeting. A beautiful blue sky spread overhead, blanched by the heat of summer.

The meeting was awkward. Sean felt his moist palms and the knot in his stomach. Betty looked down at her fried chicken. They both failed to appreciate Cordelia Knott's legendary cuisine. "I got married, Sean—the spring after you and I broke up. Cliff was a starting psychologist on his way up, working twelve-hour days. I never should have married him. He treated me like I was just an adornment on his bookshelf, less important than his rising career and his pick-up basketball games. We didn't go to church together, didn't do much of anything together. I thought I loved him, felt loved and protected by him. But, aside from our physical relationship there wasn't much there. He just penciled me in to his already-busy schedule. I was miserable and in March I asked him for a divorce. He got angry but eventually agreed, so we divorced and that's where I'm at now."

All this told matter of fact, without emotion. But Sean could see she still bled pain and anger. Clearly, she had no designs on Sean but considered him a confidant, a friend, maybe even a counselor. But he said little, except to speak his sadness.

Then, "Betty, I regret how we dated, regret how we broke up. I treated you unfairly, leading you on, giving you expectations I couldn't fulfill, didn't respect you. Will you forgive me?"

"I was just as much to blame, Sean. I was excited by our relationship, thrilled that you'd picked me out to date. Excited to grow close. But I never told you the doubts I had . . . I just couldn't imagine myself as a missionary pilot's wife in some dirty little town in the middle of Africa. Your attention flattered me and I didn't want to break up. You were right to pull back, though. If not, you would have compromised your whole future."

Her concern for his welfare impressed Sean and he felt guilty because he hadn't thought much about hers. He wondered, but didn't ask, whether their liaison had pushed her too quickly into a new relationship.

"I'm attending Fullerton Free Church, meeting with a Christian counselor. I felt so bitter against Cliff, his self-absorption, his lack of concern for me. But now I'm trying to forgive him."

"Betty, I need you to forgive me for taking advantage when I had no real commitment to you." He didn't tell her about Kathy.

She grew silent. Then, "Of course, Sean. We both need to move forward now."

He felt sorry for her and was amazed she held no resentment toward him. They shared a brief but genuine parting hug.

The languid summer days rolled by and Kathleen and Sean drew closer. They'd known each other since their sophomore year in high school and they found lots to talk about. She spoke of her Christian life, her circle of Christian friends and her bright vision to study nursing at Swedish Covenant. They did not talk about Reggie.

For his part, Sean talked aviation. This was the year that Russia's Yuri Gagarin first orbited the earth in a space capsule, pushing the U.S. to accelerate its own air and space program. When he was driving around, he craned his neck to watch every passing airplane. Commercial airlines were even hiring private pilots and training them to fly the heavy metal. But Sean had never given a thought to the airlines.

He arranged with Kathy to go together to hear the New Christy Minstrels up in the Hollywood Bowl. When he picked her up, he noticed how she appeared more relaxed, more at peace.

Kathy, in less than a month I'll return to TBI flight camp to try again. I don't know if I'll make it." His jaw turned rigid.

"Sean; you must just release it—if it is meant to be, it will happen."

She stayed with her folks that summer and Sean would often come over in the evenings. They tried to avoid too much touching because both remembered they'd violated their own moral standards in the past. They would play little games and accidentally touch but he thought too much of her, cared too deeply for her to move too fast. He saw her questioning eyes that reassured him that all would come at its appointed time.

He felt so good that they could talk about anything, even pray together. Like a living thing, their relationship grew. They saw each other on Saturdays and often another time during the week. "I wish we could go to church," Kathleen told Sean, "but I waitress on Sundays at the Jolly Roger."

"Some of these places treat their employees like disposable gloves. But maybe you can get them to change your hours."

She begged her manager and soon he changed her shift to 3 p.m. to close, so on Sundays Sean and Kathleen became an item at Calvary Church.

Kathleen felt an inner magnet pulling her back to the part of her she'd abandoned—part of her own body, part of her very soul. One night after work she parked her car in a residential area, then walked a couple blocks to the orange grove. Few cars passed at this hour but she was terrified of being discovered. The skin on her arms prickled as she turned her flashlight on the dry and sandy orchard furrows. She knew the row, the very tree she was looking for, not too far in.

Pushing aside the low-hanging branches she shined the flashlight on a small pile of stones visible above the blanket of dead brown leaves. She swept the mottled leaves away that lay around the stones and noticed the discolored dirt. Kneeling, she thought back to that awful day two winters before. She visualized the dull plastic container, the faint image of her daughter just perceptible through the lid with the white carnation lying on her tiny breast. She still felt deep regret, still struggled with seeking God's forgiveness, still agonized over the loss of her dear daughter and the night that lodged like a sunken log in her memory. She knelt in the dead leaves for a long time, sobbing, mouthing her daughter's secret name—*Angela, Angela, Angela* . . . "Dear Lord, I honor the memory of my precious *Angela*, her brief life and painful death. I thank you for kneeling here beside me, forgiving me, strengthening me for the future. O my Lord, care for this tiny child and may eternal light shine on her. My darling, I will never forget you." She rose and left the site, never to return.

Meanwhile Sean was volunteering fifteen hours a week with Winging the Word at Fullerton Airport. WTW operated about one hundred aircraft in twenty countries around the world, supporting Christian missionaries and servicing remote communities by transporting pastors, doctors and teachers. He loved meeting the pilots and mechanics. Sweeping up the hangar floor, organizing parts, washing planes—he would do anything. WTW felt so good to him—professional but compassionate.

Mid-afternoons the WTW guys would yell, "Orange break" and run out of the hangar into the adjoining orange grove to grab oranges, peel and eat them. Sean, having been raised with orange trees in his backyard, couldn't understand the excitement.

The little mechanical work he did—sheet metal, hydraulic hoses—seemed clumsy to him. He wondered if he had any mechanical aptitude at all, remembered failing flight camp two years before, feared he would fail again.

One day Sean drove over to see Dan Hardy who was home from TBI for the summer and working on his uncle's ranch. Dan walked out to greet him, smelling of manure. "Hey, Sean, good to see you. Wanna go flying?" Any money Dan had, any extra time, he poured into flying. He had his license now and one Saturday he took Sean up in an Aeronca "Airknocker" Model 7 Champ he'd rented at Huntington Beach Airport. As they flew out to ride the desert thermals, Sean envied Dan's complete control of the plane, manipulating stick and rudder as if they were appendages. He would turn around and smile at Sean. "It's easy—just keep the pointy end forward and the dirty side down." Sean thrilled when Dan let him take the controls.

The next week, Aaron called and they had a short talk about his aviation training in Pennsylvania. Sean told his mom about Aaron's problems.

"What? I can't believe they did that. Poor Aaron."

"Right. It's so harsh. TBI shoots their own wounded. He said he's taking flight lessons at a local airport."

"I hope he's able to fly for a mission," Elizabeth said.

All that brief summer Sean thought about his second and final try at flight camp. *What makes me think I'll succeed this time? Even if I'm accepted I'll have two years of hard work and the always-present possibility of washing out. And how can I stay close to Kathy if I live thirty miles away?*

The day before he left for flight camp he and Kathleen walked hand in hand down Huntington Beach, the same beach of the summer luau. "Sean, it helps me coming back here, to heal memories and feelings and make a new memory with you." The long, lambent light took its time sinking into the cloudless Pacific before the sun disappeared beneath the waves, leaving only the glow. They walked barefoot, kicking seashells, stopping to view tiny crabs stranded in the receding foam. They turned to one another, took hands, looked into each other's eyes. Kathleen teared up.

"Kathy, it's not like we're saying goodbye forever. You'll start your second year at TBI in a couple of months; I'll be thirty miles away at Maple Plain Airport if I'm accepted into the program." They drew closer. Sean leaned down and for the first time, kissed her.

Chapter 37

GREYHOUND CONNECTED IN Los Angeles, then routed through Las Vegas, Denver, Kansas City, St. Louis. Sean's long bus trip to Chicago was cheap but much less comfortable than his train ride two years before. With so many stops the trip took forever.

If he failed to get into flight camp, the constant threat of the military draft hung over his head. The Korean War had ended just a few years before, John Kennedy had been inaugurated president in January, and the US military was getting involved in some place called Vietnam. Russia's hydrogen bomb had Americans building bomb shelters and practicing "duck and cover" in schools.

But for Sean flight camp seemed more important than hydrogen bombs. He realized he'd gone to TBI mainly for flight training. The aviation program had changed—the students didn't live downtown anymore; they lived in private homes out near the airport. In a few weeks Kathy would be back at TBI. If he was accepted, he would have to get a car if he wanted to drive in to see Kathy.

He exited the Greyhound as close as he could to the airport, then, casting a weather eye at the darkening skies above, hitchhiked over and gazed at Maple Plain for the first time in two years—the same green grass, same squat control tower atop the white admin building. Like the first time, Norman Richards gave him a warm welcome and told him, "Instead of the old J-3s we're now flying Cessna 150s."

The wind quickened. The sun still streamed down hot and humid but to the northwest, huge, squally thunderclouds threatened—he stared at a black, towering hammerhead already spitting out rain.

The airport reminded Sean of a common pasture with a few yellow runway marker cones. He looked far out across the wind-bent grass and saw a red Farmall mowing back and forth. Richards told him, "Mr. Anderson mows for hours, then he sets the yellow cones along the runways. After a heavy downpour, the field turns into a soggy airplane trap; gotta watch out for the mud. For night flight he sets flare lamps to mark the runway edges."

The Farmall rolled up and Mr. Anderson jumped off wearing a crooked grin as he leaned over to whisper to Mr. Richards. "Last week I set out two flare lamps at the lip of runway one-eight so Mr. Van Dixon could land the Apache at night. But he got a little confused and almost landed on them high tension wires over to the west. After that, he asked me for more flare lamps." Guileless, transparent and a sieve for secrets, Mr. Anderson heard nothing he did not retail to others. As Sean eavesdropped, inhaling this story along with the tractor exhaust, he felt sweet Schadenfreude—an illicit rush of joy—realizing that Van Dixon, the galactico of the skies, stood on feet of clay like everybody else.

Walking back to the buildings, Richards said, "Maple Plain Airport sits three miles from the threshold of O'Hare's Runway zero-nine. On rare days when an east wind blows, Boeing 707s let down with their wheels and flaps extended, just a few hundred feet above the airport. That's why we fly our own traffic patterns at three hundred feet."

They barely got inside before the hammerhead cloud hurled down rain. Hail pounded the roof as Sean stood looking at a varnished, wood-laminated propeller hanging on the ready room wall with a clock mounted in its brass hub. "That was made out of one of our old J-3 propellers," Richards told him. Underneath hung a Chicago area aeronautical chart. They climbed the stairs to see the Link Trainer sitting in the corner with its stunted wings and bright yellow and blue fabric. Richards yelled over the noise of the pelting hail: "That's the instrument flight trainer. The student sits inside blind, with earphones that communicate with the instructor who sits there at the large table. Your flight path transfers to a moving pen that traces your path on that chart there."

A torture chamber with a stunted six-foot wingspan, Sean thought.

They went back down the stairs to the Quonset hangar. "You'll eat your meals at those tables there on the hangar floor. That's where our Cessna 180 sleeps. The Cessna 150s hangar over in the maintenance building and we still keep several J-3 Cubs out in the tee hangers."

They walked back into the admin building. At flight camp two years ago, Sean had met Mr. Dale van Dixon, chief pilot. Now his finely chiseled face stared down at him again. Behind his back, the flyboys called him the Great Stone Face. In his thirties, with sculpted arms, thicker lips and tightly curled, graying hair, he wore gray flight glasses and shiny black shoes. No-nonsense. He enjoyed a reputation as an excellent pilot. He did the stage flight checks and carried the power to wash you out of the program. When he spoke in his sonorous bass voice, the earth tremored.

It was now suppertime and Sean walked over to the Quonset hanger to join the other guys gathered around tables. The downpour stopped as abruptly as it had started. He looked out through the huge hanger doors at the scud and the white cumulus above, now gilded by the sinking sun.

At supper Sean met some of the other candidates. Donnie came from northern Minnesota. Steve, a former Navy helicopter pilot, told Sean, "When my copilot pulled out the mixture control instead of the carburetor heat, he dropped us in the Mediterranean." George, a Mennonite, came from California. Tom was an Army veteran who knew electronics. As the days passed, these men became close—working together, praying together, all sailing in the same boat.

The passing weather front had freshened the air and brought a Sunday that dawned cooler and clearer. They planned to hold a worship service in the hangar and Donnie Sanderson told Sean, "Dr. Moreau's coming out from the downtown campus to preach for us today." After the service came lunch. Then the guys walked around the grounds looking at the maintenance shop and inspecting the airplanes in the tee hangars.

On Monday morning, Sean winced when again he drew Mr. Latham for flight instructor. He thought back to his spectacular failure two years before. *How will this flight camp be any different?* he wondered. He was the only applicant back for a second try—Aaron wasn't here now. Since he hadn't improved his mechanical skills much, he wondered how he would do.

A group of the guys walked out to the flight line on this clear but windy day—the windsock stood straight out. Sean remembered how shaky his J-3 Cub flying was. Two years ago the J-3 (tailwheeled) was like a wild girlfriend. Would the Cessna 150 (nosewheeled) act more like a faithful wife? Could he settle down more in the 150?

The three Cessna 150s rocked in the wind, straining at their tiedown ropes. Mr. Latham spoke. "Walk around the airplane to look for ripples in the aluminum—wrinkles indicate damage inside." Sean wiggled the ailerons and rudder to see if they moved freely. "Make sure the tires are inflated. Check the oil." Sean smelled the Shell oil on the dipstick. "Climb up on the wheel and look into the gas tank. Drain the gascolator valve down there into this little cup and smell it to make sure it's gas, not water." Sean inhaled the pungent smell of 80/87 octane avgas as he felt the cold, red-colored fuel running down his arm.

When the time arrived for Sean to fly with Mr. Latham, they rubbed shoulders in the tiny cockpit. He struggled with Lance Latham—terse, sober, with a bleak, overcast outlook on life. Latham never praised. His favorite saying was "Ain't gonna happen." He loved to say, "Make sure you coordinate rudder and aileron in a turn or you'll bury your mortal coil in that cornfield down there." Sean couldn't discern his thoughts. He was convinced he had little chance of getting into the flight program but he would try his best.

Control wheel instead of a stick. Electric starter. Sean looked over the unfamiliar gauges. Latham raised his voice over the roar of the 100-horsepower Continental engine. "Taxi 'er out to runway three-six. You're going to fight some crosswind on takeoff—it's windy out there."

As Sean advanced the throttle, the airplane felt more stable than the old J–3 but soon the plane swerved into the left crosswind. "Use left aileron against the wind and keep 'er straight with the right rudder," Latham yelled.

The tiny 150 vaulted into the sky. *At least we didn't end up in the weeds,* Sean thought. He struggled with the unfamiliar plane and flinched when Mr. Latham yelled corrections at him. But his hands rested more lightly on the controls than with the J–3. He tried talking on the communications radio. After half an hour flying around the practice area, they returned to land. Sean watched a car whiz by on Thorndale Avenue just before they touched down.

The next day after breakfast the guys walked over to the maintenance shop. Mr. Masterson came out, smelling of solvent. He passed out coveralls with a red "TBI" embroidered on the back and again, Sean entered the strange world of aluminum, rivet guns and paint equipment. As the men took their places around the long shop tables, Masterson said, "Men, these two aluminum sheets here; I want you to rivet them together."

Sean drilled a hole, inserted the tiny rivet, backed it up with the bucking bar and pulled the rivet gun trigger. Pock, pock, pock. The air pressure was set too high and the gun dimpled a smiley face in the aluminum. Smiley faces were bad. Mr. Masterson breathed over his shoulder. Sean's sweat dripped onto the metal. On the next try, the bucking bar cocked and ruined the butt-end of the rivet. Mr. Masterson wrote in his little notebook.

At the end of two weeks came the fateful day. His face arranged to communicate nothing, Mr. Richards announced that he'd posted the names. Sean had dreaded this day for months. He clenched his teeth, thinking back two years ago to his and Aaron's devastating failure. And now Aaron wasn't here.

It was afternoon now and the northwest wind was rising. Towering cumulus filled the sky, some blackening into cumulonimbus. In the distance it was pouring sheets of rain. He hoped the weather wasn't a harbinger of another failure. What if he failed again? Mr. Latham had shattered the germ of confidence he had. How could he stay at TBI if he weren't in the flight program? He could learn to fly elsewhere but did he have the aptitude? Yet if God had led him, why would he let him fail now? Sean felt his chances slim as he walked into the ready room.

The list was alphabetical. He thought about the high hopes and prayers of his parents, especially his dad, how proud he'd been of him, how he'd encouraged him to pursue aviation. He dreaded failure, dreaded smudging the memory of his dad, dreaded having to re-start his whole education. If he wasn't accepted this time, he had no idea what he would do.

Of the twenty-four men who came to flight camp, ten names were listed. Sean wiped his sweaty hands on his coveralls, his heart pounding as he read down the list . . .

Alton, Tom

Cannon, Donald

Hershey, George . . .

He slowed his scan. His whole life flashed before him—growing up in the California orange groves, Santa Ana High School, meeting Kathy, coming to TBI, the Betty O'Shea summer . . .

Lacey, Steve

McIntosh, Sean . . .

He was accepted! He'd hoped and prayed for it but still struggled to believe it. He felt the blood coursing through his whole body—a blessed electric shock. Relief, then euphoria—an inflection point in his life.

He couldn't wait to make a couple of long-distance calls to California. His mom was elated at the news. (She'd believed in him, taken for granted that he would be accepted.) "Sean, I'm happy for you. Your dad would be so proud of you, seeing his dreams and your dreams being fulfilled."

Then Sean called Kathy who laughed, so relieved. "Oh, Sean. I'm thrilled for you. God has guided you and has given you a down payment on your future."

On the van ride back to TBI's downtown campus, the grass seemed greener, every blooming flower was turned toward him, and smiling down on him were the blue sky and white clouds. After a hard, uncertain two years, God had answered his prayer.

Chapter 38

Flight training started at once. Sean and Donnie Sandstrom were boarding with a local family so Sean bought an old car for commuting to the airport and for driving into the city on weekends to see Kathleen. He took classes and worked in the maintenance shop Monday through Friday and flew several times a week. High demands, high expectations. He still breathed the euphoria of flight camp but now his fears turned to washing out.

Sean's thoughts drifted to his dreamy California summer with Kathleen Wilberforce. On the day TBI's downtown classes started, he borrowed his landlady's telephone, called long-distance to Hargreaves Hall and asked to speak to Kathleen.

"Hello Sean. Sorry; I had to run downstairs to the phone. I'm thrilled you're accepted into the program, an answer to our prayers. Everybody at Calvary Church is excited for you—your friends, Pastor Carter, everybody."

"Thanks, Kathy. It's still hard to believe. It's great to hear your voice. I've thought of you every day. How do you feel, being back at TBI?"

"I am so grateful Dickenson let me continue. I love my organ instructor. I feel like I belong here. With my one year here, one semester's credit from Biola and taking a few overload courses, I hope to get my three-year diploma the end of this year, then go to Swedish Cov and work on my R.N. degree."

"Wonderful. I'll try to get in to see you this weekend. I can crash in Fulton's room overnight Friday and Saturday. His roommate won't mind."

The summer heat passed and soon the leaves started to turn. That same weekend and many fall weekends after that, Sean drove in to see Kathleen. One Saturday they were walking along Lake Michigan, holding hands. He'd told other girls that he loved them. He dared not tarnish the word by saying it to Kathy without meaning it. They walked in silence for a while, relaxing in the rays of the late, languid sun. Then he stopped, turned to her and took both of her hands, his heart rising into his throat.

"Kathy, I'm so glad you're back at TBI. You mean so much to me . . ."

She raised her eyes and looked into his.

"Over the summer I've realized that God sent you into my life as one of his greatest gifts. I love you and I want you to marry me."

Kathleen started, then cast her eyes down. Time stopped. Sean's proposal seemed awkward but not a surprise. She knew they were drawing closer, knew this day was coming soon but Sean had caught her off guard.

She'd already told Sean about Reggie and her; she must not conceal the rest from him. But she couldn't tell him—how could she? She hesitated, uncertain, not wanting to lose him but not wanting to keep secrets from him either.

She lifted her gaze to Sean's questioning eyes. "Sean, my feelings for you have grown. I think of you always; I'm so thankful for your friendship. [Sean's heart sank when she said 'friendship.'] Oh, Sean, you've been so kind, like a brother. You've accepted me even with what you know about me. And yet I cannot answer your proposal without revealing other things to you that are hard for me to talk about, things I've never told anyone here. Could you have patience, give me a little time?"

Time stopped for Sean. She had already told him about Reggie and her, that she'd given in to him. Sean had processed that; told her it would never come between them. What more could she possibly be holding back? She hadn't lost faith in God, had she? Impossible. In the last month they'd read the Bible together, prayed together. Kathy had more faith than he did.

His face darkened—did she have sex with Bledsoe on their trip to California? She said she hadn't but . . .

"Of course I'll give you some more time, Kathy. I'll wait as long as you need to, until you're ready."

"Oh, Sean. Thank you for understanding. I will give you my answer in a week."

They walked back to TBI like characters in a silent movie. Kathleen said goodbye at the door of Hargreaves, then walked up to the little prayer room where the failing fall light filtered through the small window. She wanted to pray and to think. She wondered, *Am I worthy of Sean's love?*

Chapter 39

Kathleen pondered Sean's proposal, knowing she would have to tell him more, dreading his reaction. The next Saturday they were again strolling through Grant Park with the proposal question lingering between them. They stopped to sit on a bench near the familiar Buckingham Fountain, tasting the cold spray. Both wore light coats and Kathleen held her dress down against the onshore wind. Sean's proposal hung over them both like the oppressive Chicago humidity. They stared ahead—she, fearing to confess; he, fearing her rejection.

Are you sure you're completely broken off with Reggie?" Sean asked.

"Yes. My parents wrote and told me that Reggie's still up at UCLA finishing his International Business degree. They don't know any more than that; he's not coming to Calvary Church anymore."

He wanted to change the subject. "I miss Aaron. He wrote me that he's working on his commercial pilot license; he'll get it before I do. Then he wants to do mission aviation. I'm still angry TBI kicked him out but he's recovered well." Sean hated to ask the next question. "What do you hear from Dean Bledsoe? I can't believe you went to California with him. Are you still in contact?" He wondered whether Kathy still had feelings for him.

"Going with him was a terrible idea. I haven't heard anything since he dropped me off last spring and disappeared into Los Angeles. He is kind of hard to figure out. His past weighs on him like a heavy backpack but I know he wants a godly life. You must admire him, trying to reconcile with his wife. I doubt she'll take him back, though."

Silence. Sean felt relieved Kathy's secret wasn't about Bledsoe.

And then, "Sean . . . I have something else to tell you."

The sun rainbowed the spray of Buckingham Fountain and Sean smelled the aroma of a passing cigar. *Kathy already told me her most embarrassing, shameful sin; what else could it be?*

Kathleen lifted her eyes. "Sean, the more I tell you the less you will understand who I am. That one night with Reggie two Augusts ago . . . I've seen him twice since that day and I hope I never see him again. It would be too painful. She closed her sad blue eyes. That night—I got pregnant."

Sean sat silent, looking down a long time. *She was right—I don't even know who she is.* Then, without looking at her—"What happened to your baby? Did you give it up for adoption?"

"She's not an 'it;' I named her Angela. I miscarried at five months, just before Christmas. I lost my baby, my little girl." Pain all over her face, tears starting down her cheeks. "I will never forget that beautiful face."

Sean sat silent as death. Angela! Kathy—a mother? Impossible. But she would never lie about a thing like that. He wanted to ask questions but knew she didn't want to elaborate.

"I'm so sorry what you've gone through, sorry about Reggie's lack of respect, sorry you lost your precious Angela."

He knew he must tell her about Betty. "Kathy, lust is an equal opportunity temptation. I never told you, but Betty O'Shea and I saw a lot of each other that first summer I returned home. It was mainly physical. She drew no boundaries. Only God's grace kept us out of bed. I knew we should break up. I feel bad about not respecting her. I talked to her this summer—life has not treated her well and I wonder how much of that is my fault."

Now Kathy grew silent. Then, "Sean, thank you for telling me this. I never realized the power of sex, how it could overwhelm my best intentions, overwhelm all my years of moral and spiritual training. I guess we've changed, become much wiser in the two years since that California summer luau—I can still smell the shish kabobs [a weak smile]. We had no idea what lay before us, did we?"

They rose and walked south toward the Field Museum, watching the seagulls wheeling about the cornices; then they circled and started back. Each carried much to think about, much to forgive. Sean pondered how they'd been hurled apart over the trajectory of time, then miraculously reunited.

Finally, "Kathy, these hard things haven't changed my mind at all. I love you." He looked at her blue eyes and quoted from an anonymous author:

> I love you
> Not only for what you are,
> But for what I am

When I am with you.
I love you,
Not only for what
You have made of yourself,
But for what
You are making of me.

And then, with trembling voice—"But I still have a question: Kathleen Wilberforce, will you marry me?"

They stopped now and took hands.

"Sean, you have been so gracious with me and the mistakes I've made. I am humbled, privileged God has brought us together. I was not sure how you would take all I told you but I'm glad I told you. And you have said these things will never come between us. I believe you."

She lifted her eyes to meet his, felt as if she had prepared all her life for this moment, felt like she had been borne by silent sails across her life's troubled sea to this good harbor. "Sean, I love you very much and with all my heart, I accept your proposal and pray God bless us as we join our futures together, forever!"

She raised her head. "See that tiny dot up there on the terrazzo of the Prudential building? I wonder what he's looking at." An anonymous tourist looked down at the tiny human figures, the hundreds of couples in Grant Park that day. Kathleen and Sean appeared as only two more young people walking together, taking hands, embracing—just a pair of insignificant dots.

But as they looked into each other's eyes, the world stopped turning on its axis. They drew closer, kissed. He felt her hair adrift against his cheek, her warm breath in the hollow of his throat. Moving apart, they gazed into the love their eyes held for each other.

Sean stood amazed at grace. He thought back, not to all his spectacular sins and failures but to all he had received—godly, loving parents, an embracing church, college in Chicago, failure, then success in aviation and the gift of restored faith. And now, improbable, against all odds, Kathy. His expanding heart rejoiced.

Walking back through the city they talked, heedless of the ashy grime and blowing trash. "I feel so much peace now," Kathleen said. "feel such a weight off my shoulders."

And then, "Sean, when do you think we should get married?"

Someone has said that marriage is the first, great event in a woman's life and the last, great event in a man's. For Sean, he saw it as God's miracle. But truth be told, he hadn't thought anything about a wedding. "How about December?"

"Oh, Sean; that's too soon. We could never get all the planning done. I know your first aviation year demands a lot. If we wait until summer to get married, we could plan better and I would be finished with my three-year diploma. Of course we'll get married at Calvary Church—our families would love it. People just think I dropped out of Biola to work, then later came back to TBI. No one knows about my pregnancy except Reggie and my family. I'm confident I can face our old friends. Right now, we don't have much money but should we shop for engagement rings? That would be fun."

Sean had thought out his proposal but he hadn't given thought to details, such as a wedding and rings. "Sure. Next time I come from the airport to see you we could look around downtown. Rings would be a great way to celebrate our love." (Remembering her 18K gold bracelet, he worried if he could afford the ring she might be expecting.)

"Oh, Sean, we need to use Kenneth Boulding's poem at our wedding." She began quoting:

> Put off the garb of woe, let mourning cease;
> Today we celebrate, solemn mirth,
> The planting in the ravaged waste of earth
> Of one small plot of heaven, a Home of peace,
> Where love unfeigned shall rule, and bring increase,
> And pure eternal joy shall come to birth . . .

Did she prepare this even before I proposed? Sean wondered. Finally, they walked through the arch, said a warm goodbye and Kathleen disappeared inside Hargreaves Hall.

Sean's faith now stood on firmer ground. He still struggled with doubt but he knew now that doubt always accompanies true faith. He had seen God amaze his life—renewing his faith, helping him enter the aviation program and now giving him the precious gift of Kathy. Kathy—who loves poetry.

The next Saturday evening Kathleen and Sean walked around TBI's city block, then turned in at an alcove of Moody-Sankey Auditorium. "Kathy, I'm so grateful now that I'm pursuing the aviation program. Grateful for my renewed faith. And grateful for you and your love." They embraced, he leaned down and kissed her and, as if for the first time, they gazed out together upon the vast city and their bright future.

THE END

Made in the USA
Monee, IL
04 March 2023

29179204R00118